EVERYMAN,

I WILL GO WITH THEE,

AND BE THY GUIDE,

IN THY MOST NEED

TO GO BY THY SIDE

✳

STORIES OF
FATHERHOOD

EDITED BY DIANA SECKER TESDELL

EVERYMAN'S POCKET CLASSICS
Alfred A. Knopf New York London Toronto

THIS IS A BORZOI BOOK
PUBLISHED BY ALFRED A. KNOPF

This selection by Diana Secker Tesdell first published in
Everyman's Library, 2014
Copyright © 2014 by Everyman's Library
A list of acknowledgments to copyright owners appears at the back
of this volume.

www.randomhouse.com/everymans
www.everymanslibrary.co.uk

ISBN: 978-0-307-71245-6 (US)
978-1-84159-615-0 (UK)

A CIP catalogue reference for this book is available from the
British Library

Typography by Peter B. Willberg
Typeset in the UK by AccComputing, Wincanton, Somerset
Printed and bound in Germany by GGP Media GmbH, Pössneck

STORIES OF
FATHERHOOD

Contents

HAROLD BRODKEY
His Son, in His Arms, in Light, Aloft   9

FRANK O'CONNOR
My Oedipus Complex   35

RAYMOND CARVER
Bicycles, Muscles, Cigarets   53

GRAHAM SWIFT
Gabor   67

RON CARLSON
The H Street Sledding Record   81

ANDRE DUBUS
A Father's Story   95

E. L. DOCTOROW
The Writer in the Family   125

VLADIMIR NABOKOV
Christmas   143

ANN PACKER
Her Firstborn   153

GUY DE MAUPASSANT
Simon's Father   181

JAMES JOYCE
A Little Cloud   195

GRACE PALEY
Anxiety   213

FRANZ KAFKA
The Judgment   219

KATHERINE MANSFIELD
The Daughters of the Late Colonel   235

HELEN SIMPSON
Sorry?   263

D. H. LAWRENCE
The Christening   273

EDITH WHARTON
His Father's Son   287

JIM SHEPARD
The Mortality of Parents   311

JOHN UPDIKE
My Father's Tears   325

WILLIAM MAXWELL
The Man Who Lost His Father   345

ACKNOWLEDGMENTS   351

HAROLD BRODKEY

HIS SON, IN HIS ARMS, IN LIGHT, ALOFT

MY FATHER IS chasing me.

My God, I feel it up and down my spine, the thumping on the turf, the approach of his hands, his giant hands, the huge ramming increment of his breath as he draws near: a widening effort. I feel it up and down my spine and in my mouth and belly – Daddy is so swift: who ever heard of such swiftness? Just as in stories . . .

I can't escape him, can't fend him off, his arms, his rapidity, his will. His interest in me.

I am being lifted into the air – and even as I pant and stare blurredly, limply, mindlessly, a map appears, of the dark ground where I ran: as I hang limply and rise anyway on the fattened bar of my father's arm, I see that there's the grass, there's the path, there's a bed of flowers.

I straighten up. There are the lighted windows of our house, some distance away. My father's face, full of noises, is near: it looms: his hidden face: is that you, old money-maker? My butt is folded on the trapeze of his arm. My father is as big as an automobile.

In the oddly shrewd-hearted torpor of being carried home in the dark, a tourist, in my father's arms, I feel myself attached by my heated-by-running dampness to him: we are attached, there are binding oval stains of warmth.

In most social talk, most politeness, most literature, most religion, it is as if violence didn't exist – except as sin, something far away. This is flattering to women. It is also conducive to grace – because the heaviness of fear, the shadowy henchmen selves that fear attaches to us, that fear sees in others, is banished.

Where am I in the web of jealousy that trembles at every human movement?

What detectives we have to be.

What if I am wrong? What if I remember incorrectly? It does not matter. This is fiction – a game – of pleasures, of truth and error, as at the sensual beginning of a sensual life.

My father, Charley, as I knew him, is invisible in any photograph I have of him. The man I hugged or ran toward or ran from is not in any photograph: a photograph shows someone of whom I think, Oh, was he like that?

But in certain memories, *he* appears, a figure, a presence, and I think, I know him.

It is embarrassing to me that I am part of what is unsayable in any account of his life.

When Momma's or my sister's excesses, of mood, or of shopping, angered or sickened Daddy, you can smell him then from two feet away: he has a dry, achy little stink of a rapidly fading interest in his life with us. At these times, the women in a spasm of wit turn to me; they comb my hair, clean my face, pat my bottom or my shoulder, and send me off; they bid me to go cheer up Daddy.

Sometimes it takes no more than a tug at his newspaper: the sight of me is enough; or I climb on his lap, mimic his depression; or I stand on his lap, press his head against my chest. . . . His face is immense, porous, complex with stubble, bits of talcum on it, unlikely colors, unlikely features, a bald brow with a curved square of lamplight in it. About his head there is a nimbus of sturdy wickedness, of unlikelihood. If his mood does not change, something tumbles and goes dead in me.

Perhaps it is more a nervous breakdown than heartbreak: I have failed him: his love for me is very limited: I must die now. I go somewhere and shudder and collapse – a corner of the dining room, the back stoop or deck: I lie there, empty, grief-stricken, literally unable to move – I have forgotten my limbs. If a memory of them comes to me, the memory is meaningless. . . .

Momma will then stalk into wherever Daddy is and say to him, 'Charley, you can be mad at me, I'm used to it, but just go take a look and see what you've done to the child. . . .'

My uselessness toward him sickens me. Anyone who fails toward him might as well be struck down, abandoned, eaten.

Perhaps it is an animal state: I-have-nothing-left, I-have-no-place-in-this-world.

Well, this is his house. Momma tells me in various ways to love him. Also, he is entrancing – he is so big, so thunderish, so smelly, and has the most extraordinary habits, reading newspapers, for instance, and wiggling his shoe: his shoe is gross: kick someone with that and they'd fall into next week.

Some memories huddle in a grainy light. What it is is a number of similar events bunching themselves, superimposing themselves, to make a false memory, a collage, a mental artifact. Within the boundaries of one such memory one plunges from year to year, is small and helpless, is a little older: one remembers it all but it is nothing that happened, that clutch of happenings, of associations, those gifts and ghosts of a meaning.

I can, if I concentrate, whiten the light – or yellow-whiten it, actually – and when the graininess goes, it is suddenly one afternoon.

I could not live without the pride and belonging-to-himness of being that man's consolation. He had the disposal of the rights to the out-of-doors – he was the other, the other-not-a-woman: he was my strength, literally, my strength if I should cry out.

Flies and swarms of the danger of being unfathered beset me when I bored my father: it was as if I were covered with flies on the animal plain where some ravening wild dog would leap up, bite and grip my muzzle, and begin to bring about my death.

I had no protection: I was subject now to the appetite of whatever inhabited the dark.

A child collapses in a sudden burst of there-is-nothing-here, and that is added onto nothingness, the nothing of being only a child concentrating on there being nothing there, no hope, no ambition: there is a despair but one without magnificence except in the face of its completeness: *I am a child and am without strength of my own.*

I have – in my grief – somehow managed to get to the back deck: I am sitting in the early-evening light; I am oblivious to the light. I did and didn't hear his footsteps, the rumble, the house thunder dimly (behind and beneath me), the thunder of his-coming-to-rescue-me. . . . I did and didn't hear him call my name.

I spoke only the gaping emptiness of grief – that tongue – I understood I had no right to the speech of fathers and sons.

My father came out on the porch. I remember how stirred he was, how beside himself that I was so unhappy, that a child, a child he liked, should suffer so. He laid aside his own mood – his disgust with life, with money, with the excesses of the women – and he took on a broad-winged, malely flustering, broad-winged optimism – he was at the center of a great beating (of the heart, a man's heart, of a man's gestures, will, concern), dust clouds rising, a beating determination to persuade me that the nature of life, of *my* life, was other than I'd thought, other than whatever had defeated me – he was about to tell me there was no need to feel defeated, he was about to tell me that I was a good, or even a wonderful, child.

He kneeled – a mountain of shirtfront and trousers; a mountain that poured, clambered down, folded itself, re-formed itself: a disorderly massiveness, near to me, fabric-hung-and-draped: Sinai. He said, 'Here, here, what is this – what is a child like you doing being so sad?' And: 'Look at me. . . . It's all right. . . . Everything is all right. . . .' The misstatements of consolation are lies about the absolute that require faith – and no memory: the truth of consolation can be investigated if one is a proper child – that is to say, affectionate – only in a nonskeptical way.

'It's not all right!'

'It is – it is.' It was and wasn't a lie: it had to do with power – and limitations: my limitations and his power: he could make it all right for me, everything, provided my everything was small enough and within his comprehension.

Sometimes he would say, 'Son' – he would say it heavily – 'don't be sad – I don't want you to be sad – I don't like it when you're sad –'

I can't look into his near and, to me, factually incredible face – incredible because so large (as at the beginning of a love affair): I mean as a *face*: it is the focus of so many emotions and wonderments: he could have been a fool or was – it was possibly the face of a fool, someone self-centered, smug, an operator, semicriminal, an intelligent psycho-analyst; it was certainly a mortal face – but what did the idea or word mean to me then – *mortal*?

There was a face; it was as large as my chest; there were eyes, inhumanly big, humid – what could they mean? How could I read them? How do you read eyes? I did not know about comparisons: how much more affectionate he was than other men, or less, how much better than common experience or how much worse in this area of being fathered my experience was with him: I cannot say even now; it is a statistical matter, after all, a matter of averages: but who at the present date can phrase the proper questions for the poll? And who will understand the hesitations, the blank looks, the odd expressions on the faces of the answerers?

The odds are he was a – median – father. He himself had usually a conviction he did pretty well; sometimes he despaired – of himself – but blamed me: my love: or something: or himself as a father: he wasn't good at managing stages between strong, clear states of feeling. Perhaps no one is.

Anyway, I knew no such terms as *median* then: I did not understand much about those parts of his emotions that extended past the rather clear area where my emotions were so often amazed. I chose, in some ways, to regard him seriously: in other ways, I had no choice – he was what was given to me.

I cannot look at him, as I said: I cannot see anything: if I look at him without seeing him, my blindness insults him: I don't want to hurt him at all: I want nothing: I am lost and have surrendered and am really dead and am waiting without hope.

* * *

He knows how to rescue people. Whatever he doesn't know, one of the things he knows in the haste and jumble of his heart, among the blither of tastes in his mouth and opinions and sympathies in his mind and so on, is the making yourself into someone who will help someone who is wounded. The dispersed and unlikely parts of him come together for a while in a clucking and focused arch of abiding concern. Oh how he plows ahead; oh how he believes in rescue! He puts – he *shoves* – he works an arm behind my shoulders, another under my legs: his arms, his powers shove at me, twist, lift, and jerk me until I am cradled in the air, in his arms: 'You don't have to be unhappy – you haven't hurt anyone – don't be sad – you're a *nice* boy. . . .'

I can't quite hear him, I can't quite believe him. I can't be *good* – the confidence game is to believe him, is to be a good child who trusts him – we will both smile then, he and I. But if I hear him, I have to believe him still. I am set up that way. He is so big; he is the possessor of so many grandeurs. If I believe him, hope and pleasure will start up again – suddenly – the blankness in me will be relieved, broken by these – meanings – that it seems he and I share in some big, attaching way.

In his pride he does not allow me to suffer: I belong to him.

He is rising, jerkily, to his feet and holding me at the same time. I do not have to stir to save myself – I only have to believe him. He rocks me into a sad-edged relief and an achingly melancholy delight with the peculiar lurch as he stands erect of establishing his balance and rectifying the way he holds me, so he can go on holding me, holding me aloft, against his chest: I am airborne: I liked to have that man hold me – in the air: I knew it was worth a great deal, the embrace, the gift of altitude. I am not exposed on the animal plain. I am not helpless.

The heat his body gives off! It is the heat of a man sweating with regret. His heartbeat, his burning, his physical force: – ah, there is a large rent in the nothingness: the mournful apparition of his regret, the proof of his loyalty wake me: I have a twin, a massive twin, mighty company: Daddy's grief is at my grief: my nothingness is echoed in him (if he is going to have to live without me): the rescue was not quite a secular thing. The evening forms itself, a classroom, a brigade of shadows, of phenomena – the tinted air slides: there are shadowy skaters everywhere; shadowy cloaked people step out from behind things that are then hidden behind their cloaks. An alteration in the air proceeds from openings in the ground, from leaks in the sunlight, which is being dis-engaged, like a stubborn hand, or is being stroked shut like my eyelids when I refuse to sleep: the dark rubs and bubbles noiselessly – and seeps – into the landscape. In the rubbed distortion of my inner air, twilight soothes: there are two of us breathing in close proximity here (he is telling me that grownups sometimes have things on their minds, he is saying mysterious things that I don't comprehend); I don't want to look at him: it takes two of my eyes to see one of his – and then I mostly see myself in his eye: he is even more unsee-able from here, this holder: my head falls against his neck. 'I know what you like – you'd like to go stand on the wall – would you like to see the sunset?' Did I nod? I think I did: I nodded gravely: but perhaps he did not need an answer since he thought he knew me well.

We are moving, this elephant and I, we are lumbering, down some steps, across grassy, uneven ground – the spoiled child in his father's arms – behind our house was a little park – we moved across the grass of the little park. There are sun's rays on the dome of the Moorish bandstand. The evening is moist, fugitive, momentarily sneaking, half welcomed in this hour of crime. My father's neck. The stubble. The skin where the stubble stops. Exhaustion has me: I am a creature of failure, a locus of childishness, an empty skull: I am this being-young. We overrun the world, he and I, with his legs, with our eyes, with our alliance. We move on in a ghostly torrent of our being like this.

My father has the smell and feel of wanting to be my father. Guilt and innocence stream and restream in him. His face, I see now in memory, held an untiring surprise: as if some grammar of deed and purpose – of comparatively easy tenderness – startled him again and again, startled him continuously for a while. He said, 'I guess we'll just have to cheer you up – we'll have to show you life isn't so bad – I guess we weren't any too careful of a little boy's feelings, were we?' I wonder if all comfort is alike.

A man's love is, after all, a fairly spectacular thing.

He said – his voice came from above me – he spoke out into the air, the twilight – 'We'll make it all right – just you wait and see. . . .'

He said, 'This is what you like,' and he placed me on the wall that ran along the edge of the park, the edge of a bluff, a wall too high for me to see over, and which I was forbidden to climb: he placed me on the stubbed stone mountains and grouting of the walltop. He put his arm around my middle: I leaned against him: and faced outward into the salt of the danger of the height, of the view (we were at least one hundred and fifty feet; we were, therefore, hundreds of feet in the air); I was flicked at by narrow, abrasive bands of wind, evening wind, veined with sunset's sun-crispness, strongly touched with coolness.

The wind would push at my eyelids, my nose, my lips. I heard a buzzing in my ears that signaled how high, how alone we were: this view of a river valley at night and of parts of four counties was audible. I looked into the hollow in front of me, a grand hole, an immense, bellying deep sheet or vast sock. There were numinous fragments in it – birds in what sunlight was left, bits of smoke faintly lit by distant light or mist, hovering inexplicably here and there: rays of yellow light, high up, touching a few high clouds.

It had a floor on which were creeks (and the big river), a little dim, a little glary at this hour, rail lines, roads, highways, houses, silos, bridges, trees, fields, everything more than half hidden in the enlarging dark: there was the shrinking glitter of far-off noises, bearded and stippled with huge and spreading shadows of my ignorance: it was panorama as a personal privilege. The sun at the end of the large, sunset-swollen sky was a glowing and urgent orange; around it were the spreading petals of pink and stratospheric gold; on the ground were occasional magenta flarings: oh, it makes you stare and gasp; a fine, astral (not a crayon) red rode in a broad, magnificent band across the Middle Western sky: below us, for miles, shadowiness tightened as we watched (it seemed); above us, tinted clouds spread across the vast shadowing sky: there were funereal lights and sinkings everywhere. I stand on the wall and lean against Daddy, only somewhat awed and abstracted: the view does not own me as it usually does: I am partly in the hands of the jolting – amusement – the conceit – of having been resurrected – by my father.

I understood that he was proffering me oblivion plus pleasure, the end of a sorrow to be henceforth remembered as Happiness. This was to be my privilege. This amazing man is going to rescue me from any anomaly or barb or sting in my existence: he is going to confer happiness on me: as a matter of fact, he has already begun.

'Just you trust me – you keep right on being cheered up – look at that sunset – that's some sunset, wouldn't you say? Everything is going to be just fine and dandy – you trust me – you'll see – just you wait and see. . . .'

Did he mean to be a swindler? He wasn't clear-minded – he often said, 'I mean well.' He did not think other people meant well.

I don't feel it would be right to adopt an Oedipal theory to explain what happened between him and me: only a sense of what he was like as a man, what certain moments were like, and what was said.

It is hard in language to get the full, irregular, heavy sound of a man.

He liked to have us 'all dressed and nice when I come home from work,' have us wait for him in attitudes of serene all-is-well contentment. As elegant as a Spanish prince, I sat on the couch toying with an oversized model truck – what a confusion of social pretensions, technologies, class disorder there was in that. My sister would sit in a chair, knees together, hair brushed: she'd doze off if Daddy was late. Aren't we happy! Actually, we often are.

One day he came in plungingly, excited to be home and to have us as an audience rather than outsiders who didn't know their lines and who often laughed at him as part of their struggle to improve their parts in his scenes. We were waiting to have him approve of our tableau – he usually said something about what a nice family we looked like or how well we looked or what a pretty group or some such thing – and we didn't realize he was the tableau tonight. We held our positions, but we stared at him in a kind of mindless

21

what-should-we-do-besides-sit-here-and-be-happy-and-nice? Impatiently he said, 'I have a surprise for you, Charlotte – Abe Last has a heart after all.' My father said something on that order: or 'a conscience after all'; and then he walked across the carpet, a man somewhat jerky with success – a man redolent of vaudeville, of grotesque and sentimental movies (he liked grotesquerie, prettiness, sentiment). As he walked, he pulled banded packs of currency out of his pockets, two or three in each hand. 'There,' he said, dropping one, then three, in Momma's dressed-up lap. 'There,' he said, dropping another two: he uttered a 'there' for each subsequent pack. 'Oh, let me!' my sister cried, and ran over to look – and then she grabbed two packs and said, 'Oh, Daddy, how much *is* this?'

It was eight or ten thousand dollars, he said. Momma said, 'Charley, what if someone sees – we could be robbed – why do you take chances like this?'

Daddy harrumphed and said, 'You have no sense of fun – if you ask me, you're afraid to be happy. I'll put it in the bank tomorrow – if I can find an honest banker. Here, young lady, put that money down: you don't want to prove your mother right, do you?'

Then he said, 'I know one person around here who knows how to enjoy himself –' and he lifted me up, held me in his arms.

He said, 'We're going outside, this young man and I.'

'What should I do with this money!'

'Put it under your mattress – make a salad out of it: you're always the one who worries about money,' he said in a voice solid with authority and masculinity, totally pieced out with various self-satisfactions – as if he had gained a kingdom and the assurance of appearing as glorious in the histories of his time; I put my head back and smiled at the superb animal, at the rosy – and cowardly – panther leaping; and then I glanced over his shoulder and tilted my head and looked sympathetically at Momma.

My sister shouted, 'I know how to enjoy myself – I'll come, too! ...'

'Yes, yes,' said Daddy, who was *never* averse to enlarging spheres of happiness and areas of sentiment. He held her hand and held me on his arm.

'Let him walk,' my sister said. And: 'He's getting bigger – you'll make a sissy out of him, Daddy....'

Daddy said, 'Shut up and enjoy the light – it's as beautiful as Paris, and in our own backyard.'

Out of folly, or a wish to steal his attention, or greed, my sister kept on: she asked if she could get something with some of the money; he dodged her question; and she kept on; and he grew peevish, so peevish he returned to the house and accused Momma of having never taught her daughter not to be greedy – he sprawled, impetuous, displeased, semi-frantic in a chair: 'I can't enjoy myself – there is no way a man can live in this house with all of you – I swear to God this will kill me soon....'

Momma said to him, 'I can't believe in the things you believe in – I'm not a girl anymore: when I play the fool, it isn't convincing – you get angry with me when I try. You shouldn't get angry with her – you've spoiled her more than I have – and how do you expect her to act when you show her all that money – how do you think money affects people?'

I looked at him to see what the answer was, to see what he would answer. He said, 'Charlotte, try being a rose and not a thorn.'

At all times, and in all places, there is always the possibility that I will start to speak or will be looking at something and

I will feel his face covering mine, as in a kiss and as a mask, turned both ways like that: and I am inside him, his presence, his thoughts, his language: *I* am languageless then for a moment, an automaton of repetition, a bagged piece of an imaginary river of descent.

I can't invent everything for myself: some always has to be what I already know: some of me always has to be him.

When he picked me up, my consciousness fitted itself to that position: I remember it – clearly. He could punish me – and did – by refusing to lift me, by denying me that union with him. Of course, the union was not one-sided: I was his innocence – as long as I was not an accusation, that is. I censored him – in that when he felt himself being, consciously, a father, he held back part of his other life, of his whole self: his shadows, his impressions, his adventures would not readily fit into me – what a gross and absurd rape that would have been.

So he was *careful* – he *walked on eggs* – there was an odd courtesy of his withdrawal behind his secrets, his secret sorrows and horrors, behind the curtain of what-is-suitable-for-a-child.

Sometimes he becomes simply a set of limits, of walls, inside which there is the caroming and echoing of my astounding sensibility amplified by being his son and in his arms and aloft; and he lays his sensibility aside or models his on mine, on my joy, takes his emotional coloring from me, like a mirror or a twin: his incomprehensible life, with its strengths, ordeals, triumphs, crimes, horrors, his sadness and disgust, is enveloped and momentarily assuaged by my direct and indirect childish consolation. My gaze, my enjoying him, my willingness to be him, my joy at it, supported the baroque tower of his necessary but limited and maybe dishonest optimism.

* * *

One time, he and Momma fought over money and he left: he packed a bag and went. Oh, it was sad and heavy at home. I started to be upset, but then I retreated into an impenetrable stupidity: not knowing was better than being despairing. I was put to bed and I did fall asleep; I woke in the middle of the night: he had returned and was sitting on my bed – in the dark – a huge shadow in the shadows. He was stroking my forehead. When he saw my eyes open, he said in a sentimental, heavy voice, 'I could never leave *you* –'

He didn't really mean it: I was an excuse; but he did mean it – the meaning and not-meaning were like the rise and fall of a wave in me, in the dark outside of me, between the two of us, between him and me (at other moments he would think of other truths, other than the one of he-couldn't-leave-me). He bent over sentimentally, painedly, not nicely, and he began to hug me; he put his head down, on my chest; my small heartbeat vanished into the near, sizable, anguished, angular, emotion-swollen one that was his. I kept advancing swiftly into wakefulness, my consciousness came rushing and widening blurredly, embracing the dark, his presence, his embrace. It's Daddy, it's Daddy – it's dark still – wakefulness rushed into the dark grave or grove of his hugely extended presence. His affection. My arms stumbled: there was no adequate embrace in me – I couldn't lift *him*. I had no adequacy yet except that of my charm or what-have-you, except things the grownups gave me – not things: traits, qualities. I mean, my hugging his head was nothing until he said, 'Oh, you love me. . . . You're all right. . . .'

Momma said: 'They are as close as two peas in a pod – they are just alike – that child and Charley. That child is God to Charley. . . .'

25

He didn't always love me.

In the middle of the night that time, he picked me up after a while, he wrapped me in a blanket, held me close, took me downstairs in the dark; we went outside, into the night; it was dark and chilly but there was a moon – I thought he would take me to the wall but he just stood on our back deck. He grew tired of loving me; he grew abstracted and forgot me: the love that had just a moment before been so intently and tightly clasping and nestling went away, and I found myself released, into the cool night air, the floating damp, the silence, with the darkened houses around us.

I saw the silver moon, heard my father's breath, felt the itchiness of the woolen blanket on my hands, noticed its wool smell. I did this alone and I waited. Then, when he didn't come back, I grew sleepy and put my head down against his neck: he was nowhere near me. Alone in his arms, I slept.

Over and over a moment seems to recur, something seems to return in its entirety, a name seems to be accurate: and we say it always happens like this. But we are wrong, of course.

I was a weird choice as someone for him to love.

So different from him in the way I was surprised by things.

I am a child with this mind. I am a child he has often rescued.

Our attachment to each other manifests itself in sudden swoops and grabs and rubs of attention, of being entertained, by each other, at the present moment.

I ask you, how is it possible it's going to last?

Sometimes when we are entertained by each other, we are bold about it, but just as frequently it seems embarrassing, and we turn our faces aside.

His recollections of horror are more certain than mine. His suspicions are more terrible. There are darknesses in me I'm afraid of, but the ones in him don't frighten me but are like the dark in the yard, a dark a child like me might sneak into (and has) – a dark full of unseen shadowy almost glowing presences: the fear, the danger, are desirable – difficult – with the call-to-be-brave: the childish bravura of *I must endure this* (knowing I can run away if I choose).

The child touches with his pursed, jutting, ignorant lips the large, handsome, odd, humid face of his father, who can run away too. More dangerously.

He gave away a car of his that he was about to trade in on a new one: he gave it to a man in financial trouble; he did it after seeing a movie about crazy people being loving and gentle with each other and everyone else: Momma said to Daddy, 'You can't do anything you want – you can't listen to your feelings – you have a family. . . .'

After seeing a movie in which a child cheered up an old man, he took me to visit an old man who probably was a distant relative, and who hated me at sight, my high coloring, the noise I might make, my father's affection for me: 'Will he sit still? I can't stand noise. Charley, listen, I'm in bad shape – I think I have cancer and they won't tell me –'

'Nothing can kill a tough old bird like you, Ike. . . .'

The old man wanted all of Charley's attention – and strength – while he talked about how the small threads and thicker ropes that tied him to life were being cruelly tampered with.

Daddy patted me afterward, but oddly he was bored and disappointed in me, as if I'd failed at something.

He could not seem to keep it straight about my value to him or to the world in general; he lived at the center of his own intellectual shortcomings and his moral pride: he needed it to be true, as an essential fact, that goodness – or innocence – was in him or was protected by him, and that, therefore, he was a good *man* and superior to other men, and did not deserve certain common masculine fates – horrors – tests of his courage – certain pains. It was necessary to him to have it be true that he knew what real goodness was and had it in his life.

Perhaps that was because he didn't believe in God, and because he felt (with a certain self-love) that people, out in the world, didn't appreciate him and were needlessly difficult – 'unloving': he said it often – and because it was true he was shocked and guilty and even enraged when he was 'forced' into being unloving himself, or when he caught sight in himself of such a thing as cruelty, or cruel nosiness, or physical cowardice – God, how he hated being a coward – or hatred, physical hatred, even for me, if I was coy or evasive or disinterested or tired of him: it tore him apart literally – bits of madness, in varying degrees, would grip him as in a Greek play: I see his mouth, his salmon-colored mouth, showing various degrees of sarcasm – sarcasm mounting into bitterness and even a ferocity without tears that always suggested to me, as a child, that he was near tears but had forgotten in his ferocity that he was about to cry.

Or he would catch sight of some evidence, momentarily inescapable – in contradictory or foolish statements of his or in unkept promises that it was clear he had never meant to keep, had never made any effort to keep – that he was a fraud; and sometimes he would laugh because he was a fraud – a good-hearted fraud, he believed – or he would be sullen or angry, a fraud caught either by the tricks of language, so that in expressing affection absentmindedly he had expressed too much; or caught by greed and self-concern:

he hated the evidence that he was mutable as hell: that he loved sporadically and egoistically, and often with rage and vengeance, and that madness I mentioned earlier: he couldn't stand those things; he usually forgot them, but sometimes when he was being tender, or noble, or self-sacrificing, he would sigh and be very sad – maybe because the good stuff was temporary. I don't know. Or sad that he did it only when he had the time and was in the mood. Sometimes he forgot such things and was superbly confident – or was that a bluff?

I don't know. I really can't speak for him.

I look at my hand and then at his; it is not really conceivable to me that both are hands: mine is a sort of hand. He tells me over and over that I must not upset him – he tells me of my power over him – I don't know how to take such a fact – is it a fact? I stare at him. I gasp with the ache of life stirring in me – again: again: *again* – I ache with tentative and complete and then again tentative belief.

For a long time piety was anything at all sitting still or moving slowly and not rushing at me or away from me but letting me look at it or be near it without there being any issue of safety-about-to-be-lost.

This world is evasive.

But someone who lets you observe him is not evasive, is not hurtful, at that moment: it is like in sleep where *the other* waits – the Master of Dreams – and there are doors, doorways opening into farther rooms where there is an altered light, and which I enter to find – what? That someone is gone? That the room is empty? Or perhaps I find a vista, of rooms, of archways, and a window, and a peach tree in flower – a tree with peach-colored flowers in the solitude of night.

* * *

I am dying of grief, Daddy. I am waiting here, limp with abandonment, with exhaustion: perhaps I'd better believe in God. . . .

My father's virtues, those I dreamed about, those I saw when I was awake, those I understood and misunderstood, were, as I felt them, in dreams or wakefulness, when I was a child, like a broad highway opening into a small dusty town that was myself; and down that road came bishops and slogans, Chinese processions, Hasidim in a dance, the nation's honor and glory *in its young people*, baseball players, singers who sang 'with their whole hearts,' automobiles and automobile grilles, and grave or comic bits of instruction. This man is attached to me and makes me light up with festal affluence and oddity; he says, 'I think you love me.'

He was right.

He would move his head – his giant face – and you could observe in his eyes the small town that was me in its temporary sophistication, a small town giving proof on every side of its arrogance and its prosperity and its puzzled contentment.

He also instructed me in hatred: he didn't mean to, not openly: but I saw and picked up the curious buzzing of his puckered distastes, a nastiness of dismissal that he had: a fetor of let-them-all-kill-each-other. He hated lots of people, whole races: he hated ugly women.

He conferred an odd inverted splendor on awfulness – because *he* knew about it: he went into it every day. He told me not to want that, not to want to know about that: he told me to go on being just the way I was – 'a nice boy.'

When he said something was unbearable, he meant it; he meant he could not bear it.

In my memories of this time of my life, it seems to be

summer all the time, even when the ground is white: I suppose it seems like summer because I was never cold.

Ah: I wanted to see. . . .

My father, when he was low (in spirit), would make rounds, inside his head, checking on his consciousness, to see if it was safe from inroads by *the unbearable*: he found an all-is-well in a quiet emptiness. . . .

In an uninvadedness, he found the weary complacency and self-importance of All is Well.

(The women liked invasions – up to a point.)

One day he came home, mysterious, exalted, hatted and suited, roseate, handsome, a little sweaty – it really was summer that day. He was exalted – as I said – but nervous toward me, anxious with promises.

And he was, oh, somewhat angry, justified, toward the world, toward me, not exactly as a threat (in case I didn't respond) but as a jumble.

He woke me from a nap, an uneasy nap, lifted me out of bed, me, a child who had not expected to see him that afternoon – I was not particularly happy that day, not particularly pleased with him, not pleased with him at all, really.

He dressed me himself. At first he kept his hat on. After a while, he took it off. When I was dressed, he said, 'You're pretty sour today,' and he put his hat back on.

He hustled me down the stairs; he held my wrist in his enormous palm – immediate and gigantic to me and blankly suggestive of a meaning I could do nothing about except stare at blankly from time to time in my childish life.

We went outside into the devastating heat and glare, the blathering, humming afternoon light of a Midwestern summer day: a familiar furnace.

We walked along the street, past the large, silent houses, set, each one, in hard, pure light. You could not look directly at anything; the glare, the reflections were too strong.

Then he lifted me in his arms – aloft.

He was carrying me to help me because the heat was bad – and worse near the sidewalk, which reflected it upward into my face – and because my legs were short and I was struggling, because he was in a hurry and because he liked carrying me, and because I was sour and blackmailed him with my unhappiness, and he was being kind with a certain – limited – mixture of exasperation-turning-into-a-degree-of-mortal-love.

Or it was another time, really early in the morning, when the air was partly asleep, partly adance, but in veils, trembling with heavy moisture. Here and there, the air broke into a string of beads of pastel colors, pink, pale green, small rainbows, really small, and very narrow. Daddy walked rapidly. I bounced in his arms. My eyesight was unforced – it bounced, too. Things were more than merely present: they pressed against me: they had the aliveness of myth, of the beginning of an adventure when nothing is explained as yet.

All at once we were at the edge of a bankless river of yellow light. To be truthful, it was like a big, wooden beam of fresh, unweathered wood: but we entered it: and then it turned into light, cooler light than in the hot humming afternoon but full of bits of heat that stuck to me and then were blown away, a semiheat, not really friendly, yet reassuring: and very dimly sweaty; and it grew, it spread: this light turned into a knitted cap of light, fuzzy, warm, woven, itchy: it was pulled over my head, my hair, my forehead, my eyes, my nose, my mouth.

So I turned my face away from the sun – I turned it so it was pressed against my father's neck mostly – and then I knew, in a childish way, knew from the heat (of his neck, of his shirt collar), knew by childish deduction, that his face was unprotected from the luminousness all around us: and I looked; and it was so: his face, for the moment unembarrassedly, was caught in that light. In an accidental glory.

FRANK O'CONNOR

MY OEDIPUS COMPLEX

FATHER WAS IN the army all through the war – the first war, I mean – so, up to the age of five, I never saw much of him, and what I saw did not worry me. Sometimes I woke and there was a big figure in khaki peering down at me in the candlelight. Sometimes in the early morning I heard the slamming of the front door and the clatter of nailed boots down the cobbles of the lane. These were Father's entrances and exits. Like Santa Claus he came and went mysteriously.

In fact, I rather liked his visits, though it was an uncomfortable squeeze between Mother and him when I got into the big bed in the early morning. He smoked, which gave him a pleasant musty smell, and shaved, an operation of astounding interest. Each time he left a trail of souvenirs – model tanks and Gurkha knives with handles made of bullet cases, and German helmets and cap badges and buttonsticks, and all sorts of military equipment – carefully stowed away in a long box on top of the wardrobe, in case they ever came in handy. There was a bit of the magpie about Father; he expected everything to come in handy. When his back was turned, Mother let me get a chair and rummage through his treasures. She didn't seem to think so highly of them as he did.

The war was the most peaceful period of my life. The window of my attic faced southeast. My mother had curtained it, but that had small effect. I always woke with the first light and, with all the responsibilities of the previous day melted, feeling myself rather like the sun, ready to illumine and rejoice. Life never seemed so simple and clear and full of possibilities as then. I put my feet out from under the clothes – I called them Mrs Left and Mrs Right – and invented dramatic situations for them in which they discussed the problems of the day. At least Mrs Right did; she was very demonstrative, but I hadn't the same control of Mrs Left, so she mostly contented herself with nodding agreement.

They discussed what Mother and I should do during the day, what Santa Claus should give a fellow for Christmas, and what steps should be taken to brighten the home. There was that little matter of the baby, for instance. Mother and I could never agree about that. Ours was the only house in the terrace without a new baby, and Mother said we couldn't afford one till Father came back from the war because they cost seventeen and six. That showed how simple she was. The Geneys up the road had a baby, and everyone knew they couldn't afford seventeen and six. It was probably a cheap baby, and Mother wanted something really good, but I felt she was too exclusive. The Geneys' baby would have done us fine.

Having settled my plans for the day, I got up, put a chair under the attic window, and lifted the frame high enough to stick out my head. The window overlooked the front gardens of the terrace behind ours, and beyond these it looked over a deep valley to the tall, red-brick houses terraced up the opposite hillside, which were all still in shadow, while those at our side of the valley were all lit up, though with long strange shadows that made them seem unfamiliar; rigid and painted.

After that I went into Mother's room and climbed into the big bed. She woke and I began to tell her of my schemes. By this time, though I never seem to have noticed it, I was petrified in my nightshirt, and I thawed as I talked until, the last frost melted, I fell asleep beside her and woke again only when I heard her below in the kitchen, making the breakfast.

After breakfast we went into town; heard Mass at St Augustine's and said a prayer for Father, and did the shopping. If the afternoon was fine we either went for a walk in the country or a visit to Mother's great friend in the convent, Mother St Dominic. Mother had them all praying for Father, and every night, going to bed, I asked God to send him back safe from the war to us. Little, indeed, did I know what I was praying for!

One morning, I got into the big bed, and there, sure enough, was Father in his usual Santa Claus manner, but later, instead of uniform, he put on his best blue suit, and Mother was as pleased as anything. I saw nothing to be pleased about, because, out of uniform, Father was altogether less interesting, but she only beamed, and explained that our prayers had been answered, and off we went to Mass to thank God for having brought Father safely home.

The irony of it! That very day when he came in to dinner he took off his boots and put on his slippers, donned the dirty old cap he wore about the house to save him from colds, crossed his legs, and began to talk gravely to Mother, who looked anxious. Naturally, I disliked her looking anxious, because it destroyed her good looks, so I interrupted him.

'Just a moment, Larry!' she said gently.

This was only what she said when we had boring visitors, so I attached no importance to it and went on talking.

'Do be quiet, Larry!' she said impatiently. 'Don't you hear me talking to Daddy?'

This was the first time I had heard those ominous words, 'talking to Daddy', and I couldn't help feeling that if this was how God answered prayers, he couldn't listen to them very attentively.

'Why are you talking to Daddy?' I asked with as great a show of indifference as I could muster.

'Because Daddy and I have business to discuss. Now, don't interrupt again!'

In the afternoon, at Mother's request, Father took me for a walk. This time we went into town instead of out the country, and I thought at first, in my usual optimistic way, that it might be an improvement. It was nothing of the sort. Father and I had quite different notions of a walk in town. He had no proper interest in trams, ships, and horses, and the only thing that seemed to divert him was talking to fellows as old as himself. When I wanted to stop he simply went on, dragging me behind him by the hand; when he wanted to stop I had no alternative but to do the same. I noticed that it seemed to be a sign that he wanted to stop for a long time whenever he leaned against a wall. The second time I saw him do it I got wild. He seemed to be settling himself forever. I pulled him by the coat and trousers, but, unlike Mother who, if you were too persistent, got into a wax and said: 'Larry, if you don't behave yourself, I'll give you a good slap,' Father had an extraordinary capacity for amiable inattention. I sized him up and wondered would I cry, but he seemed to be too remote to be annoyed even by that. Really, it was like going for a walk with a mountain! He either ignored the wrenching and pummelling entirely, or else glanced down with a grin of amusement from his peak. I had never met anyone so absorbed in himself as he seemed.

At teatime, 'talking to Daddy' began again, complicated this time by the fact that he had an evening paper, and every few minutes he put it down and told Mother something new out of it. I felt this was foul play. Man for man, I was prepared to compete with him any time for Mother's attention, but when he had it all made up for him by other people it left me no chance. Several times I tried to change the subject without success.

'You must be quiet while Daddy is reading, Larry,' Mother said impatiently.

It was clear that she either genuinely liked talking to Father better than talking to me, or else that he had some terrible hold on her which made her afraid to admit the truth.

'Mummy,' I said that night when she was tucking me up, 'do you think if I prayed hard God would send Daddy back to the war?'

She seemed to think about that for a moment.

'No, dear,' she said with a smile. 'I don't think he would.'

'Why wouldn't he, Mummy?'

'Because there isn't a war any longer, dear.'

'But, Mummy, couldn't God make another war, if He liked?'

'He wouldn't like to, dear. It's not God who makes wars, but bad people.'

'Oh!' I said.

I was disappointed about that. I began to think that God wasn't quite what he was cracked up to be.

Next morning I woke at my usual hour, feeling like a bottle of champagne. I put out my feet and invented a long conversation in which Mrs Right talked of the trouble she had with her own father till she put him in the Home. I didn't quite know what the Home was but it sounded the right place for Father. Then I got my chair and stuck my head out of the attic window. Dawn was just breaking, with a guilty air that made me feel I had caught it in the act. My head bursting with stories and schemes, I stumbled in next door, and in the half-darkness scrambled into the big bed. There was no room at Mother's side so I had to get between her and Father. For the time being I had forgotten about him, and for several minutes I sat bolt upright, racking my brains to know what I could do with him. He was taking up more than his fair share of the bed, and I couldn't get comfortable, so I gave him several kicks that made him grunt and stretch. He made room all right, though. Mother waked and felt for me. I settled back comfortably in the warmth of the bed with my thumb in my mouth.

'Mummy!' I hummed, loudly and contentedly.

'Sssh! dear,' she whispered. 'Don't wake Daddy!'

This was a new development, which threatened to be even more serious than 'talking to Daddy.' Life without my early-morning conferences was unthinkable.

'Why?' I asked severely.

'Because poor Daddy is tired.'

This seemed to me a quite inadequate reason, and I was sickened by the sentimentality of her 'poor Daddy.' I never liked that sort of gush; it always struck me as insincere.

'Oh!' I said lightly. Then in my most winning tone: 'Do you know where I want to go with you today, Mummy?'

'No, dear,' she sighed.

'I want to go down the Glen and fish for thornybacks with my new net, and then I want to go out to the Fox and Hounds, and –'

'Don't-wake-Daddy!' she hissed angrily, clapping her hand across my mouth.

But it was too late. He was awake, or nearly so. He grunted and reached for the matches. Then he stared incredulously at his watch.

'Like a cup of tea, dear?' asked Mother in a meek, hushed voice I had never heard her use before. It sounded almost as though she were afraid.

'Tea?' he exclaimed indignantly. 'Do you know what the time is?'

'And after that I want to go up the Rathcooney Road,' I said loudly, afraid I'd forget something in all those interruptions.

'Go to sleep at once, Larry!' she said sharply.

I began to snivel. I couldn't concentrate, the way that pair went on, and smothering my early-morning schemes was like burying a family from the cradle.

Father said nothing, but lit his pipe and sucked it, looking out into the shadows without minding Mother or me. I knew he was mad. Every time I made a remark Mother hushed me irritably. I was mortified. I felt it wasn't fair; there was even something sinister in it. Every time I had pointed out to her the waste of making two beds when we could both sleep in one, she had told me it was healthier like that, and now here was this man, this stranger, sleeping with her without the least regard for her health!

He got up early and made tea, but though he brought Mother a cup he brought none for me.

'Mummy,' I shouted, 'I want a cup of tea, too.'

'Yes, dear,' she said patiently. 'You can drink from Mummy's saucer.'

That settled it. Either Father or I would have to leave the house. I didn't want to drink from Mother's saucer; I wanted to be treated as an equal in my own home, so, just to spite her, I drank it all and left none for her. She took that quietly, too.

But that night when she was putting me to bed she said gently:

'Larry, I want you to promise me something.'

'What is it?' I asked.

'Not to come in and disturb poor Daddy in the morning. Promise?'

'Poor Daddy' again! I was becoming suspicious of everything involving that quite impossible man.

'Why?' I asked.

'Because poor Daddy is worried and tired and he doesn't sleep well.'

'Why doesn't he, Mummy?'

'Well, you know, don't you, that while he was at the war Mummy got the pennies from the Post Office?'

'From Miss MacCarthy?'

'That's right. But now, you see, Miss MacCarthy hasn't any more pennies, so Daddy must go out and find us some. You know what would happen if he couldn't?'

'No,' I said, 'tell us.'

'Well, I think we might have to go out and beg for them like the poor old woman on Fridays. We wouldn't like that, would we?'

'No,' I agreed. 'We wouldn't.'

'So you'll promise not to come in and wake him?'

'Promise.'

Mind you, I meant that. I knew pennies were a serious matter, and I was all against having to go out and beg like the old woman on Fridays. Mother laid out all my toys in a complete ring round the bed so that, whatever way I got out, I was bound to fall over one of them.

When I woke I remembered my promise all right. I got up and sat on the floor and played – for hours, it seemed to me. Then I got my chair and looked out the attic window for more hours. I wished it was time for Father to wake; I wished someone would make me a cup of tea. I didn't feel in the least like the sun; instead, I was bored and so very, very cold! I simply longed for the warmth and depth of the big featherbed.

At last I could stand it no longer. I went into the next

44

room. As there was still no room at Mother's side I climbed over her and she woke with a start.

'Larry,' she whispered, gripping my arm very tightly, 'what did you promise?'

'But I did, Mummy,' I wailed, caught in the very act. 'I was quiet for ever so long.'

'Oh, dear, and you're perished!' she said sadly, feeling me all over. 'Now, if I let you stay will you promise not to talk?'

'But I want to talk, Mummy,' I wailed.

'That has nothing to do with it,' she said with a firmness that was new to me. 'Daddy wants to sleep. Now, do you understand that?'

I understood it only too well. I wanted to talk, he wanted to sleep – whose house was it, anyway?

'Mummy,' I said with equal firmness, 'I think it would be healthier for Daddy to sleep in his own bed.'

That seemed to stagger her, because she said nothing for a while.

'Now, once for all,' she went on, 'you're to be perfectly quiet or go back to your own bed. Which is it to be?'

The injustice of it got me down. I had convicted her out of her own mouth of inconsistency and unreasonableness, and she hadn't even attempted to reply. Full of spite, I gave Father a kick, which she didn't notice but which made him grunt and open his eyes in alarm.

'What time is it?' he asked in a panic-stricken voice, not looking at Mother but at the door, as if he saw someone there.

'It's early yet,' she replied soothingly. 'It's only the child. Go to sleep again. . . . Now, Larry,' she added, getting out of bed, 'you've wakened Daddy and you must go back.'

This time, for all her quiet air, I knew she meant it, and knew that my principal rights and privileges were as good as lost unless I asserted them at once. As she lifted me, I gave a screech, enough to wake the dead, not to mind Father. He groaned.

'That damn child! Doesn't he ever sleep?'

'It's only a habit, dear,' she said quietly, though I could see she was vexed.

'Well, it's time he got out of it,' shouted Father, beginning to heave in the bed. He suddenly gathered all the bedclothes about him, turned to the wall, and then looked back over his shoulder with nothing showing only two small, spiteful, dark eyes. The man looked very wicked.

To open the bedroom door, Mother had to let me down, and I broke free and dashed for the farthest corner, screeching. Father sat bolt upright in bed.

'Shut up, you little puppy!' he said in a choking voice.

I was so astonished that I stopped screeching. Never, never had anyone spoken to me in that tone before. I looked at him incredulously and saw his face convulsed with rage. It was only then that I fully realized how God had codded me, listening to my prayers for the safe return of this monster.

'Shut up, you!' I bawled, beside myself.

'What's that you said?' shouted Father, making a wild leap out of the bed.

'Mick, Mick!' cried Mother. 'Don't you see the child isn't used to you?'

'I see he's better fed than taught,' snarled Father, waving his arms wildly. 'He wants his bottom smacked.'

All his previous shouting was as nothing to these obscene words referring to my person. They really made my blood boil.

'Smack your own!' I screamed hysterically. 'Smack your own! Shut up! Shut up!'

At this he lost his patience and let fly at me. He did it with the lack of conviction you'd expect of a man under Mother's horrified eyes, and it ended up as a mere tap, but the sheer indignity of being struck at all by a stranger, a total stranger who had cajoled his way back from the war into our big bed as a result of my innocent intercession, made me completely dotty. I shrieked and shrieked, and danced in my bare feet, and Father, looking awkward and hairy in nothing but a short gray army shirt, glared down at me like a mountain out for murder. I think it must have been then that I realized he was jealous too. And there stood Mother in her nightdress, looking as if her heart was broken between us. I hoped she felt as she looked. It seemed to me that she deserved it all.

From that morning out my life was a hell. Father and I were enemies, open and avowed. We conducted a series of skirmishes against one another, he trying to steal my time with Mother and I his. When she was sitting on my bed, telling me a story, he took to looking for some pair of old boots which he alleged he had left behind him at the beginning of the war. While he talked to Mother I played loudly with my toys to show my total lack of concern. He created a terrible scene one evening when he came in from work and found me at his box, playing with his regimental badges, Gurkha knives and button-sticks. Mother got up and took the box from me.

'You mustn't play with Daddy's toys unless he lets you, Larry,' she said severely. 'Daddy doesn't play with yours.'

For some reason Father looked at her as if she had struck him and then turned away with a scowl.

'Those are not toys,' he growled, taking down the box again to see had I lifted anything. 'Some of those curios are very rare and valuable.'

But as time went on I saw more and more how he managed to alienate Mother and me. What made it worse was that I couldn't grasp his method or see what attraction he had for Mother. In every possible way he was less winning than I. He had a common accent and made noises at his tea. I thought for a while that it might be the newspapers she was interested in, so I made up bits of news of my own to read to her. Then I thought it might be the smoking, which I personally thought attractive, and took his pipes and went round the house dribbling into them till he caught me. I even made noises at my tea, but Mother only told me I was disgusting. It all seemed to hinge round that unhealthy habit of sleeping together, so I made a point of dropping into their bedroom and nosing round, talking to myself, so that they wouldn't know I was watching them, but they were never up to anything that I could see. In the end it beat me. It seemed to depend on being grown-up and giving people rings, and I realized I'd have to wait.

But at the same time I wanted him to see that I was only waiting, not giving up the fight. One evening when he was being particularly obnoxious, chattering away well above my head, I let him have it.

'Mummy,' I said, 'do you know what I'm going to do when I grow up?'

'No, dear,' she replied. 'What?'

'I'm going to marry you,' I said quietly.

Father gave a great guffaw out of him, but he didn't take me in. I knew it must only be pretense. And Mother, in spite of everything, was pleased. I felt she was probably relieved to know that one day Father's hold on her would be broken.

'Won't that be nice?' she said with a smile.

'It'll be very nice,' I said confidently. 'Because we're going to have lots and lots of babies.'

'That's right, dear,' she said placidly. 'I think we'll have one soon, and then you'll have plenty of company.'

I was no end pleased about that because it showed that in spite of the way she gave in to Father she still considered my wishes. Besides, it would put the Geneys in their place.

It didn't turn out like that, though. To begin with, she was very preoccupied – I supposed about where she would get the seventeen and six – and though Father took to staying out late in the evenings it did me no particular good. She stopped taking me for walks, became as touchy as blazes, and smacked me for nothing at all. Sometimes I wished I'd never mentioned the confounded baby – I seemed to have a genius for bringing calamity on myself.

And calamity it was! Sonny arrived in the most appalling hullabaloo – even that much he couldn't do without a fuss – and from the first moment I disliked him. He was a difficult child – so far as I was concerned he was always difficult – and demanded far too much attention. Mother was simply silly about him, and couldn't see when he was only showing off. As company he was worse than useless. He slept all day, and I had to go round the house on tiptoe to avoid waking him. It wasn't any longer a question of not waking Father. The slogan now was 'Don't-wake-Sonny!' I couldn't understand why the child wouldn't sleep at the proper time, so whenever Mother's back was turned I woke him. Sometimes to keep him awake I pinched him as well. Mother caught me at it one day and gave me a most unmerciful flaking.

One evening, when Father was coming in from work, I was playing trains in the front garden. I let on not to notice him; instead, I pretended to be talking to myself, and said in a loud voice: 'If another bloody baby comes into this house, I'm going out.'

Father stopped dead and looked at me over his shoulder.

'What's that you said?' he asked sternly.

'I was only talking to myself,' I replied, trying to conceal my panic. 'It's private.'

He turned and went in without a word. Mind you, I intended it as a solemn warning, but its effect was quite different. Father started being quite nice to me. I could understand that, of course. Mother was quite sickening about Sonny. Even at mealtimes she'd get up and gawk at him in the cradle with an idiotic smile, and tell Father to do the same. He was always polite about it, but he looked so puzzled you could see he didn't know what she was talking about. He complained of the way Sonny cried at night, but she only got cross and said that Sonny never cried except when there was something up with him – which was a flaming lie, because Sonny never had anything up with him, and only cried for attention. It was really painful to see how simple-minded she was. Father wasn't attractive, but he had a fine intelligence. He saw through Sonny, and now he knew that I saw through him as well.

One night I woke with a start. There was someone beside me in bed. For one wild moment I felt sure it must be Mother, having come to her senses and left Father for good, but then I heard Sonny in convulsions in the next room, and Mother saying: 'There! There! There!' and I knew it wasn't she. It was Father. He was lying beside me, wide awake, breathing hard and apparently as mad as hell.

After a while it came to me what he was mad about. It was his turn now. After turning me out of the big bed, he had been turned out himself. Mother had no consideration now for anyone but that poisonous pup, Sonny. I couldn't help feeling sorry for Father. I had been through it all myself, and even at that age I was magnanimous. I began to stroke him down and say: 'There! There!' He wasn't exactly responsive.

'Aren't you asleep either?' he snarled.

'Ah, come on and put your arm around us, can't you?' I said, and he did, in a sort of way. Gingerly, I suppose, is how you'd describe it. He was very bony but better than nothing.

At Christmas he went out of his way to buy me a really nice model railway.

RAYMOND CARVER

BICYCLES, MUSCLES, CIGARETS

IT HAD BEEN two days since Evan Hamilton had stopped smoking, and it seemed to him everything he'd said and thought for the two days somehow suggested cigarets. He looked at his hands under the kitchen light. He sniffed his knuckles and his fingers.

'I can smell it,' he said.

'I know. It's as if it sweats out of you,' Ann Hamilton said. 'For three days after I stopped I could smell it on me. Even when I got out of the bath. It was disgusting.' She was putting plates on the table for dinner. 'I'm so sorry, dear. I know what you're going through. But, if it's any consolation, the second day is always the hardest. The third day is hard, too, of course, but from then on, if you can stay with it that long, you're over the hump. But I'm so happy you're serious about quitting, I can't tell you.' She touched his arm. 'Now, if you'll just call Roger, we'll eat.'

Hamilton opened the front door. It was already dark. It was early in November and the days were short and cool. An older boy he had never seen before was sitting on a small, well-equipped bicycle in the driveway. The boy leaned forward just off the seat, the toes of his shoes touching the pavement and keeping him upright.

'You Mr Hamilton?' the boy said.

'Yes, I am,' Hamilton said. 'What is it? Is it Roger?'

'I guess Roger is down at my house talking to my mother. Kip is there and this boy named Gary Berman. It is about

55

my brother's bike. I don't know for sure,' the boy said, twisting the handle grips, 'but my mother asked me to come and get you. One of Roger's parents.'

'But he's all right?' Hamilton said. 'Yes, of course, I'll be right with you.'

He went into the house to put his shoes on.

'Did you find him?' Ann Hamilton said.

'He's in some kind of jam,' Hamilton answered. 'Over a bicycle. Some boy – I didn't catch his name – is outside. He wants one of us to go back with him to his house.'

'Is he all right?' Ann Hamilton said and took her apron off.

'Sure, he's all right.' Hamilton looked at her and shook his head. 'It sounds like it's just a childish argument, and the boy's mother is getting herself involved.'

'Do you want me to go?' Ann Hamilton asked.

He thought for a minute. 'Yes, I'd rather you went, but I'll go. Just hold dinner until we're back. We shouldn't be long.'

'I don't like his being out after dark,' Ann Hamilton said. 'I don't like it.'

The boy was sitting on his bicycle and working the hand-brake now.

'How far?' Hamilton said as they started down the sidewalk.

'Over in Arbuckle Court,' the boy answered, and when Hamilton looked at him, the boy added, 'Not far. About two blocks from here.'

'What seems to be the trouble?' Hamilton asked.

'I don't know for sure. I don't understand all of it. He and Kip and this Gary Berman are supposed to have used my brother's bike while we were on vacation, and I guess they wrecked it. On purpose. But I don't know. Anyway, that's what they're talking about. My brother can't find his bike and they had it last, Kip and Roger. My mom is trying to find out where it's at.'

'I know Kip,' Hamilton said. 'Who's this other boy?'

'Gary Berman. I guess he's new in the neighborhood. His dad is coming as soon as he gets home.'

They turned a corner. The boy pushed himself along, keeping just slightly ahead. Hamilton saw an orchard, and then they turned another corner onto a dead-end street. He hadn't known of the existence of this street and was sure he would not recognize any of the people who lived here. He looked around him at the unfamiliar houses and was struck with the range of his son's personal life.

The boy turned into a driveway and got off the bicycle and leaned it against the house. When the boy opened the front door, Hamilton followed him through the living room and into the kitchen, where he saw his son sitting on one side of a table along with Kip Hollister and another boy. Hamilton looked closely at Roger and then he turned to the stout, dark-haired woman at the head of the table.

'You're Roger's father?' the woman said to him.

'Yes, my name is Evan Hamilton. Good evening.'

'I'm Mrs Miller, Gilbert's mother,' she said. 'Sorry to ask you over here, but we have a problem.'

Hamilton sat down in a chair at the other end of the table and looked around. A boy of nine or ten, the boy whose bicycle was missing, Hamilton supposed, sat next to the woman. Another boy, fourteen or so, sat on the draining board, legs dangling, and watched another boy who was talking on the telephone. Grinning slyly at something that had just been said to him over the line, the boy reached over to the sink with a cigaret. Hamilton heard the sound of the cigaret sputting out in a glass of water. The boy who had brought him leaned against the refrigerator and crossed his arms.

'Did you get one of Kip's parents?' the woman said to the boy.

'His sister said they were shopping. I went to Gary Berman's and his father will be here in a few minutes. I left the address.'

'Mr Hamilton,' the woman said, 'I'll tell you what happened. We were on vacation last month and Kip wanted to borrow Gilbert's bike so that Roger could help him with Kip's paper route. I guess Roger's bike had a flat tire or something. Well, as it turns out –'

'Gary was choking me, Dad,' Roger said.

'What?' Hamilton said, looking at his son carefully.

'He was choking me. I got the marks.' His son pulled down the collar of his T-shirt to show his neck.

'They were out in the garage,' the woman continued. 'I didn't know what they were doing until Curt, my oldest, went out to see.'

'He started it!' Gary Berman said to Hamilton. 'He called me a jerk.' Gary Berman looked toward the front door.

'I think my bike cost about sixty dollars, you guys,' the boy named Gilbert said. 'You can pay me for it.'

'You keep out of this, Gilbert,' the woman said to him.

Hamilton took a breath. 'Go on,' he said.

'Well, as it turns out, Kip and Roger used Gilbert's bike to help Kip deliver his papers, and then the two of them, and Gary too, they say, took turns rolling it.'

'What do you mean "rolling it"?' Hamilton said.

'Rolling it,' the woman said. 'Sending it down the street with a push and letting it fall over. Then, mind you – and they just admitted this a few minutes ago – Kip and Roger took it up to the school and threw it against a goalpost.'

'Is that true, Roger?' Hamilton said, looking at his son again.

'Part of it's true, Dad,' Roger said, looking down and rubbing his finger over the table. 'But we only rolled it once. Kip did it, then Gary, and then I did it.'

'Once is too much,' Hamilton said. 'Once is one too many times, Roger. I'm surprised and disappointed in you. And you too, Kip,' Hamilton said.

'But you see,' the woman said, 'someone's fibbing tonight or else not telling all he knows, for the fact is the bike's still missing.'

The older boys in the kitchen laughed and kidded with the boy who still talked on the telephone.

'We don't know where the bike is, Mrs Miller,' the boy named Kip said. 'We told you already. The last time we saw it was when me and Roger took it to my house after we had it at school. I mean that was the next to last time. The very last time was when I took it back here the next morning and parked it behind the house.' He shook his head. 'We don't know where it is,' the boy said.

'Sixty dollars,' the boy named Gilbert said to the boy named Kip. 'You can pay me off like five dollars a week.'

'Gilbert, I'm warning you,' the woman said. 'You see, *they* claim,' the woman went on, frowning now, 'it disappeared from *here*, from behind the house. But how can we believe them when they haven't been all that truthful this evening?'

'We've told the truth,' Roger said. 'Everything.'

Gilbert leaned back in his chair and shook his head at Hamilton's son.

The doorbell sounded and the boy on the draining board jumped down and went into the living room.

A stiff-shouldered man with a crew haircut and sharp gray eyes entered the kitchen without speaking. He glanced at the woman and moved over behind Gary Berman's chair.

'You must be Mr Berman?' the woman said. 'Happy to

meet you. I'm Gilbert's mother, and this is Mr Hamilton, Roger's father.'

The man inclined his head at Hamilton but did not offer his hand.

'What's all this about?' Berman said to his son.

The boys at the table began to speak at once.

'Quiet down!' Berman said. 'I'm talking to Gary. You'll get your turn.'

The boy began his account of the affair. His father listened closely, now and then narrowing his eyes to study the other two boys.

When Gary Berman had finished, the woman said, 'I'd like to get to the bottom of this. I'm not accusing any one of them, you understand, Mr Hamilton, Mr Berman – I'd just like to get to the bottom of this.' She looked steadily at Roger and Kip, who were shaking their heads at Gary Berman.

'It's not true, Gary,' Roger said.

'Dad, can I talk to you in private?' Gary Berman said.

'Let's go,' the man said, and they walked into the living room.

Hamilton watched them go. He had the feeling he should stop them, this secrecy. His palms were wet, and he reached to his shirt pocket for a cigaret. Then, breathing deeply, he passed the back of his hand under his nose and said, 'Roger, do you know any more about this, other than what you've already said? Do you know where Gilbert's bike is?'

'No, I don't,' the boy said. 'I swear it.'

'When was the last time you saw the bicycle?' Hamilton said.

'When we brought it home from school and left it at Kip's house.'

'Kip,' Hamilton said, 'do you know where Gilbert's bicycle is now?'

'I swear I don't, either,' the boy answered. 'I brought it back the next morning after we had it at school and I parked it behind the garage.'

'I thought you said you left it behind the *house*,' the woman said quickly.

'I mean the house! That's what I meant,' the boy said.

'Did you come back here some other day to ride it?' she asked, leaning forward.

'No, I didn't,' Kip answered.

'Kip?' she said.

'I didn't! I don't know where it is!' the boy shouted.

The woman raised her shoulders and let them drop. 'How do you know who or what to believe?' she said to Hamilton. 'All I know is, Gilbert's missing a bicycle.'

Gary Berman and his father returned to the kitchen.

'It was Roger's idea to roll it,' Gary Berman said.

'It was yours!' Roger said, coming out of his chair. 'You wanted to! Then you wanted to take it to the orchard and strip it!'

'You shut up!' Berman said to Roger. 'You can speak when spoken to, young man, not before. Gary, I'll handle this – dragged out at night because of a couple of roughnecks! Now if either of you,' Berman said, looking first at Kip and then Roger, 'know where this kid's bicycle is, I'd advise you to start talking.'

'I think you're getting out of line,' Hamilton said.

'What?' Berman said, his forehead darkening. 'And I think you'd do better to mind your own business!'

'Let's go, Roger,' Hamilton said, standing up. 'Kip, you come now or stay.' He turned to the woman. 'I don't know what else we can do tonight. I intend to talk this over more with Roger, but if there is a question of restitution I feel since

Roger did help manhandle the bike, he can pay a third if it comes to that.'

'I don't know what to say,' the woman replied, following Hamilton through the living room. 'I'll talk to Gilbert's father – he's out of town now. We'll see. It's probably one of those things finally, but I'll talk to his father.'

Hamilton moved to one side so that the boys could pass ahead of him onto the porch, and from behind him he heard Gary Berman say, 'He called me a jerk, Dad.'

'He did, did he?' Hamilton heard Berman say. 'Well, he's the jerk. He looks like a jerk.'

Hamilton turned and said, 'I think you're seriously out of line here tonight, Mr Berman. Why don't you get control of yourself?'

'And I told you I think you should keep out of it!' Berman said.

'You get home, Roger,' Hamilton said, moistening his lips. 'I mean it,' he said, 'get going!' Roger and Kip moved out to the sidewalk. Hamilton stood in the doorway and looked at Berman, who was crossing the living room with his son.

'Mr Hamilton,' the woman began nervously but did not finish.

'What do you want?' Berman said to him. 'Watch out now, get out of my way!' Berman brushed Hamilton's shoulder and Hamilton stepped off the porch into some prickly cracking bushes. He couldn't believe it was happening. He moved out of the bushes and lunged at the man where he stood on the porch. They fell heavily onto the lawn. They rolled on the lawn, Hamilton wrestling Berman onto his back and coming down hard with his knees on the man's biceps. He had Berman by the collar now and began to pound his head against the lawn while the woman cried, 'God almighty, someone stop them! For God's sake, someone call the police!'

Hamilton stopped.

Berman looked up at him and said, 'Get off me.'

'Are you all right?' the woman called to the men as they separated. 'For God's sake,' she said. She looked at the men, who stood a few feet apart, backs to each other, breathing hard. The older boys had crowded onto the porch to watch; now that it was over, they waited, watching the men, and then they began feinting and punching each other on the arms and ribs.

'You boys get back in the house,' the woman said. 'I never thought I'd see,' she said and put her hand on her breast.

Hamilton was sweating and his lungs burned when he tried to take a deep breath. There was a ball of something in his throat so that he couldn't swallow for a minute. He started walking, his son and the boy named Kip at his sides. He heard car doors slam, an engine start. Headlights swept over him as he walked.

Roger sobbed once, and Hamilton put his arm around the boy's shoulders.

'I better get home,' Kip said and began to cry. 'My dad'll be looking for me,' and the boy ran.

'I'm sorry,' Hamilton said. 'I'm sorry you had to see something like that,' Hamilton said to his son.

They kept walking and when they reached their block, Hamilton took his arm away.

'What if he'd picked up a knife, Dad? Or a club?'

'He wouldn't have done anything like that,' Hamilton said.

'But what if he had?' his son said.

'It's hard to say what people will do when they're angry,' Hamilton said.

They started up the walk to their door. His heart moved when Hamilton saw the lighted windows.

'Let me feel your muscle,' his son said.

'Not now,' Hamilton said. 'You just go in now and have your dinner and hurry up to bed. Tell your mother I'm all right and I'm going to sit on the porch for a few minutes.'

The boy rocked from one foot to the other and looked at his father, and then he dashed into the house and began calling, 'Mom! Mom!'

He sat on the porch and leaned against the garage wall and stretched his legs. The sweat had dried on his forehead. He felt clammy under his clothes.

He had once seen his father – a pale, slow-talking man with slumped shoulders – in something like this. It was a bad one, and both men had been hurt. It had happened in a café. The other man was a farmhand. Hamilton had loved his father and could recall many things about him. But now he recalled his father's one fistfight as if it were all there was to the man.

He was still sitting on the porch when his wife came out.

'Dear God,' she said and took his head in her hands. 'Come in and shower and then have something to eat and tell me about it. Everything is still warm. Roger has gone to bed.'

But he heard his son calling him.

'He's still awake,' she said.

'I'll be down in a minute,' Hamilton said. 'Then maybe we should have a drink.'

She shook her head. 'I really don't believe any of this yet.'

He went into the boy's room and sat down at the foot of the bed.

'It's pretty late and you're still up, so I'll say good night,' Hamilton said.

'Good night,' the boy said, hands behind his neck, elbows jutting.

He was in his pajamas and had a warm fresh smell about him that Hamilton breathed deeply. He patted his son through the covers.

'You take it easy from now on. Stay away from that part of the neighborhood, and don't let me ever hear of you damaging a bicycle or any other personal property. Is that clear?' Hamilton said.

The boy nodded. He took his hands from behind his neck and began picking at something on the bedspread.

'Okay, then,' Hamilton said, 'I'll say good night.'

He moved to kiss his son, but the boy began talking.

'Dad, was Grandfather strong like you? When he was your age, I mean, you know, and you –'

'And I was nine years old? Is that what you mean? Yes, I guess he was,' Hamilton said.

'Sometimes I can hardly remember him,' the boy said. 'I don't want to forget him or anything, you know? You know what I mean, Dad?'

When Hamilton did not answer at once, the boy went on. 'When you were young, was it like it is with you and me? Did you love him more than me? Or just the same?' The boy said this abruptly. He moved his feet under the covers and looked away. When Hamilton still did not answer, the boy said, 'Did he smoke? I think I remember a pipe or something.'

'He started smoking a pipe before he died, that's true,' Hamilton said. 'He used to smoke cigarets a long time ago and then he'd get depressed with something or other and quit, but later he'd change brands and start in again. Let me show you something,' Hamilton said. 'Smell the back of my hand.'

The boy took the hand in his, sniffed it, and said, 'I guess I don't smell anything, Dad. What is it?'

Hamilton sniffed the hand and then the fingers. 'Now I can't smell anything, either,' he said. 'It was there before, but now it's gone.' Maybe it was scared out of me, he thought. 'I wanted to show you something. All right, it's late now. You better go to sleep,' Hamilton said.

The boy rolled onto his side and watched his father walk to the door and watched him put his hand to the switch. And then the boy said, 'Dad? You'll think I'm pretty crazy, but I wish I'd known you when you were little. I mean, about as old as I am right now. I don't know how to say it, but I'm lonesome about it. It's like – it's like I miss you already if I think about it now. That's pretty crazy, isn't it? Anyway, please leave the door open.'

Hamilton left the door open, and then he thought better of it and closed it halfway.

GRAHAM SWIFT

GABOR

'THIS IS GABOR,' said my father in a solemn, rehearsed, slightly wavering voice.

This was early in 1957. The war was still then quite fresh in the memory – even of those, like myself, who were born after it. Most households seemed to have framed photographs of figures in uniform, younger Dads, jauntily posed astride gun barrels, sitting on wings. Across the asphalt playground of my County Primary School the tireless struggle between English and Germans was regularly enacted. This was the only war, and its mythology ousted other, lesser intrusions into peace. I was too young to be aware of Korea. Then there was Suez, and Hungary.

'Gabor, this is Mrs Everett,' continued my father, enunciating slowly, 'Roger's Mummy. And this is Roger.'

Gabor was a lanky, dark-haired boy. He was dressed in a worn black jacket, a navy blue jumper, grey shorts, long grey socks and black shoes. Only the jacket and limp haversack, which he held in one hand, looked as if they were his. He had a thick, pale, straight-sided face, dark, horizontal eyes and a heavy mouth. Above his upper lip – I found this remarkable because he was only my age – was a crescent of gossamer, blackish hairs, like a faint moustache.

'Hello,' said my mother. Poised in the doorway, a fixed smile on her face, she was not at all clear what was to be done on occasions like this – whether motherly hugs or formality were required. She had half expected to be ready with blankets and soup.

Father and the newcomer stood pathetically immobile on the doorstep.

'Hello Gabor,' I said. One adult custom which seemed to me, for once, eminently practical, and vindicated by moments like this, was to shake hands. I reached out and took the visitor's wrist. Gabor went a salmony colour under his pale skin and spoke, for the first time, something incomprehensible. Mother and Father beamed benignly.

Gabor was a refugee from Budapest.

He was largely Father's doing. As I see it now, he was the sort of ideal foster-child he had always wanted; the answer to his forlorn, lugubrious, strangely martyrish prayers. Father had been an infantry officer during the war. He had been in North Africa and Normandy and at the liberation of concentration camps. He had seen almost all his friends killed around him. These experiences had given him the sense that suffering was the reality of life and that he had, in its presence, a peculiarly privileged understanding and power to reassure. Peace was for him a brittle veneer. He was not happy with his steady job in marine insurance, with the welfare state blandishments of those post-ration years. The contentments of fatherhood were equivocal. Now, as I look back, I see him waiting, watching over me, the corners of his stern mouth melancholically down-turned, waiting for me to encounter pain, grief, to discover that the world was not the sunny playground I thought it to be; so that he could bestow on me at last – with love I am sure – the benefits of his own experience, of his sorrow and strength, the large, tobaccoey palms of his protection.

I must have hurt him. While he lived with his war-time

ghosts, I was Richard Todd as Guy Gibson, with an RT mask made from my cupped hand, skimming ecstatically over our back lawn to bomb the Möhne Dam; or Kenneth More as Douglas Bader, cheerily cannonading the Luftwaffe.

Father scanned the newspapers. At headlines of trouble and disaster he looked wise. When the news broke of the uprising in Hungary and its suppression, and later the stories of orphaned Hungarian children of my generation coming to our shores, who needed to be found homes, he acquired a new mission in life.

I did not take kindly to Gabor's arrival. Though he was not a proper adoption and was to be with us at first only on what the authorities called a 'trial basis', I was envious of him as a substitute child – a replacement for myself. A minor war, of a kind unenvisaged, between England and Hungary, might have ensued in our house. But I saw how – from the very start – I had a facility with Gabor which my parents did not, and the pride I derived from this checked my resentment. Besides, Gabor had the appeal of someone who – like my father – had lived through real bloodshed and conflict, though in his case the experience was of the present, not of the past, and belonged moreover to a boy my own age. Perhaps – unlike my father – he would share in, and enhance, the flavour of my war games.

Should this happen it would assuage another long-standing grievance against my father. I could not understand why, seasoned veteran as he was, he did not participate in, at least smile on, my imaginary battles. I began to regard him as a bad sport and – more serious – to doubt his own quite authentic credentials. I tried to see in my father the features of my cinema heroes but failed to do so. He lacked their sun-burned cragginess or devil-may-care nonchalance. His own face was pasty, almost clerical. Consequently I suspected that his real exploits in the war (which I had only heard about vaguely) were lies.

The first lesson in English manners I taught Gabor was how to shoot Germans.

When I reflect on this, it was remarkable that he grasped what was required of him. Not only did he scarcely know a word of English, but there was an historical difficulty. I had absolutely no knowledge of Hungary's role in the Second World War (I was ignorant of its collaboration with the Nazis), which I took to be a national duel between England and Germany. Nonetheless, when the smoke from our bren guns or hand grenades had cleared, and I informed Gabor, after bravely reconnoitring, of another knocked out Panzer, another slaughtered infantry patrol, he would look up at me with implicit trust and grin, manically, jubilantly.

'*Jó*,' he would say. 'Good, good.'

Father was horrified at the careless zeal with which Gabor took part in my games. He could not understand how a boy who had known real violence, whose own parents (for all we knew) had been brutally killed, could lend a part so blithely to these fantasies. Some impenetrable barrier – like a glass wall which gave to my father the forlorn qualities of a goldfish – existed for him between reality and illusion so that he could not cross from one to the other. But it was not just this that distressed him. He saw how Gabor looked to me and not to him, how when he returned from our forays at the end of the garden Gabor would follow me like a trusted commander; how, from the very beginning, that affinity which he had hoped to have with this child of suffering had eluded him. I often wondered how they had managed together on that first day, when Father had gone up to 'collect' Gabor, like

72

some new purchase. I pictured them coming home, sitting mutely on opposite seats in the train compartment as they bounced through suburbia, like two lost souls.

'Gabor,' Father would say as he lit his cigarette after dinner, with the air of being about to make some vital announcement or to ask some searching question.

'*Igen?*' Gabor would say. 'Yes?'

Father would open his lips and look into Gabor's face, but something, some obstacle greater than that of language, would leave his words trapped.

'Nothing.'

'Yes?'

Gabor would go pink; his eyes would swivel in my direction.

Later, when Gabor had acquired a little more English, I asked him whether he liked my father. He gave a rambling, inarticulate answer, but I understood it to mean from the manner in which it was spoken that he was afraid of him. 'Tell me about your own mother and father,' I asked. Gabor's chin trembled, his lips twisted, his eyes went oily. For two days not even the prospect of Messerschmitts to be shot down persuaded him to smile.

Gabor went to my primary school with me. Except when he had special language tuition he was scarcely ever out of my company. He was an intelligent boy and after eighteen months his English was remarkably fluent. He had a way of sitting in the class with a sad expression on his face which made all the teachers fall for him. I alone knew he was not really sad. My closeness to Gabor gave me a superior standing among my English friends. Gabor would now and then mutter phrases in Hungarian because he knew this gave him a certain charisma; I would acquire even more charisma by casually translating them. In our newly-built brick school, with its grass verges and laburnums, its pictures of the Queen, maps of the Commonwealth and catkins in jam-jars, there was very little to disturb our lives. Only the eleven-plus hung, like a precipice, at the end of it all.

In the summer holidays Gabor and I would play till dark. At the end of our garden were the ramshackle plots of some old small holdings, and beyond that open fields and hedges sloping down to a road. These provided limitless scope for the waging of all types of warfare. We would scale the fence at the end of the garden, steal venturously past the tumbled sheds and smashed cucumber frames of the small holdings (still technically private property) and into the long grass beyond (later they built a housing estate over all this). At one point there was a sizeable crater in the ground, made by an actual flying-bomb in the war, filled with old paint cans and discarded prams. We would crouch in it and pretend we were being blown up; after each grisly death our bodies would be miraculously reconstituted. And everywhere, amongst the brambles and ground-ivy, there were little oddities, and discoveries, holes, tree-stumps, rusted tools, shattered porcelain, debris of former existences (I believed it was this ground-eye view of things which adults lacked), which gave to our patch of territory infinite imaginary depths.

A few impressions are sufficient to recapture that time: my mother's thin wail, as if she herself were lost, coming to us from the garden fence as the dark gathered: 'Roger! Gabor!'; Gabor's hoarse breath as we stalked, watching for enemy snipers, through the undergrowth, and the sporadic accompaniment, as if we shared a code, of his Hungarian: '*Menjünk! Megvárj!*'; Father, trying to restrain his anger, his disappointment, as we trailed in finally through our back door. He would scan disapprovingly our sweaty frames. He would furrow his brows at me as if I was Gabor's corruptor, and avoid Gabor's eyes. He would not dare raise his voice or lay a finger on me because of Gabor's presence. But even if Gabor had not been there he would have been afraid to use violence against me.

Father would not believe that Gabor was happy.

In the summer in which I waited with foreboding to hear the result of my eleven-plus, and Gabor also waited for his own fate to be sealed (he had not sat the exam, the education committee deciding he was a 'special case'), something happened to distract us from our usual bellicose games. We had taken to ranging far into the field and to the slopes leading down to the road, from which, camouflaged by bushes or the tall grass, we would machine-gun passing cars. The July weather was fine. One day we saw the motor-bike – an old BSA model (its enemy insignia visible through imaginary field-glasses) – lying near the road by a clump of hawthorn. Then there was the man and the girl, coming up one of the chalk gulleys to where the slope flattened off – talking, disappearing and reappearing, as they drew level with us, behind the banks and troughs of grass, like swimmers behind waves. They dipped for some time behind one of the grass billows, then appeared again, returning. The man held the girl's hand so she would not slip down the gulley. The girl drew her pleated skirt between her legs before mounting the pillion.

The motor-cycle appeared the next day at the same time, about five in the hot afternoon. Without saying anything to each other, we returned to the same vantage point the following day, and our attention turned from bombarding cars to stalking the man and the girl. On the fourth day we hid ourselves in a bed of ferns along the way the couple usually took, from which we could just see, through the fronds, a section of road, the top of the gulley and, in the other direction, at eye level, the waving ears of grass. Amongst the grass there were pink spears of willow herb. We heard the motor-bike, heard its engine cut, and saw the couple appear at the top of the gulley. The girl had a cotton skirt and a red blouse. The man wore a T-shirt with sweat at the arm-pits. They passed within a few feet of our look-out then settled some yards away in the grass. For a good while we saw just the tops of their heads or were aware of their presence only by the signs of movement in the taller stems of grass. Sounds of an indistinct and sometimes hectic kind reached us through the buzzing of bees and flies, the flutter of the breeze.

'*Mi az?*' whispered Gabor. '*Mit csinálnak?*' Something had made him forget his English.

After a silence we saw the girl sit up, her back towards us. Her shoulders were bare. She said something and laughed. She tilted her head back, shaking her dark hair, raising her face to the sun. Then, abruptly turning round and quite unwittingly smiling straight at us as if we had called her, she presented to us two white, sunlit, pink-flowered globes.

On the way back I suddenly realized that Gabor was trying not to cry. Bravely and wordlessly he was fighting back tears.

It so happened that that day was my parents' wedding anniversary. Every July this occasion was observed with punctilious sentimentality. Father would buy, on his way home from work, a bottle of my mother's favourite sweet white wine. My mother would cook 'Steak au Poivre' or 'Duck à l'Orange' and put on her organdie summer frock with bits of tulle around the neckline. They would eat. After the meal my father would wash up, sportingly wearing my mother's frilled apron. If the evening was fine they would sit outside, as if on some colonial patio. My father would fetch the Martell. My mother would put on the gramophone so that its sound wafted through the open window, 'Love is a Many Splendoured Thing' by Nat King Cole.

In previous years, given an early supper and packed off to bed, I had viewed this ritual from a distance, but now, perhaps for Gabor's sake, we were allowed to partake. Solemnly we sipped our half-glasses of sweet wine; solemnly we watched my parents. Inside, we still crouched, eyes wide, amongst the ferns.

'Fifteen years ago,' Father explained to Gabor, 'Roger's mother and I were married. Wed-ding ann-i-versary,' he articulated slowly so that Gabor might learn the expression.

I looked at Gabor. He kept his head lowered towards the tablecloth. His eyes were dry but I could see that at any moment they might start to gush.

Mother and Father ate their steaks. Their cutlery snipped and scraped meticulously. 'Gorgeous,' my father said after the second mouthful, 'beautiful.' My mother blinked and drew back her lips obligingly. I noticed that, despite her puffy dress, her chest was quite flat.

Gabor caught my eyes. Some sorrow, some memory of which none of us knew, could no longer be contained. Father intercepted the glance and turned with sudden heed towards Gabor. For the first time that evening something like anima-tion awoke in his eyes. I could imagine him, in a moment or so, pushing aside the remainder of his steak, rejecting with a knitting of his brows the bottle of Barsac, the bowl of roses in the middle of the table, grasping Gabor's hand and saying: 'Yes, of course, this is all nonsense . . .'

But this was not to be. I was determined, if only to defy Father, that Gabor would not cry. There was something in our experience of that afternoon, I recognized, for which tears were only one response. Gabor relowered his head, but I pinned my gaze, like a mind-reader, on his black mop of hair, and now and then his eyes flashed up at me. A nervous, expectant silence hung over the dinner table, in which my parents resumed eating, their elbows and jaws moving as if on wires. I saw them suddenly as Gabor must have seen them – as though they were not my parents at all. Each time Gabor looked up I caught his eyes, willing them not to moisten, to read my thoughts, to follow my own glance as I looked, now at my father's slack jowl, now at Mother's thin throat.

Gabor sat in front of the window. With the evening light behind him and his head bent forward, his infant moustache showed distinctly.

Then suddenly, like boys in church who cannot restrain a joke, he and I began to laugh.

I learnt that I was to be accepted at a new grammar school. Gabor, by some inept piece of administration, was granted a place at a similar, but not the same institution, and arrangements were made for continuing his private tuition. The whole question of Gabor's future, whether or not he was to be formally adopted into our family, was at this stage 'under review'. We had till September to pretend we were free. We watched for the couple on their motor-bike. They did not reappear. Somehow the final defeat or destruction of the last remnants of the German army, accomplished that summer, did not compensate for this. But our future advance in status brought with it new liberties. Father, whose face had become more dour (I sometimes wondered if he would be glad or sorry if the authorities decided that he could legally be Gabor's father), suggested that I might spend a day or two of our holiday showing Gabor round London. I knew this was a sacrifice. We had gone to London before, as a family, to show Gabor the sights. Gabor had trailed sheepishly after my parents, showing a token, dutiful interest. I knew that Father had had a dream once, which he had abandoned now, of taking Gabor by himself up to London, of showing him buildings and monuments, of extending to him his grown man's knowledge of the world, his shrewdness in its ways, of seeing his eyes kindle and warm as to a new-found father.

I took Gabor up on the train to London Bridge. I knew my way about from the times Father had taken me, and was a confident guide. We had fun. We rode on the Underground and on the top decks of buses. In the City and around St Paul's there were bomb-sites with willow-herb sprouting in the rubble. We bought ice-creams at the Tower and took each other's photo in Trafalgar Square. We watched Life Guards riding like toys down the Mall. When we got home (not long before Father himself came in from work) Father asked, seeing our contented faces: 'Well, and how was the big city?' Gabor replied, with the grave, wise expression he always had when concentrating on his English: 'I like London. Iss full history. Iss full history.'

RON CARLSON

THE H STREET
SLEDDING RECORD

THE LAST THING I do every Christmas Eve is go out in the yard and throw the horse manure onto the roof. It is a ritual. After we return from making our attempt at the H Street Sledding Record, and we sit in the kitchen sipping Egg Nog and listening to Elise recount the sled ride, and Elise then finally goes to bed happily, reluctantly, and we finish placing Elise's presents under the tree and we pin her stocking to the mantel – with care – and Drew brings out two other wrapped boxes which anyone could see are for me, and I slap my forehead having forgotten to get her anything at all for Christmas (except the prizes hidden behind the glider on the front porch), I go into the garage and put on the gloves and then into the yard where I throw the horse manure on the roof.

Drew always uses this occasion to call my mother. They exchange all the Christmas news, but the main purpose of the calls the last few years has been for Drew to stand in the window where she can see me out there lobbing the great turds up into the snow on the roof, and describe what I am doing to my mother. The two women take amusement from this. They say things like: 'You married him' and 'He's your son.' I take their responses to my rituals as a kind of fond, subtle support, which it is. Drew had said when she first discovered me throwing the manure on the roof, the Christmas that Elise was four, 'You're the only man I've ever known who did that.' See: a compliment.

83

But, now that Elise is eight, Drew has become cautious: 'You're fostering her fantasies.' I answer: 'Kids grow up too soon these days.' And then Drew has this: 'What do you want her to do, come home from school in tears when she's fifteen? Some kid in her class will have said – *Oh, sure, Santa's reindeer shit on your roof, eh?*' All I can say to Drew then is: 'Some kid in her class! Fine! I don't care what he says. I'm her father!'

I have thrown horse manure on our roof for four years now, and I plan to do it every Christmas Eve until my arm gives out. It satisfies me as a homeowner to do so, for the wonderful amber stain that is developing between the swamp cooler and the chimney and is visible all spring-summer-fall as you drive down the hill by our house, and for the way the two rose-bushes by the gutterspout have raged into new and profound growth during the milder months. And as a father, it satisfies me as a ritual that keeps my family together.

Drew has said, 'You want to create evidence? Let's put out milk and a cookie and then drink the milk and eat a bite out of the cookie.'

I looked at her. 'Drew,' I had said, 'I don't like cookies. I never ate a dessert in my life.'

And like I said, Drew has been a good sport, even the year I threw one gob short and ran a hideous smear down the kitchen window screen that hovered over all of us until March when I was able to take it down and go to the carwash.

I obtain the manure from my friend Bob, more specifically from his horse, Power, who lives just west of Heber. I drive out there the week before Christmas and retrieve about a bushel. I throw it on the roof a lump at a time, wearing a pair of welding gloves my father gave me.

*   *   *

I put the brake on the sled in 1975 when Drew was pregnant with Elise so we could still make our annual attempt on the W Street Record on Christmas Eve. It was the handle of a broken Louisville Slugger baseball bat, and still had the precise '34' stamped into the bottom. I sawed it off square and drilled and bolted it to the rear of the sled, so that when I pulled back on it, the stump would drag us to a stop. As it turned out, it was one of the two years when there was no snow, so we walked up to Eleventh Avenue and H Street (as we promised: rain or shine), sat on the Flexible Flyer in the middle of the dry street on a starry Christmas Eve, and I held her in my lap. We sat on the sled like two basketball players contesting possession of her belly. We talked a little about what it would be like when she took her leave from the firm and I had her home all day with the baby, and we talked remotely about whether we wanted any more babies, and we talked about the Record, which was set on December 24, 1969, the first Christmas of our marriage, when we lived in the neighborhood, on Fifth Avenue in an old barn of a house the total rent on which was seventy-two fifty, honest, and Drew had given me the sled that very night and we had walked out about midnight and been surprised by the blizzard. No wonder we took the sled and walked around the corner up H Street, up, up, up to Eleventh Avenue, and without speaking or knowing what we were doing, opening the door on the second ritual of our marriage, the annual sled ride (the first ritual was the word 'condition' and the activities it engendered in our droopy old bed).

At the top we scanned the city blurred in snow, sat on my brand new Christmas sled, and set off. The sled rode high and effortlessly through the deep snow, and suddenly, as our hearts started and our eyes began to burn against the snowy air, we were going faster than we'd planned. We crossed Tenth Avenue, nearly taking flight in the dip, and then descended in a dark rush: Ninth, Eighth, Seventh, soaring across each avenue, my arms wrapped around Drew like a straitjacket to drag her off with me if a car should cross in front of us on Sixth, Fifth Avenue, Fourth (this all took seconds, do you see?) until a car did turn onto H Street, headed our way, and we veered the new sled sharply, up over the curb, dousing our speed in the snowy yard one house from the corner of Third Avenue. Drew took a real faceful of snow, which she squirmed around and pressed into my neck, saying the words: 'Now, that's a record!'

And it was the Record: Eleventh to Third, and it stood partly because there had been two Christmas Eves with no snow, partly because of assorted spills brought on by too much speed, too much laughter, sometimes too much caution, and by a light blue Mercedes that crossed Sixth Avenue just in front of us in 1973. And though some years were flops, there was nothing about Christmas that Elise looked forward to as much as our one annual attempt at the H Street Sledding Record.

I think Drew wants another baby. I'm not sure, but I think she wants another child. The signs are so subtle they barely seem to add up, but she says things like, 'Remember before Elise went to school?' and 'There sure are a lot of women in their mid-thirties having babies.' I should ask her. But for some reason, I don't. We talk about everything, *everything*. But I've avoided this topic. I've avoided talking to Drew about this topic because I want another child too badly to have her not want one. I want a little boy to come into the yard on Christmas morning and say: 'See, there on the roof! The reindeers were there!' I want another kid to throw horse manure for. I'll wait. It will come up one of these days; I'll find a way to bring it up. Christmas is coming.

Every year on the day after Halloween, I tip the sled out of the rafters in the garage and Elise and I sponge it off, clean the beautiful dark blond wood with furniture polish, enamel the nicked spots on the runner supports with black engine paint, and rub the runners themselves with waxed paper. It is a ritual done on the same plaid blanket in the garage and it takes all afternoon. When we are finished, we lean the sled against the wall, and Elise marches into the house. 'Okay now,' she says to her mother: 'Let it snow.'

On the first Friday night in December, every year, Elise and Drew and I go buy our tree. This too is ritual. Like those families that bundle up and head for the wilderness so they can trudge through the deep, pristine snow, chop down their own little tree, and drag it, step by step, all the way home, we venture forth in the same spirit. Only we take the old pickup down to South State and find some joker who has thrown up two strings of colored lights around the corner of the parking lot of a burned-out Safeway and is proffering trees to the general public.

There is something magical and sad about this little forest just sprung up across from City Tacos, and Drew and Elise and I wander the wooded paths, waiting for some lopsided piñon to leap into our hearts.

The winter Drew and I became serious, when I was a senior and she was already in her first year at law school, I sold Christmas trees during vacation. I answered a card on a dorm bulletin board and went to work for a guy named Geer, who had cut two thousand squat piñons from the hills east of Cedar City and was selling them from a dirt lot on Redwood Road. Drew's mother invited me to stay with them for the holidays, and it gave me the chance to help Drew make up her mind about me. I would sell trees until midnight with Geer, and then drive back to Drew's and watch every old movie in the world and wrestle with Drew until our faces were mashed blue. I wanted to complicate things wonderfully by having her sleep with me. She wanted to keep the couch cushions between us and think it over. It was a crazy Christmas; we'd steam up the windows in the entire living room, but she never gave in. We did develop the joke about 'condition,' which we still use as a code word for desire. And later, I won't say if it was spring or fall, when Drew said to me, 'I'd like to see you about this condition,' I knew everything was going to be all right, and that we'd spend every Christmas together for the rest of our lives.

One night during that period, I delivered a tree to University Village, the married students' housing off Sunnyside. The woman was waiting for me with the door open as I dragged the pine up the steps to the second floor. She was a girl, really, about twenty, and her son, about three, watched the arrival from behind her. When I had the tree squeezed into the apartment, she asked if I could just hold it for a minute while she found her tree stand. If you ever need to stall for a couple of hours, just say you're looking for your tree stand; I mean the girl was gone for about twenty minutes. I stood and exchanged stares with the kid, who was scared; he didn't understand why some strange man had brought a tree into his home. 'Christmas,' I told him. 'Christmas. Can you say "Merry Christmas"?' I was an idiot.

When the girl returned with her tree stand, she didn't seem in any hurry to set it up. She came over to me and showed me the tree stand, holding it up for an explanation as to how it worked. Close up the girl's large eyes had an odd look in them, and then I understood it when she leaned through the boughs and kissed me. It was a great move; I had to hand it to her. There I was holding the tree; I couldn't make a move either way. It has never been among my policies to kiss strangers, but I held the kiss and the tree. Something about her eyes. She stepped back with the sweetest look of embarrassment and hope on her pretty face that I'd ever seen. 'Just loosen the turn-screws in the side of that stand,' I said, finally. 'And we can put this tree up.'

By the time I had the tree secured, she had returned again with a box of ornaments, lights, junk like that, and I headed for the door. 'Thanks,' I said. 'Merry Christmas.'

Her son had caught on by now and was fully involved in unloading the ornaments. The girl looked up at me, and this time I saw it all: her husband coming home in his cap and gown last June, saying, 'Thanks for law school, honey, but I met Doris at the Juris-Prudence Ball and I gotta be me. Keep the kid.'

The girl said to me, 'You could stay and help.'

It seemed like two statements to me, and so I answered them separately: 'Thank you. But I can't stay; that's the best help. Have a good Christmas.'

And I left them there together, decorating that tree; a ritual against the cold.

'How do you like it?' Elise says to me. She has selected a short broad bush which seems to have grown in two directions at once and then given up. She sees the look on my face and says, 'If you can't say anything nice, don't say anything at all. Besides, I've already decided: this is the tree for us.'

'It's a beautiful tree,' Drew says.

'Quasimodo,' I whisper to Drew. 'This tree's name is Quasimodo.'

'No whispering,' Elise says from behind us. 'What's he saying now, Mom?'

'He said he likes the tree, too.'

Elise is not convinced and after a pause she says, 'Dad. It's Christmas. Behave yourself.'

When we go to pay for the tree, the master of ceremonies is busy negotiating a deal with two kids, a punk couple. The tree man stands with his hands in his change apron and says, 'I gotta get thirty-five bucks for that tree.' The boy, a skinny kid in a leather jacket, shrugs and says he's only got twenty-eight bucks. His girlfriend, a large person with a bowl haircut and a monstrous black overcoat festooned with buttons, is wailing, 'Please! Oh no! Jimmy! Jimmy! I love that tree! I want that tree!' The tree itself stands aside, a noble pine of about twelve feet. Unless these kids live in a gymnasium, they're buying a tree bigger than their needs.

Jimmy retreats to his car, an old Plymouth big as a boat. 'Police Rule' is spraypainted across both doors in balloon letters. He returns instantly and opens a hand full of coins. 'I'll give you thirty-one bucks, fifty-five cents, and my watch.' To our surprise, the wily tree man takes the watch to examine it. When I see that, I give Elise four dollars and tell her to give it to Kid Jimmy and say, 'Merry Christmas.' His girlfriend is still wailing but now a minor refrain of 'Oh Jimmy, that tree! Oh Jimmy, etc.' I haven't seen a public display of emotion and longing of this magnitude in Salt Lake City, ever. I watch Elise give the boy the money, but instead of saying, 'Merry Christmas,' I hear her say instead: 'Here, Jimmy. Santa says keep your watch.'

Jimmy pays for the tree, and his girl – and this is the truth – jumps on him, wrestles him to the ground in gratitude and smothers him for nearly a minute. There have never been people happier about a Christmas tree. We pay quickly and head out before Jimmy or his girlfriend can think to begin thanking us.

On the way home in the truck, I say to Elise, 'Santa says keep your watch, eh?'

'Yes, he does,' she smiles.

'How old are you, anyway?'

'Eight.'

It's an old joke, and Drew finishes it for me: 'When he was your age, he was seven.'

We will go home and while the two women begin decorating the tree with the artifacts of our many Christmases together, I will thread popcorn onto a long string. It is a ritual I prefer for its uniqueness; the fact that once a year I get to sit and watch the two girls I am related to move about a tree inside our home, while I sit nearby and sew food.

On the morning of the twenty-fourth of December, Elise comes into our bedroom, already dressed for sledding. 'Good news,' she says. 'We've got a shot at the record.'

Drew rises from the pillow and peeks out the blind. 'It's snowing,' she says.

Christmas Eve, we drive back along the snowy Avenues, and park on Fifth, as always. 'I know,' Elise says, hopping out of the car. 'You two used to live right over there before you had me and it was a swell place and only cost seventy-two fifty a month, honest.'

Drew looks at me and smiles.

'How old are you?' I ask Elise, but she is busy towing the sled away, around the corner, up toward Eleventh Avenue. It is still snowing, petal flakes, teeming by the streetlamps, trying to carry the world away. I take Drew's hand and we walk up the middle of H Street behind our daughter. There is no traffic, but the few cars have packed the tender snow perfectly. It *could* be a record. On Ninth Avenue, Drew stops me in the intersection, the world still as snow, and kisses me. 'I love you,' she says.

'What a planet,' I whisper. 'To allow such a thing.'

By the time we climb to Eleventh Avenue, Elise is seated on the sled, ready to go. 'What are you guys waiting for, Christmas?' she says and then laughs at her own joke. Then she becomes all business: 'Listen, Dad, I figure if you stay just a little to the left of the tire tracks we could go all the way. And no wobbling!' She's referring to last year's record attempt, which was extinguished in the Eighth Avenue block when we laughed ourselves into a fatal wobble and ended in a slush heap.

We arrange ourselves on the sled, as we have each Christmas Eve for eight years. As I reach my long legs around these two women, I sense their excitement. 'It's going to be a record!' Elise whispers into the whispering snow.

'Do you think so?' Drew asks. She also feels this could be the night.

'Oh yeah!' Elise says. 'The conditions are perfect!'

'What do you think?' Drew turns to me.

'Well, the conditions are perfect.'

When I say *conditions*, Drew leans back and kisses me. So I press: 'There's still room on the sled,' I say, pointing to the 'F' in Flexible Flyer that is visible between Elise's legs. 'There's still room for another person.'

'Who?' Elise asks.

'Your little brother,' Drew says, squeezing my knees.

And that's about all that was said, sitting up there on Eleventh Avenue on Christmas Eve on a sled which is as old as my marriage with a brake that is as old as my daughter. Later tonight I will stand in my yard and throw this year's reindeer droppings on my very own home. I love Christmas.

Now the snow spirals around us softly. I put my arms around my family and lift my feet onto the steering bar. We begin to slip down H Street. We are trying for the record. The conditions, as you know by now, are perfect.

ANDRE DUBUS

A FATHER'S STORY

MY NAME IS Luke Ripley, and here is what I call my life: I own a stable of thirty horses, and I have young people who teach riding, and we board some horses too. This is in north-eastern Massachusetts. I have a barn with an indoor ring, and outside I've got two fenced-in rings and a pasture that ends at a woods with trails. I call it my life because it looks like it is, and people I know call it that, but it's a life I can get away from when I hunt and fish, and some nights after dinner when I sit in the dark in the front room and listen to opera. The room faces the lawn and the road, a two-lane country road. When cars come around the curve northwest of the house, they light up the lawn for an instant, the leaves of the maple out by the road and the hemlock closer to the window. Then I'm alone again, or I'd appear to be if someone crept up to the house and looked through a window: a big-gutted grey-haired guy, drinking tea and smoking cigarettes, staring out at the dark woods across the road, listening to a grieving soprano.

My real life is the one nobody talks about anymore, except Father Paul LeBoeuf, another old buck. He has a decade on me: he's sixty-four, a big man, bald on top with grey at the sides; when he had hair, it was black. His face is ruddy, and he jokes about being a whiskey priest, though he's not. He gets outdoors as much as he can, goes for a long walk every morning, and hunts and fishes with me. But I can't get him on a horse anymore. Ten years ago I could badger him into

97

a trail ride; I had to give him a western saddle, and he'd hold the pommel and bounce through the woods with me, and be sore for days. He's looking at seventy with eyes that are younger than many I've seen in people in their twenties. I do not remember ever feeling the way they seem to; but I was lucky, because even as a child I knew that life would try me, and I must be strong to endure, though in those early days I expected to be tortured and killed for my faith, like the saints I learned about in school.

Father Paul's family came down from Canada, and he grew up speaking more French than English, so he is different from the Irish priests who abound up here. I do not like to make general statements, or even to hold general beliefs, about people's blood, but the Irish do seem happiest when they're dealing with misfortune or guilt, either their own or somebody else's, and if you think you're not a victim of either one, you can count on certain Irish priests to try to change your mind. On Wednesday nights Father Paul comes to dinner. Often he comes on other nights too, and once, in the old days when we couldn't eat meat on Fridays, we bagged our first ducks of the season on a Friday, and as we drove home from the marsh, he said: For the purposes of Holy Mother Church, I believe a duck is more a creature of water than land, and is not rightly meat. Sometimes he teases me about never putting anything in his Sunday collection, which he would not know about if I hadn't told him years ago. I would like to believe I told him so we could have philosophical talk at dinner, but probably the truth is I suspected he knew, and I did not want him to think I so loved money that I would not even give his church a coin on Sunday. Certainly the ushers who pass the baskets know me as a miser.

I don't feel right about giving money for buildings, places. This starts with the Pope, and I cannot respect one of them till he sells his house and everything in it, and that church too, and uses the money to feed the poor. I have rarely, and maybe never, come across saintliness, but I feel certain it cannot exist in such a place. But I admit, also, that I know very little, and maybe the popes live on a different plane and are tried in ways I don't know about. Father Paul says his own church, St John's, is hardly the Vatican. I like his church: it is made of wood, and has a simple altar and crucifix, and no padding on the kneelers. He does not have to lock its doors at night. Still it is a place. He could say Mass in my barn. I know this is stubborn, but I can find no mention by Christ of maintaining buildings, much less erecting them of stone or brick, and decorating them with pieces of metal and mineral and elements that people still fight over like barbarians. We had a Maltese woman taking riding lessons, she came over on the boat when she was ten, and once she told me how the nuns in Malta used to tell the little girls that if they wore jewelry, rings and bracelets and necklaces, in purgatory snakes would coil around their fingers and wrists and throats. I do not believe in frightening children or telling them lies, but if those nuns saved a few girls from devotion to things, maybe they were right. That Maltese woman laughed about it, but I noticed she wore only a watch, and that with a leather strap.

The money I give to the church goes in people's stomachs, and on their backs, down in New York City. I have no delusions about the worth of what I do, but I feel it's better to feed somebody than not. There's a priest in Times Square giving shelter to runaway kids, and some Franciscans who run a bread line; actually it's a morning line for coffee and a roll, and Father Paul calls it the continental breakfast for winos and bag ladies. He is curious about how much I am sending, and I know why: he guesses I send a lot, he has said probably more than tithing, and he is right; he wants to know how much because he believes I'm generous and good, and he is wrong about that; he has never had much money and does not know how easy it is to write a check when you have everything you will ever need, and the figures are mere numbers, and represent no sacrifice at all. Being a real Catholic is too hard; if I were one, I would do with my house and barn what I want the Pope to do with his. So I do not want to impress Father Paul, and when he asks me how much, I say I can't let my left hand know what my right is doing.

He came on Wednesday nights when Gloria and I were married, and the kids were young; Gloria was a very good cook (I assume she still is, but it is difficult to think of her in the present), and I liked sitting at the table with a friend who was also a priest. I was proud of my handsome and healthy children. This was long ago, and they were all very young and cheerful and often funny, and the three boys took care of their baby sister, and did not bully or tease her. Of course they did sometimes, with that excited cruelty children are prone to, but not enough so that it was part of her days. On the Wednesday after Gloria left with the kids and a U-Haul trailer, I was sitting on the front steps, it was summer, and I was watching cars go by on the road, when Father Paul drove around the curve and into the driveway. I was ashamed to see him because he is a priest and my family was gone, but I was relieved too. I went to the car to greet him. He got out smiling, with a bottle of wine, and shook my hand, then pulled me to him, gave me a quick hug, and said: 'It's Wednesday, isn't it? Let's open some cans.'

With arms about each other we walked to the house, and it was good to know he was doing his work but coming as a friend too, and I thought what good work he had. I have no calling. It is for me to keep horses.

In that other life, anyway. In my real one I go to bed early and sleep well and wake at four forty-five, for an hour of silence. I never want to get out of bed then, and every morning I know I can sleep for another four hours, and still not fail at any of my duties. But I get up, so have come to believe my life can be seen in miniature in that struggle in the dark of morning. While making the bed and boiling water for coffee, I talk to God: I offer Him my day, every act of my body and spirit, my thoughts and moods, as a prayer of thanksgiving, and for Gloria and my children and my friends and two women I made love with after Gloria left. This morning offertory is a habit from my boyhood in a Catholic school; or then it was a habit, but as I kept it and grew older it became a ritual. Then I say the Lord's Prayer, trying not to recite it, and one morning it occurred to me that a prayer, whether recited or said with concentration, is always an act of faith.

I sit in the kitchen at the rear of the house and drink coffee and smoke and watch the sky growing light before sunrise, the trees of the woods near the barn taking shape, becoming single pines and elms and oaks and maples. Sometimes a rabbit comes out of the treeline, or is already sitting there, invisible till the light finds him. The birds are awake in the trees and feeding on the ground, and the little ones, the purple finches and titmice and chickadees, are at the feeder I rigged outside the kitchen window; it is too small for pigeons to get a purchase. I sit and give myself to coffee and tobacco, that get me brisk again, and I watch and listen. In the first year or so after I lost my family, I played the radio in the mornings. But I overcame that, and now I rarely play it at all. Once in the mail I received a questionnaire asking me to write down everything I watched on television during the week they had chosen. At the end of those seven days

I wrote in *The Wizard of Oz* and returned it. That was in winter and was actually a busy week for my television, which normally sits out the cold months without once warming up. Had they sent the questionnaire during baseball season, they would have found me at my set. People at the stables talk about shows and performers I have never heard of, but I cannot get interested; when I am in the mood to watch television, I go to a movie or read a detective novel. There are always good detective novels to be found, and I like remembering them next morning with my coffee.

I also think of baseball and hunting and fishing, and of my children. It is not painful to think about them anymore, because even if we had lived together, they would be gone now, grown into their own lives, except Jennifer. I think of death too, not sadly, or with fear, though something like excitement does run through me, something more quickening than the coffee and tobacco. I suppose it is an intense interest, and an outright distrust: I never feel certain that I'll be here watching birds eating at tomorrow's daylight. Sometimes I try to think of other things, like the rabbit that is warm and breathing but not there till twilight. I feel on the brink of something about the life of the senses, but either am not equipped to go further or am not interested enough to concentrate. I have called all of this thinking, but it is not, because it is unintentional; what I'm really doing is feeling the day, in silence, and that is what Father Paul is doing too on his five-to-ten-mile walks.

When the hour ends I take an apple or carrot and I go to the stable and tack up a horse. We take good care of these horses, and no one rides them but students, instructors, and me, and nobody rides the horses we board unless an owner asks me to. The barn is dark and I turn on lights and take some deep breaths, smelling the hay and horses and their manure, both fresh and dried, a combined odor that you either like or you don't. I walk down the wide space of dirt between stalls, greeting the horses, joking with them about their quirks, and choose one for no reason at all other than the way it looks at me that morning. I get my old English saddle that has smoothed and darkened through the years, and go into the stall, talking to this beautiful creature who'll swerve out of a canter if a piece of paper blows in front of him, and if the barn catches fire and you manage to get him out he will, if he can get away from you, run back into the fire, to his stall. Like the smells that surround them, you either like them or you don't. I love them, so am spared having to try to explain why. I feed one the carrot or apple and tack up and lead him outside, where I mount, and we go down the driveway to the road and cross it and turn northwest and walk then trot then canter to St John's.

A few cars are on the road, their drivers looking serious about going to work. It is always strange for me to see a woman dressed for work so early in the morning. You know how long it takes them, with the makeup and hair and clothes, and I think of them waking in the dark of winter or early light of other seasons, and dressing as they might for an evening's entertainment. Probably this strikes me because I grew up seeing my father put on those suits he never wore on weekends or his two weeks off, and so am accustomed to the men, but when I see these women I think something went wrong, to send all those dressed-up people out on the road when the dew hasn't dried yet. Maybe it's because I so dislike getting up early, but am also doing what I choose to do, while they have no choice. At heart I am lazy, yet I find such peace and delight in it that I believe it is a natural state, and in what looks like my laziest periods I am closest to my center. The ride to St John's is fifteen minutes. The horses and I do it in all weather; the road is well plowed in winter, and there are only a few days a year when ice makes me drive the pickup. People always look at someone on horseback, and for a moment their faces change and many drivers and I wave to each other. Then at St John's, Father Paul and five or six regulars and I celebrate the Mass.

Do not think of me as a spiritual man whose every thought during those twenty-five minutes is at one with the words of the Mass. Each morning I try, each morning I fail, and know that always I will be a creature who, looking at Father Paul and the altar, and uttering prayers, will be distracted by scrambled eggs, horses, the weather, and memories and day-dreams that have nothing to do with the sacrament I am about to receive. I can receive, though: the Eucharist, and also, at Mass and at other times, moments and even minutes of contemplation. But I cannot achieve contemplation, as some can; and so, having to face and forgive my own failures, I have learned from them both the necessity and wonder of ritual. For ritual allows those who cannot will themselves out of the secular to perform the spiritual, as dancing allows the tongue-tied man a ceremony of love. And, while my mind dwells on breakfast, or Major or Duchess tethered under the church eave, there is, as I take the Host from Father Paul and place it on my tongue and return to the pew, a feeling that I am thankful I have not lost in the forty-eight years since my first Communion. At its center is excitement; spreading out from it is the peace of certainty. Or the certainty of peace. One night Father Paul and I talked about faith. It was long ago, and all I remember is him saying: Belief is believing in God; faith is believing that God believes in you. That is the excitement, and the peace; then the Mass is over, and I go into the sacristy and we have a cigarette and chat, the mystery ends, we are two men talking like any two men on a morning in America, about baseball, plane crashes, presidents, governors, murders, the sun, the clouds. Then I go to the horse and ride back to the life people see, the one in which I move and talk, and most days I enjoy it.

It is late summer now, the time between fishing and hunting, but a good time for baseball. It has been two weeks since Jennifer left, to drive home to Gloria's after her summer visit. She is the only one who still visits; the boys are married and have children, and sometimes fly up for a holiday, or I fly down or west to visit one of them. Jennifer is twenty, and I worry about her the way fathers worry about daughters but not sons. I want to know what she's up to, and at the same time I don't. She looks athletic, and she is: she swims and runs and of course rides. All my children do. When she comes for six weeks in summer, the house is loud with girls, friends of hers since childhood, and new ones. I am glad she kept the girl friends. They have been young company for me and, being with them, I have been able to gauge her growth between summers. On their riding days, I'd take them back to the house when their lessons were over and they had walked the horses and put them back in the stalls, and we'd have lemonade or Coke, and cookies if I had some, and talk until their parents came to drive them home. One year their breasts grew, so I wasn't startled when I saw Jennifer in July. Then they were driving cars to the stable, and beginning to look like young women, and I was passing out beer and ashtrays and they were talking about college.

When Jennifer was here in summer, they were at the house most days. I would say generally that as they got older they became quieter, and though I enjoyed both, I sometimes missed the giggles and shouts. The quiet voices, just low enough for me not to hear from wherever I was, rising and falling in proportion to my distance from them, frightened me. Not that I believed they were planning or recounting anything really wicked, but there was a female seriousness about them, and it was secretive, and of course I thought: love, sex. But it was more than that: it was womanhood they were entering, the deep forest of it, and no matter how many women and men too are saying these days that there is little difference between us, the truth is that men find their way into that forest only on clearly marked trails, while women move about in it like birds. So hearing Jennifer and her friends talking so quietly, yet intensely, I wanted very much to have a wife.

But not as much as in the old days, when Gloria had left but her presence was still in the house as strongly as if she had only gone to visit her folks for a week. There were no clothes or cosmetics, but potted plants endured my neglectful care as long as they could, and slowly died; I did not kill them on purpose, to exorcise the house of her, but I could not remember to water them. For weeks, because I did not use it much, the house was as neat as she had kept it, though dust layered the order she had made. The kitchen went first: I got the dishes in and out of the dishwasher and wiped the top of the stove, but did not return cooking spoons and pot holders to their hooks on the wall, and soon the burners and oven were caked with spillings, the refrigerator had more space and was spotted with juices. The living room and my bedroom went next; I did not go into the children's rooms except on bad nights when I went from room to room and looked and touched and smelled, so they did not lose their order until a year later when the kids came for six weeks. It was three months before I ate the last of the food Gloria had cooked and frozen: I remember it was a beef stew, and very good. By then I had four cookbooks, and was boasting a bit, and talking about recipes with the women at the stables, and looking forward to cooking for Father Paul. But I never looked forward to cooking at night only for myself, though I made myself do it; on some nights I gave in to my daily temptation, and took a newspaper or detective novel to a restaurant. By the end of the second year, though, I had stopped turning on the radio as soon as I woke in the morning, and was able to be silent and alone in the evening too, and then I enjoyed my dinners.

It is not hard to live through a day, if you can live through a moment. What creates despair is the imagination, which pretends there is a future, and insists on predicting millions of moments, thousands of days, and so drains you that you cannot live the moment at hand. That is what Father Paul told me in those first two years, on some of the bad nights when I believed I could not bear what I had to: the most painful loss was my children, then the loss of Gloria, whom I still loved despite or maybe because of our long periods of sadness that rendered us helpless, so neither of us could break out of it to give a hand to the other. Twelve years later I believe ritual would have healed us more quickly than the repetitious talks we had, perhaps even kept us healed. Marriages have lost that, and I wish I had known then what I know now, and we had performed certain acts together every day, no matter how we felt, and perhaps then we could have subordinated feeling to action, for surely that is the essence of love. I know this from my distractions during Mass, and during everything else I do, so that my actions and feelings are seldom one. It does happen every day, but in proportion to everything else in a day, it is rare, like joy. The third most painful loss, which became second and sometimes first as months passed, was the knowledge that I could never marry again, and so dared not even keep company with a woman.

On some of the bad nights I was bitter about this with Father Paul, and I so pitied myself that I cried, or nearly did, speaking with damp eyes and breaking voice. I believe that celibacy is for him the same trial it is for me, not of the flesh, but the spirit: the heart longing to love. But the difference is he chose it, and did not wake one day to a life with thirty horses. In my anger I said I had done my service to love and chastity, and I told him of the actual physical and spiritual pain of practicing rhythm: nights of striking the mattress with a fist, two young animals lying side by side in heat, leaving the bed to pace, to smoke, to curse, and too passionate to question, for we were so angered and oppressed by our passion that we could see no further than our loins. So now I understand how people can be enslaved for generations before they throw down their tools or use them as weapons, the form of their slavery – the cotton fields, the shacks and puny cupboards and untended illnesses – absorbing their emotions and thoughts until finally they have little or none at all to direct with clarity and energy at the owners and legislators. And I told him of the trick of passion and its slaking: how during what we had to believe were safe periods, though all four children were conceived at those times, we were able with some coherence to question the tradition and reason and justice of the law against birth control, but not with enough conviction to soberly act against it, as though regular satisfaction in bed tempered our revolutionary as well as our erotic desires. Only when abstinence drove us hotly away from each other did we receive an urge so strong it lasted all the way to the drugstore and back; but always, after release, we threw away the remaining condoms; and after going through this a few times, we knew what would happen, and from then on we submitted to the calendar she so precisely marked on the bedroom wall. I told him that living two lives each month, one as celibates, one as lovers, made us tense and short-tempered, so we snapped at each other like dogs.

To have endured that, to have reached a time when we burned slowly and could gain from bed the comfort of lying down at night with one who loves you and whom you love, could for weeks on end go to bed tired and peacefully sleep after a kiss, a touch of the hands, and then to be thrown out of the marriage like a bundle from a moving freight car, was unjust, was intolerable, and I could not or would not muster the strength to endure it. But I did, a moment at a time, a day, a night, except twice, each time with a different woman and more than a year apart, and this was so long ago that I clearly see their faces in my memory, can hear the pitch of their voices, and the way they pronounced words, one with a Massachusetts accent, one midwestern, but I feel as though I only heard about them from someone else. Each rode at the stables and was with me for part of an evening; one was badly married, one divorced, so none of us was free. They did not understand this Catholic view, but they were understanding about my having it, and I remained friends with both of them until the married one left her husband and went to Boston, and the divorced one moved to Maine. After both those evenings, those good women, I went to Mass early while Father Paul was still in the confessional, and received his absolution. I did not tell him who I was, but of course he knew, though I never saw it in his eyes. Now my longing for a wife comes only once in a while, like a cold: on some late afternoons when I am alone in the barn, then I lock up and walk to the house, daydreaming, then suddenly look at it and see it empty, as though for the first time, and all at once I'm weary and feel I do not have the energy to broil meat, and I think of driving to a restaurant, then shake my head and go on to the house, the refrigerator, the oven; and some mornings when I wake in the dark and listen to the silence and run my hand over the cold sheet beside me; and some days in summer when Jennifer is here.

Gloria left first me, then the Church, and that was the end of religion for the children, though on visits they went to Sunday Mass with me, and still do, out of a respect for my life that they manage to keep free of patronage. Jennifer is an agnostic, though I doubt she would call herself that, any more than she would call herself any other name that implied she had made a decision, a choice, about existence, death, and God. In truth she tends to pantheism, a good sign, I think; but not wanting to be a father who tells his children what they ought to believe, I do not say to her that Catholicism includes pantheism, like onions in a stew. Besides, I have no missionary instincts and do not believe everyone should or even could live with the Catholic faith. It is Jennifer's womanhood that renders me awkward. And womanhood now is frank, not like when Gloria was twenty and there were symbols: high heels and cosmetics and dresses, a cigarette, a cocktail. I am glad that women are free now of false modesty and all its attention paid the flesh; but, still, it is difficult to see so much of your daughter, to hear her talk as only men and bawdy women used to, and most of all to see in her face the deep and unabashed sensuality of women, with no tricks of the eyes and mouth to hide the pleasure she feels at having a strong young body. I am certain, with the way things are now, that she has very happily not been a virgin for years. That does not bother me. What bothers me is my certainty about it, just from watching her walk across a room or light a cigarette or pour milk on cereal.

She told me all of it, waking me that night when I had gone to sleep listening to the wind in the trees and against the house, a wind so strong that I had to shut all but the lee windows, and still the house cooled; told it to me in such detail and so clearly that now, when she has driven the car to Florida, I remember it all as though I had been a passenger in the front seat, or even at the wheel. It started with a movie, then beer and driving to the sea to look at the waves in the night and the wind, Jennifer and Betsy and Liz. They drank a beer on the beach and wanted to go in naked but were afraid they would drown in the high surf. They bought another six-pack at a grocery store in New Hampshire, and drove home. I can see it now, feel it: the three girls and the beer and the ride on country roads where pines curved in the wind and the big deciduous trees swayed and shook as if they might leap from the earth. They would have some windows partly open so they could feel the wind; Jennifer would be playing a cassette, the music stirring them, as it does the young, to memories of another time, other people and places in what is for them the past.

She took Betsy home, then Liz, and sang with her cassette as she left the town west of us and started home, a twenty-minute drive on the road that passes my house. They had each had four beers, but now there were twelve empty bottles in the bag on the floor at the passenger seat, and I keep focusing on their sound against each other when the car shifted speeds or changed directions. For I want to understand that one moment out of all her heart's time on earth, and whether her history had any bearing on it, or whether her heart was then isolated from all it had known, and the sound of those bottles urged it. She was just leaving the town, accelerating past a night club on the right, gaining speed to climb a long, gradual hill, then she went up it, singing, patting the beat on the steering wheel, the wind loud through her few inches of open window, blowing her hair as it did the high branches alongside the road, and she looked up at them and watched the top of the hill for someone drunk or heedless coming over it in part of her lane. She crested to an open black road, and there he was: a bulk, a blur, a thing running across her headlights, and she swerved left and her foot went for the brake and was stomping air above its pedal when she hit him, saw his legs and body in the air, flying out of her light, into the dark. Her brakes were screaming into the wind, bottles clinking in the fallen bag, and with the music and wind inside the car was his sound, already a memory but as real as an echo, that car-shuddering thump as though she had struck a tree. Her foot was back on the accelerator. Then she shifted gears and pushed it. She ejected the cassette and closed the window. She did not start to cry until she knocked on my bedroom door, then called: 'Dad?'

Her voice, her tears, broke through my dream and the wind I heard in my sleep, and I stepped into jeans and hurried to the door, thinking harm, rape, death. All were in her face, and I hugged her and pressed her cheek to my chest and smoothed her blown hair, then led her, weeping, to the kitchen and sat her at the table where still she could not speak, nor look at me; when she raised her face it fell forward again, as of its own weight, into her palms. I offered tea and she shook her head, so I offered beer twice, then she shook her head, so I offered whiskey and she nodded. I had some rye that Father Paul and I had not finished last hunting season, and I poured some over ice and set it in front of her and was putting away the ice but stopped and got another glass and poured one for myself too, and brought the ice and bottle to the table where she was trying to get one of her long menthols out of the pack, but her fingers jerked like severed snakes, and I took the pack and lit one for her and took one for myself. I watched her shudder with her first swallow of rye, and push hair back from her face, it is auburn and gleamed in the overhead light, and I remembered how beautiful she looked riding a sorrel; she was smoking fast, then the sobs in her throat stopped, and she looked at me and said it, the words coming out with smoke: 'I hit somebody. With the *car.*'

Then she was crying and I was on my feet, moving back and forth, looking down at her, asking *Who? Where? Where?* She was pointing at the wall over the stove, jabbing her fingers and cigarette at it, her other hand at her eyes, and twice in horror I actually looked at the wall. She finished the whiskey in a swallow and I stopped pacing and asking and poured another, and either the drink or the exhaustion of tears quieted her, even the dry sobs, and she told me; not as I tell it now, for that was later as again and again we relived it in the kitchen or living room, and, if in daylight, fled it on horseback out on the trails through the woods and, if at night, walked quietly around in the moonlit pasture, walked around and around it, sweating through our clothes. She told it in bursts, like she was a child again, running to me, injured from play. I put on boots and a shirt and left her with the bottle and her streaked face and a cigarette twitching between her fingers, pushed the door open against the wind, and eased it shut. The wind squinted and watered my eyes as I leaned into it and went to the pickup.

When I passed St John's I looked at it, and Father Paul's little white rectory in the rear, and wanted to stop, wished I could as I could if he were simply a friend who sold hardware or something. I had forgotten my watch but I always know the time within minutes, even when a sound or dream or my bladder wakes me in the night. It was nearly two; we had been in the kitchen about twenty minutes; she had hit him around one-fifteen. Or her. The road was empty and

I drove between blowing trees; caught for an instant in my lights, they seemed to be in panic. I smoked and let hope play its tricks on me; it was neither man nor woman but an animal, a goat or calf or deer on the road; it was a man who had jumped away in time, the collision of metal and body glancing not direct, and he had limped home to nurse bruises and cuts. Then I threw the cigarette and hope both out the window and prayed that he was alive, while beneath that prayer, a reserve deeper in my heart, another one stirred: that if he were dead, they would not get Jennifer.

From our direction, east and a bit south, the road to that hill and the night club beyond it and finally the town is, for its last four or five miles, straight through farming country. When I reached that stretch I slowed the truck and opened my window for the fierce air; on both sides were scattered farmhouses and barns and sometimes a silo, looking not like shelters but like unsheltered things the wind would flatten. Corn bent toward the road from a field on my right, and always something blew in front of me: paper, leaves, dried weeds, branches. I slowed approaching the hill, and went up it in second, staring through my open window at the ditch on the left side of the road, its weeds alive, whipping, a mad dance with the trees above them. I went over the hill and down and, opposite the club, turned right onto a side street of houses, and parked there, in the leaping shadows of trees. I walked back across the road to the club's parking lot, the wind behind me, lifting me as I strode, and I could not hear my boots on pavement. I walked up the hill, on the shoulder, watching the branches above me, hearing their leaves and the creaking trunks and the wind. Then I was at the top, looking down the road and at the farms and fields; the night was clear, and I could see a long way; clouds scudded past the half-moon and stars, blown out to sea.

I started down, watching the tall grass under the trees to my right, glancing into the dark of the ditch, listening for cars behind me; but as soon as I cleared one tree, its sound was gone, its flapping leaves and rattling branches far behind me, as though the greatest distance I had at my back was a matter of feet, while ahead of me I could see a barn two miles off. Then I saw her skid marks: short, and going left and downhill, into the other lane. I stood at the ditch, its weeds blowing; across it were trees and their moving shadows, like the clouds. I stepped onto its slope, and it took me sliding on my feet, then rump, to the bottom, where I sat still, my body gathered to itself, lest a part of me should touch him. But there was only tall grass, and I stood, my shoulders reaching the sides of the ditch, and I walked uphill, wishing for the flashlight in the pickup, walking slowly, and down in the ditch I could hear my feet in the grass and on the earth, and kicking cans and bottles. At the top of the hill I turned and went down, watching the ground above the ditch on my right, praying my prayer from the truck again, the first one, the one I would admit, that he was not dead, was in fact home, and began to hope again, memory telling me of lost pheasants and grouse I had shot, but they were small and the colors of their home, while a man was either there or not; and from that memory I left where I was and while walking in the ditch under the wind was in the deceit of imagination with Jennifer in the kitchen, telling her she had hit no one, or at least had not badly hurt anyone, when I realized he could be in the hospital now and I would have to think of a way to check there, something to say on the phone. I see now that, once hope returned, I should have been certain what it prepared me for: ahead of me, in high grass and the shadows of trees, I saw his shirt. Or that is all my mind would allow itself: a shirt, and I stood looking at it for the moments it took my mind to admit the arm and head and the dark length covered by pants. He lay face down, the arm I could see near his side, his head turned from me, on its cheek.

'Fella?' I said. I had meant to call, but it came out quiet and high, lost inches from my face in the wind. Then I said, 'Oh God,' and felt Him in the wind and the sky moving past the stars and moon and the fields around me, but only watching me as He might have watched Cain or Job, I did not know which, and I said it again, and wanted to sink to the earth and weep till I slept there in the weeds. I climbed, scrambling up the side of the ditch, pulling at clutched grass, gained the top on hands and knees, and went to him like that, panting, moving through the grass as high and higher than my face, crawling under that sky, making sounds too, like some animal, there being no words to let him know I was here with him now. He was long; that is the word that came to me, not tall. I kneeled beside him, my hands on my legs. His right arm was by his side, his left arm straight out from the shoulder, but turned, so his palm was open to the tree above us. His left cheek was clean-shaven, his eye closed, and there was no blood. I leaned forward to look at his open mouth and saw the blood on it, going down into the grass. I straightened and looked ahead at the wind blowing past me through grass and trees to a distant light, and I stared at the light, imagining someone awake out there, wanting someone to be, a gathering of old friends, or someone alone listening to music or painting a picture, then I figured it was a night light at a farmyard whose house I couldn't see. *Going,* I thought. *Still going.* I leaned over again and looked at dripping blood.

So I had to touch his wrist, a thick one with a watch and expansion band that I pushed up his arm, thinking *he's left-handed,* my three fingers pressing his wrist, and all I felt was my tough fingertips on that smooth underside flesh and small bones, then relief, then certainty. But against my will, or only because of it, I still don't know, I touched his neck, ran my fingers down it as if petting, then pressed, and my hand sprang back as from fire. I lowered it again, held it there until it felt that faint beating that I could not believe. There was too much wind. Nothing could make a sound in it. A pulse could not be felt in it, nor could mere fingers in that wind feel the absolute silence of a dead man's artery. I was making sounds again; I grabbed his left arm and his waist, and pulled him toward me, and that side of him rose, turned, and I lowered him to his back, his face tilted up toward the tree that was groaning, the tree and I the only sounds in the wind. Turning my face from his, looking down the length of him at his sneakers, I placed my ear on his heart, and heard not that but something else, and I clamped a hand over my exposed ear, heard something liquid and alive, like when you pump a well and after a few strokes you hear air and water moving in the pipe, and I knew I must raise his legs and cover him and run to a phone, while still I listened to his chest, thinking *raise with what? cover with what?* and amid the liquid sound I heard the heart, then lost it, and pressed my ear against bone, but his chest was quiet, and I did not know when the liquid had stopped, and do not know now when I heard air, a faint rush of it, and whether under my ear or at his mouth or whether I heard it at all. I straightened and looked at the light, dim and yellow. Then I touched his throat, looking him full in the face. He was blond and young. He could have been sleeping in the shade of a tree, but for the smear of blood from his mouth to his hair, and the night sky, and the weeds blowing against his head, and the leaves shaking in the dark above us.

I stood. Then I kneeled again and prayed for his soul to

join in peace and joy all the dead and living; and, doing so, confronted my first sin against him, not stopping for Father Paul, who could have given him the last rites, and immediately then my second one, or I saw then, my first, not calling an ambulance to meet me there, and I stood and turned into the wind, slid down the ditch and crawled out of it, and went up the hill and down it, across the road to the street of houses whose people I had left behind forever, so that I moved with stealth in the shadows to my truck.

When I came around the bend near my house, I saw the kitchen light at the rear. She sat as I had left her, the ashtray filled, and I looked at the bottle, felt her eyes on me, felt what she was seeing too: the dirt from my crawling. She had not drunk much of the rye. I poured some in my glass, with the water from melted ice, and sat down and swallowed some and looked at her and swallowed some more, and said: 'He's dead.'

She rubbed her eyes with the heels of her hands, rubbed the cheeks under them, but she was dry now.

'He was probably dead when he hit the ground. I mean, that's probably what killed –'

'Where was he?'

'Across the ditch, under a tree.'

'Was he – did you see his face?'

'No. Not really. I just felt. For life, pulse. I'm going out to the car.'

'What for? Oh.'

I finished the rye, and pushed back the chair, then she was standing too.

'I'll go with you.'

'There's no need.'

'I'll go.'

I took a flashlight from a drawer and pushed open the

door and held it while she went out. We turned our faces from the wind. It was like on the hill, when I was walking, and the wind closed the distance behind me: after three or four steps I felt there was no house back there. She took my hand, as I was reaching for hers. In the garage we let go, and squeezed between the pickup and her little car, to the front of it, where we had more room, and we stepped back from the grille and I shone the light on the fender, the smashed headlight turned into it, the concave chrome staring to the right, at the garage wall.

'We ought to get the bottles,' I said.

She moved between the garage and the car, on the passenger side, and had room to open the door and lift the bag. I reached out, and she gave me the bag and backed up and shut the door and came around the car. We sidled to the doorway, and she put her arm around my waist and I hugged her shoulders.

'I thought you'd call the police,' she said.

We crossed the yard, faces bowed from the wind, her hair blowing away from her neck, and in the kitchen I put the bag of bottles in the garbage basket. She was working at the table: capping the rye and putting it away, filling the ice tray, washing the glasses, emptying the ashtray, sponging the table.

'Try to sleep now,' I said.

She nodded at the sponge circling under her hand, gathering ashes. Then she dropped it in the sink and, looking me full in the face, as I had never seen her look, as perhaps she never had, being for so long a daughter on visits (or so it seemed to me and still does: that until then our eyes had never seriously met), she crossed to me from the sink and kissed my lips, then held me so tightly I lost balance, and would have stumbled forward had she not held me so hard.

*　　*　　*

I sat in the living room, the house darkened, and watched the maple and the hemlock. When I believed she was asleep I put on *La Bohème*, and kept it at the same volume as the wind so it would not wake her. Then I listened to *Madame Butterfly*, and in the third act had to rise quickly to lower the sound: the wind was gone. I looked at the still maple near the window, and thought of the wind leaving farms and towns and the coast, going out over the sea to die on the waves. I smoked and gazed out the window. The sky was darker, and at daybreak the rain came. I listened to *Tosca*, and at six-fifteen went to the kitchen where Jennifer's purse lay on the table, a leather shoulder purse crammed with the things of an adult woman, things she had begun accumulating only a few years back, and I nearly wept, thinking of what sandy foundations they were: driver's license, credit card, disposable lighter, cigarettes, checkbook, ballpoint pen, cash, cosmetics, comb, brush, Kleenex, these the rite of passage from childhood, and I took one of them – her keys – and went out, remembering a jacket and hat when the rain struck me, but I kept going to the car, and squeezed and lowered myself into it, pulled the seat belt over my shoulder and fastened it and backed out, turning in the drive, going forward into the road, toward St John's and Father Paul.

Cars were on the road, the workers, and I did not worry about any of them noticing the fender and light. Only a horse distracted them from what they drove to. In front of St John's is a parking lot; at its far side, past the church and at the edge of the lawn, is an old pine, taller than the steeple now. I shifted to third, left the road, and, aiming the right headlight at the tree, accelerated past the white blur of church, into the black trunk growing bigger till it was all I could see, then I rocked in that resonant thump she had heard, had felt, and when I turned off the ignition it was still in my ears, my blood, and I saw the boy flying in the wind. I lowered my forehead to the wheel. Father Paul opened the door, his face white in the rain.

'I'm all right.'

'What happened?'

'I don't know. I fainted.'

I got out and went around to the front of the car, looked at the smashed light, the crumpled and torn fender.

'Come to the house and lie down.'

'I'm all right.'

'When was your last physical?'

'I'm due for one. Let's get out of this rain.'

'You'd better lie down.'

'No. I want to receive.'

That was the time to say I want to confess, but I have not and will not. Though I could now, for Jennifer is in Florida, and weeks have passed, and perhaps now Father Paul would not feel that he must tell me to go to the police. And, for that very reason, to confess now would be unfair. It is a world of secrets, and now I have one from my best, in truth my only, friend. I have one from Jennifer too, but that is the nature of fatherhood.

Most of that day it rained, so it was only in early evening, when the sky cleared, with a setting sun, that two little boys, leaving their confinement for some play before dinner, found him. Jennifer and I got that on the local news, which we listened to every hour, meeting at the radio, standing with cigarettes, until the one at eight o'clock; when she stopped crying, we went out and walked on the wet grass, around the pasture, the last of sunlight still in the air and trees. His name was Patrick Mitchell, he was nineteen years old, was employed by CETA, lived at home with his parents and brother and sister. The paper next day said he had been at a friend's house and was walking home, and I thought of that light I had seen, then knew it was not for him; he lived on one of the streets behind the club. The paper did not say then, or in the next few days, anything to make Jennifer think he was alive while she was with me in the kitchen. Nor do I know if we – I – could have saved him.

In keeping her secret from her friends, Jennifer had to perform so often, as I did with Father Paul and at the stables, that I believe the acting, which took more of her than our daylight trail rides and our night walks in the pasture, was her healing. Her friends teased me about wrecking her car. When I carried her luggage out to the car on that last morning, we spoke only of the weather for her trip – the day was clear, with a dry cool breeze – and hugged and kissed, and I stood watching as she started the car and turned it around. But then she shifted to neutral and put on the parking brake and unclasped the belt, looking at me all the while, then she was coming to me, as she had that night in the kitchen, and I opened my arms.

I have said I talk with God in the mornings, as I start my day, and sometimes as I sit with coffee, looking at the birds, and the woods. Of course He has never spoken to me, but that is not something I require. Nor does He need to. I know Him, as I know the part of myself that knows Him, that felt Him watching from the wind and the night as I kneeled over the dying boy. Lately I have taken to arguing with Him, as I can't with Father Paul, who, when he hears my monthly confession, has not heard and will not hear anything of failure to do all that one can to save an anonymous life, of injustice to a family in their grief, of deepening their pain at the chance and mystery of death by giving them nothing – no one – to hate. With Father Paul I feel lonely about this, but not with God. When I received the Eucharist while

Jennifer's car sat twice-damaged, so redeemed, in the rain, I felt neither loneliness nor shame, but as though He were watching me, even from my tongue, intestines, blood, as I have watched my sons at times in their young lives when I was able to judge but without anger, and so keep silent while they, in the agony of their youth, decided how they must act; or found reasons, after their actions, for what they had done. Their reasons were never as good or as bad as their actions, but they needed to find them, to believe they were living by them, instead of the awful solitude of the heart.

I do not feel the peace I once did: not with God, nor the earth, or anyone on it. I have begun to prefer this state, to remember with fondness the other one as a period of peace I neither earned nor deserved. Now in the mornings while I watch purple finches driving larger titmice from the feeder, I say to Him: I would do it again. For when she knocked on my door, then called me, she woke what had flowed dormant in my blood since her birth, so that what rose from the bed was not a stable owner or a Catholic or any other Luke Ripley I had lived with for a long time, but the father of a girl.

And He says: I am a Father too.

Yes, I say, as You are a Son Whom this morning I will receive; unless You kill me on the way to church, then I trust You will receive me. And as a Son You made Your plea.

Yes, He says, but I would not lift the cup.

True, and I don't want You to lift it from me either. And if one of my sons had come to me that night, I would have phoned the police and told them to meet us with an ambulance at the top of the hill.

Why? Do you love them less?

I tell Him no, it is not that I love them less, but that I could bear the pain of watching and knowing my sons' pain, could bear it with pride as they took the whip and nails.

But You never had a daughter and, if You had, You could not have borne her passion.

So, He says, you love her more than you love Me.

I love her more than I love truth.

Then you love in weakness, He says.

As You love me, I say, and I go with an apple or carrot out to the barn.

E. L. DOCTOROW

THE WRITER IN THE FAMILY

IN 1955 MY father died with his ancient mother still alive in a nursing home. The old lady was ninety and hadn't even known he was ill. Thinking the shock might kill her, my aunts told her that he had moved to Arizona for his bronchitis. To the immigrant generation of my grandmother, Arizona was the American equivalent of the Alps, it was where you went for your health. More accurately, it was where you went if you had the money. Since my father had failed in all the business enterprises of his life, this was the aspect of the news my grandmother dwelled on, that he had finally had some success. And so it came about that as we mourned him at home in our stocking feet, my grandmother was bragging to her cronies about her son's new life in the dry air of the desert.

My aunts had decided on their course of action without consulting us. It meant neither my mother nor my brother nor I could visit Grandma because we were supposed to have moved west too, a family, after all. My brother Harold and I didn't mind – it was always a nightmare at the old people's home, where they all sat around staring at us while we tried to make conversation with Grandma. She looked terrible, had numbers of ailments, and her mind wandered. Not seeing her was no disappointment either for my mother, who had never gotten along with the old woman and did not visit when she could have. But what was disturbing was that my aunts had acted in the manner of that side of the family of making government on everyone's behalf, the true citizens by blood and the lesser citizens by marriage. It was exactly this attitude that had tormented my mother all her married life. She claimed Jack's family had never accepted her. She had battled them for twenty-five years as an outsider.

A few weeks after the end of our ritual mourning my aunt Frances phoned us from her home in Larchmont. Aunt Frances was the wealthier of my father's sisters. Her husband was a lawyer, and both her sons were at Amherst. She had called to say that Grandma was asking why she didn't hear from Jack. I had answered the phone. 'You're the writer in the family,' my aunt said. 'Your father had so much faith in you. Would you mind making up something? Send it to me and I'll read it to her. She won't know the difference.'

That evening, at the kitchen table, I pushed my homework aside and composed a letter. I tried to imagine my father's response to his new life. He had never been west. He had never traveled anywhere. In his generation the great journey was from the working class to the professional class. He hadn't managed that either. But he loved New York, where he had been born and lived his life, and he was always discovering new things about it. He especially loved the old parts of the city below Canal Street, where he would find ships' chandlers or firms that wholesaled in spices and teas. He was a salesman for an appliance jobber with accounts all over the city. He liked to bring home rare cheeses or exotic foreign vegetables that were sold only in certain neighborhoods. Once he brought home a barometer, another time an antique ship's telescope in a wooden case with a brass snap.

'Dear Mama,' I wrote. 'Arizona is beautiful. The sun shines all day and the air is warm and I feel better than I have in years. The desert is not as barren as you would expect, but filled with wild-flowers and cactus plants and peculiar crooked trees that look like men holding their arms out. You can see great distances in whatever direction you turn and to the west is a range of mountains maybe fifty miles from here, but in the morning with the sun on them you can see the snow on their crests.'

My aunt called some days later and told me it was when she read this letter aloud to the old lady that the full effect of Jack's death came over her. She had to excuse herself and went out in the parking lot to cry. 'I wept so,' she said. 'I felt such terrible longing for him. You're so right, he loved to go places, he loved life, he loved everything.'

We began trying to organize our lives. My father had borrowed money against his insurance and there was very little left. Some commissions were still due but it didn't look as if his firm would honor them. There was a couple of thousand dollars in a savings bank that had to be maintained there until the estate was settled. The lawyer involved was Aunt Frances' husband and he was very proper. 'The estate!' my mother muttered, gesturing as if to pull out her hair. 'The estate!' She applied for a job part-time in the admissions office of the hospital where my father's terminal illness had been diagnosed, and where he had spent some months until they had sent him home to die. She knew a lot of the doctors and staff and she had learned 'from bitter experience,' as she told them, about the hospital routine. She was hired.

I hated that hospital, it was dark and grim and full of tortured people. I thought it was masochistic of my mother to seek out a job there, but did not tell her so.

We lived in an apartment on the corner of 175th Street and the Grand Concourse, one flight up. Three rooms. I shared the bedroom with my brother. It was jammed with furniture because when my father had required a hospital bed in the last weeks of his illness we had moved some of the living-room pieces into the bedroom and made over the living room for him. We had to navigate bookcases, beds, a gateleg table, bureaus, a record player and radio console, stacks of 78 albums, my brother's trombone and music stand, and so on. My mother continued to sleep on the convertible sofa in the living room that had been their bed before his illness. The two rooms were connected by a narrow hall made even narrower by bookcases along the wall. Off the hall were a small kitchen and dinette and a bathroom. There were lots of appliances in the kitchen – broiler, toaster, pressure cooker, countertop dishwasher, blender – that my father had gotten through his job, at cost. A treasured phrase in our house: *at cost*. But most of these fixtures went unused because my mother did not care for them. Chromium devices with timers or gauges that required the reading of elaborate instructions were not for her. They were in part responsible for the awful clutter of our lives and now she wanted to get rid of them. 'We're being buried,' she said. 'Who needs them!'

So we agreed to throw out or sell anything inessential. While I found boxes for the appliances and my brother tied the boxes with twine, my mother opened my father's closet and took out his clothes. He had several suits because as a salesman he needed to look his best. My mother wanted us to try on his suits to see which of them could be altered and used. My brother refused to try them on. I tried on one jacket, which was too large for me. The lining inside the sleeves chilled my arms and the vaguest scent of my father's being came to me.

'This is way too big,' I said.

'Don't worry,' my mother said. 'I had it cleaned. Would I let you wear it if I hadn't?'

It was the evening, the end of winter, and snow was coming down on the windowsill and melting as it settled.

The ceiling bulb glared on a pile of my father's suits and trousers on hangers flung across the bed in the shape of a dead man. We refused to try on anything more, and my mother began to cry.

'What are you crying for?' my brother shouted. 'You wanted to get rid of things, didn't you?'

A few weeks later my aunt phoned again and said she thought it would be necessary to have another letter from Jack. Grandma had fallen out of her chair and bruised herself and was very depressed.

'How long does this go on?' my mother said.

'It's not so terrible,' my aunt said, 'for the little time left to make things easier for her.'

My mother slammed down the phone. 'He can't even die when he wants to!' she cried. 'Even death comes second to Mama! What are they afraid of, the shock will kill her? Nothing can kill her. She's indestructible! A stake through the heart couldn't kill her!'

When I sat down in the kitchen to write the letter I found it more difficult than the first one. 'Don't watch me,' I said to my brother. 'It's hard enough.'

'You don't have to do something just because someone wants you to,' Harold said. He was two years older than me and had started at City College; but when my father became ill he had switched to night school and gotten a job in a record store.

'Dear Mama,' I wrote. 'I hope you're feeling well. We're all fit as a fiddle. The life here is good and the people are very friendly and informal. Nobody wears suits and ties here. Just a pair of slacks and a short-sleeved shirt. Perhaps a sweater in the evening. I have bought into a very successful radio and record business and I'm doing very well. You remember Jack's

Electric, my old place on Forty-third Street? Well, now it's Jack's Arizona Electric and we have a line of television sets as well.'

I sent that letter off to my aunt Frances, and as we all knew she would, she phoned soon after. My brother held his hand over the mouthpiece. 'It's Frances with her latest review,' he said.

'Jonathan? You're a very talented young man. I just wanted to tell you what a blessing your letter was. Her whole face lit up when I read the part about Jack's store. That would be an excellent way to continue.'

'Well, I hope I don't have to do this anymore, Aunt Frances. It's not very honest.'

Her tone changed. 'Is your mother there? Let me talk to her.'

'She's not here,' I said.

'Tell her not to worry,' my aunt said. 'A poor old lady who has never wished anything but the best for her will soon die.'

I did not repeat this to my mother, for whom it would have been one more in the family anthology of unforgivable remarks. But then I had to suffer it myself for the possible truth it might embody. Each side defended its position with rhetoric, but I, who wanted peace, rationalized the snubs and rebuffs each inflicted on the other, taking no stands, like my father himself.

Years ago his life had fallen into a pattern of business failures and missed opportunities. The great debate between his family on the one side, and my mother Ruth on the other, was this: who was responsible for the fact that he had not lived up to anyone's expectations?

As to the prophecies, when spring came my mother's prevailed. Grandma was still alive.

One balmy Sunday my mother and brother and I took the

bus to the Beth El cemetery in New Jersey to visit my father's grave. It was situated on a slight rise. We stood looking over rolling fields embedded with monuments. Here and there processions of black cars wound their way through the lanes, or clusters of people stood at open graves. My father's grave was planted with tiny shoots of evergreen but it lacked a headstone. We had chosen one and paid for it and then the stonecutters had gone on strike. Without a headstone my father did not seem to be honorably dead. He didn't seem to me properly buried.

My mother gazed at the plot beside his, reserved for her coffin. 'They were always too fine for other people,' she said. 'Even in the old days on Stanton Street. They put on airs. Nobody was ever good enough for them. Finally Jack himself was not good enough for them. Except to get them things wholesale. Then he was good enough for them.'

'Mom, please,' my brother said.

'If I had known. Before I ever met him he was tied to his mama's apron strings. And Essie's apron strings were like chains, let me tell you. We had to live where we could be near them for the Sunday visits. Every Sunday, that was my life, a visit to Mamaleh. Whatever she knew I wanted, a better apartment, a stick of furniture, a summer camp for the boys, she spoke against it. You know your father, every decision had to be considered and reconsidered. And nothing changed. Nothing ever changed.'

She began to cry. We sat her down on a nearby bench. My brother walked off and read the names on stones. I looked at my mother, who was crying, and I went off after my brother.

'Mom's still crying,' I said. 'Shouldn't we do something?'

'It's all right,' he said. 'It's what she came here for.'

'Yes,' I said, and then a sob escaped from my throat. 'But I feel like crying too.'

My brother Harold put his arm around me. 'Look at this old black stone here,' he said. 'The way it's carved. You can see the changing fashion in monuments – just like everything else.'

Somewhere in this time I began dreaming of my father. Not the robust father of my childhood, the handsome man with healthy pink skin and brown eyes and a mustache and the thinning hair parted in the middle. My dead father. We were taking him home from the hospital. It was understood that he had come back from death. This was amazing and joyous. On the other hand, he was terribly mysteriously damaged, or, more accurately, spoiled and unclean. He was very yellowed and debilitated by his death, and there were no guarantees that he wouldn't soon die again. He seemed aware of this and his entire personality was changed. He was angry and impatient with all of us. We were trying to help him in some way, struggling to get him home, but something prevented us, something we had to fix, a tattered suitcase that had sprung open, some mechanical thing: he had a car but it wouldn't start; or the car was made of wood; or his clothes, which had become too large for him, had caught in the door. In one version he was all bandaged and as we tried to lift him from his wheelchair into a taxi the bandage began to unroll and catch in the spokes of the wheelchair. This seemed to be some unreasonableness on his part. My mother looked on sadly and tried to get him to cooperate.

That was the dream. I shared it with no one. Once when I woke, crying out, my brother turned on the light. He wanted to know what I'd been dreaming but I pretended I didn't remember. The dream made me feel guilty. I felt guilty *in* the dream too because my enraged father knew we didn't want to live with him. The dream represented us taking him home, or trying to, but it was nevertheless under-stood by all of us that he was to live alone. He was this derelict back from death, but what we were doing was taking him to some place where he would live by himself without help from anyone until he died again.

At one point I became so fearful of this dream that I tried not to go to sleep. I tried to think of good things about my father and to remember him before his illness. He used to call me 'matey.' 'Hello, matey,' he would say when he came home from work. He always wanted us to go someplace – to the store, to the park, to a ball game. He loved to walk. When I went walking with him he would say: 'Hold your shoulders back, don't slump. Hold your head up and look at the world. Walk as if you meant it!' As he strode down the street his shoulders moved from side to side, as if he was hearing some kind of cakewalk. He moved with a bounce. He was always eager to see what was around the corner.

The next request for a letter coincided with a special occasion in the house: my brother Harold had met a girl he liked and had gone out with her several times. Now she was coming to our house for dinner.

We had prepared for this for days, cleaning everything in sight, giving the house a going-over, washing the dust of dis-use from the glasses and good dishes. My mother came home early from work to get the dinner going. We opened the gate-leg table in the living room and brought in the kitchen chairs. My mother spread the table with a laundered white cloth and put out her silver. It was the first family occasion since my father's illness.

I liked my brother's girlfriend a lot. She was a thin girl with very straight hair and she had a terrific smile. Her presence seemed to excite the air. It was amazing to have a living breathing girl in our house. She looked around and what she said was: 'Oh, I've never seen so many books!' While she and my brother sat at the table my mother was in the kitchen putting the food into serving bowls and I was going from the kitchen to the living room, kidding around like a waiter, with a white cloth over my arm and a high style of service, placing the serving dish of green beans on the table with a flourish. In the kitchen my mother's eyes were sparkling. She looked at me and nodded and mimed the words: 'She's adorable!'

My brother suffered himself to be waited on. He was wary of what we might say. He kept glancing at the girl – her name was Susan – to see if we met with her approval. She worked in an insurance office and was taking courses in accounting at City College. Harold was under a terrible strain but he was excited and happy too. He had bought a bottle of Concord-grape wine to go with the roast chicken. He held up his glass and proposed a toast. My mother said: 'To good health and happiness,' and we all drank, even I. At that moment the phone rang and I went into the bedroom to get it.

'Jonathan? This is your aunt Frances. How is everyone?'

'Fine, thank you.'

'I want to ask one last favor of you. I need a letter from Jack. Your grandma's very ill. Do you think you can?'

'Who is it?' my mother called from the living room.

'Okay, Aunt Frances,' I said quickly. 'I have to go now, we're eating dinner.' And I hung up the phone.

'It was my friend Louie,' I said, sitting back down. 'He didn't know the math pages to review.'

The dinner was very fine. Harold and Susan washed the dishes and by the time they were done my mother and I had folded up the gateleg table and put it back against the wall and I had swept the crumbs up with the carpet sweeper. We all sat and talked and listened to records for a while and then my brother took Susan home. The evening had gone very well.

Once when my mother wasn't home my brother had pointed out something: the letters from Jack weren't really necessary. 'What is this ritual?' he said, holding his palms up. 'Grandma is almost totally blind, she's half deaf and crippled. Does the situation really call for a literary composition? Does it need verisimilitude? Would the old lady know the difference if she was read the phone book?'

'Then why did Aunt Frances ask me?'

'That is the question, Jonathan. Why did she? After all, she could write the letter herself – what difference would it make? And if not Frances, why not Frances' sons, the Amherst students? They should have learned by now to write.'

'But they're not Jack's sons,' I said.

'That's exactly the point,' my brother said. 'The idea is *service*. Dad used to bust his balls getting them things whole-sale, getting them deals on things. Frances of Westchester really needed things at cost. And Aunt Molly. And Aunt Molly's husband, and Aunt Molly's ex-husband. Grandma, if she needed an errand done. He was always on the hook for something. They never thought his time was important. They never thought every favor he got was one he had to pay back. Appliances, records, watches, china, opera tickets, any goddamn thing. Call Jack.'

'It was a matter of pride to him to be able to do things for them,' I said. 'To have connections.'

'Yeah, I wonder why,' my brother said. He looked out the window.

Then suddenly it dawned on me that I was being implicated.

'You should use your head more,' my brother said.

137

*   *   *

Yet I had agreed once again to write a letter from the desert and so I did. I mailed it off to Aunt Frances. A few days later, when I came home from school, I thought I saw her sitting in her car in front of our house. She drove a black Buick Roadmaster, a very large clean car with whitewall tires. It was Aunt Frances all right. She blew the horn when she saw me. I went over and leaned in at the window.

'Hello, Jonathan,' she said. 'I haven't long. Can you get in the car?'

'Mom's not home,' I said. 'She's working.'

'I know that. I came to talk to you.'

'Would you like to come upstairs?'

'I can't, I have to get back to Larchmont. Can you get in for a moment, please?'

I got in the car. My aunt Frances was a very pretty white-haired woman, very elegant, and she wore tasteful clothes. I had always liked her and from the time I was a child she had enjoyed pointing out to everyone that I looked more like her son than Jack's. She wore white gloves and held the steering wheel and looked straight ahead as she talked, as if the car was in traffic and not sitting at the curb.

'Jonathan,' she said, 'there is your letter on the seat. Needless to say I didn't read it to Grandma. I'm giving it back to you and I won't ever say a word to anyone. This is just between us. I never expected cruelty from you. I never thought you were capable of doing something so deliberately cruel and perverse.'

I said nothing.

'Your mother has very bitter feelings and now I see she has poisoned you with them. She has always resented the family. She is a very strong-willed, selfish person.'

'No she isn't,' I said.

'I wouldn't expect you to agree. She drove poor Jack crazy with her demands. She always had the highest aspirations and he could never fulfill them to her satisfaction. When he still had his store he kept your mother's brother, who drank, on salary. After the war when he began to make a little money he had to buy Ruth a mink jacket because she was so desperate to have one. He had debts to pay but she wanted a mink. He was a very special person, my brother, he should have accomplished something special, but he loved your mother and devoted his life to her. And all she ever thought about was keeping up with the Joneses.'

I watched the traffic going up the Grand Concourse. A bunch of kids were waiting at the bus stop at the corner. They had put their books on the ground and were horsing around.

'I'm sorry I have to descend to this,' Aunt Frances said. 'I don't like talking about people this way. If I have nothing good to say about someone, I'd rather not say anything. How is Harold?'

'Fine.'

'Did he help you write this marvelous letter?'

'No.'

After a moment she said more softly: 'How are you all getting along?'

'Fine.'

'I would invite you up for Passover if I thought your mother would accept.'

I didn't answer.

She turned on the engine. 'I'll say goodbye now, Jonathan. Take your letter. I hope you give some time to thinking about what you've done.'

*   *   *

That evening when my mother came home from work I saw that she wasn't as pretty as my aunt Frances. I usually thought my mother was a good-looking woman, but I saw now that she was too heavy and that her hair was undistinguished.

'Why are you looking at me?' she said.

'I'm not.'

'I learned something interesting today,' my mother said. 'We may be eligible for a VA pension because of the time your father spent in the navy.'

That took me by surprise. Nobody had ever told me my father was in the navy.

'In World War I,' she said, 'he went to Webb's Naval Academy on the Harlem River. He was training to be an ensign. But the war ended and he never got his commission.'

After dinner the three of us went through the closets looking for my father's papers, hoping to find some proof that could be filed with the Veterans Administration. We came up with two things, a Victory medal, which my brother said everyone got for being in the service during the Great War, and an astounding sepia photograph of my father and his shipmates on the deck of a ship. They were dressed in bell-bottoms and T-shirts and armed with mops and pails, brooms and brushes.

'I never knew this,' I found myself saying. 'I never knew this.'

'You just don't remember,' my brother said.

I was able to pick out my father. He stood at the end of the row, a thin, handsome boy with a full head of hair, a mustache, and an intelligent smiling countenance.

'He had a joke,' my mother said. 'They called their training ship the SS *Constipation* because it never moved.'

Neither the picture nor the medal was proof of anything, but my brother thought a duplicate of my father's service record had to be in Washington somewhere and that it was just a matter of learning how to go about finding it.

'The pension wouldn't amount to much,' my mother said. 'Twenty or thirty dollars. But it would certainly help.'

I took the picture of my father and his shipmates and propped it against the lamp at my bedside. I looked into his youthful face and tried to relate it to the father I knew. I looked at the picture a long time. Only gradually did my eye connect it to the set of Great Sea Novels in the bottom shelf of the bookcase a few feet away. My father had given that set to me: it was uniformly bound in green with gilt lettering and it included works by Melville, Conrad, Victor Hugo, and Captain Marryat. And lying across the top of the books, jammed in under the sagging shelf above, was his old ship's telescope in its wooden case with the brass snap.

I thought how stupid, and imperceptive, and self-centered I had been never to have understood while he was alive what my father's dream for his life had been.

On the other hand, I had written in my last letter from Arizona – the one that had so angered Aunt Frances – something that might allow me, the writer in the family, to soften my judgment of myself. I will conclude by giving the letter here in its entirety.

Dear Mama,

This will be my final letter to you since I have been told by the doctors that I am dying.

I have sold my store at a very fine profit and am sending Frances a check for five thousand dollars to be deposited in your account. My present to you, Mamaleh. Let Frances show you the passbook.

As for the nature of my ailment, the doctors haven't told me what it is, but I know that I am simply dying of the wrong life. I should never have come to the desert. It wasn't the place for me.

I have asked Ruth and the boys to have my body cremated and the ashes scattered in the ocean.

Your loving son,
Jack

VLADIMIR NABOKOV

CHRISTMAS

I

AFTER WALKING BACK from the village to his manor across the dimming snows, Sleptsov sat down in a corner, on a plush-covered chair which he never remembered using before. It was the kind of thing that happens after some great calamity. Not your brother but a chance acquaintance, a vague country neighbor to whom you never paid much attention, with whom in normal times you exchange scarcely a word, is the one who comforts you wisely and gently, and hands you your dropped hat after the funeral service is over, and you are reeling from grief, your teeth chattering, your eyes blinded by tears. The same can be said of inanimate objects. Any room, even the coziest and the most absurdly small, in the little-used wing of a great country house has an unlived-in corner. And it was such a corner in which Sleptsov sat.

The wing was connected by a wooden gallery, now encumbered with our huge north Russian snowdrifts, to the master house, used only in summer. There was no need to awaken it, to heat it: the master had come from Petersburg for only a couple of days and had settled in the annex where it was a simple matter to get the stoves of white Dutch tile going.

The master sat in his corner, on that plush chair, as in a doctor's waiting room. The room floated in darkness; the dense blue of early evening filtered through the crystal feathers of frost on the windowpane. Ivan, the quiet, portly valet, who had recently shaved off his mustache and now looked like his late father, the family butler, brought in a kerosene lamp, all trimmed and brimming with light. He set it on a small table, and noiselessly caged it within its pink silk shade. For an instant a tilted mirror reflected his lit ear and cropped gray hair. Then he withdrew and the door gave a subdued creak.

Sleptsov raised his hand from his knee and slowly examined it. A drop of candle wax had stuck and hardened in the thin fold of skin between two fingers. He spread his fingers and the little white scale cracked.

II

The following morning, after a night spent in nonsensical, fragmentary dreams totally unrelated to his grief, as Sleptsov stepped out into the cold veranda, a floorboard emitted a merry pistol crack underfoot, and the reflections of the many-colored panes formed paradisal lozenges on the white-washed cushionless window seats. The outer door resisted at first, then opened with a luscious crunch, and the dazzling frost hit his face. The reddish sand providently sprinkled on the ice coating the porch steps resembled cinnamon, and thick icicles shot with greenish blue hung from the eaves. The snowdrifts reached all the way to the windows of the annex, tightly gripping the snug little wooden structure in their frosty clutches. The creamy white mounds of what were flower beds in summer swelled slightly above the level snow in front of the porch, and farther off loomed the radiance of the park, where every black branchlet was rimmed with silver, and the firs seemed to draw in their green paws under their bright plump load.

Wearing high felt boots and a short fur-lined coat with a

karakul collar, Sleptsov strode off slowly along a straight path, the only one cleared of snow, into that blinding distant landscape. He was amazed to be still alive, and able to perceive the brilliance of the snow and feel his front teeth ache from the cold. He even noticed that a snow-covered bush resembled a fountain and that a dog had left a series of saffron marks on the slope of a snowdrift, which had burned through its crust. A little farther, the supports of a footbridge stuck out of the snow, and there Sleptsov stopped. Bitterly, angrily, he pushed the thick, fluffy covering off the parapet. He vividly recalled how this bridge looked in summer. There was his son walking along the slippery planks, flecked with aments, and deftly plucking off with his net a butterfly that had settled on the railing. Now the boy sees his father. Forever-lost laughter plays on his face, under the turned-down brim of a straw hat burned dark by the sun; his hand toys with the chainlet of the leather purse attached to his belt, his dear, smooth, sun-tanned legs in their serge shorts and soaked sandals assume their usual cheerful widespread stance. Just recently, in Petersburg, after having babbled in his delirium about school, about his bicycle, about some great Oriental moth, he died, and yesterday Sleptsov had taken the coffin – weighed down, it seemed, with an entire lifetime – to the country, into the family vault near the village church.

It was quiet as it can only be on a bright, frosty day. Sleptsov raised his leg high, stepped off the path and, leaving blue pits behind him in the snow, made his way among the trunks of amazingly white trees to the spot where the park dropped off toward the river. Far below, ice blocks sparkled near a hole cut in the smooth expanse of white and, on the opposite bank, very straight columns of pink smoke stood above the snowy roofs of log cabins. Sleptsov took off his karakul cap and leaned against a tree trunk. Somewhere far away peasants were chopping wood – every blow bounced resonantly skyward – and beyond the light silver mist of trees, high above the squat isbas, the sun caught the equanimous radiance of the cross on the church.

III

That was where he headed after lunch, in an old sleigh with a high straight back. The cod of the black stallion clacked strongly in the frosty air, the white plumes of low branches glided overhead, and the ruts in front gave off a silvery blue sheen. When he arrived he sat for an hour or so by the grave, resting a heavy, woolen-gloved hand on the iron of the railing that burned his hand through the wool. He came home with a slight sense of disappointment, as if there, in the burial vault, he had been even further removed from his son than here, where the countless summer tracks of his rapid sandals were preserved beneath the snow.

In the evening, overcome by a fit of intense sadness, he had the main house unlocked. When the door swung open with a weighty wail, and a whiff of special, unwintery coolness came from the sonorous iron-barred vestibule, Sleptsov took the lamp with its tin reflector from the watchman's hand and entered the house alone. The parquet floors crackled eerily under his step. Room after room filled with yellow light, and the shrouded furniture seemed unfamiliar; instead of a tinkling chandelier, a soundless bag hung from the ceiling; and Sleptsov's enormous shadow, slowly extending one arm, floated across the wall and over the gray squares of curtained paintings.

He went into the room which had been his son's study in summer, set the lamp on the window ledge, and, breaking his fingernails as he did so, opened the folding shutters, even though all was darkness outside. In the blue glass the yellow flame of the slightly smoky lamp appeared, and his large, bearded face showed momentarily.

He sat down at the bare desk and sternly, from under bent brows, examined the pale wallpaper with its garlands of bluish roses; a narrow office-like cabinet, with sliding drawers from top to bottom; the couch and armchairs under slip-covers; and suddenly, dropping his head onto the desk, he started to shake, passionately, noisily, pressing first his lips, then his wet cheek, to the cold, dusty wood and clutching at its far corners.

In the desk he found a notebook, spreading boards, sup-plies of black pins, and an English biscuit tin that contained a large exotic cocoon which had cost three rubles. It was papery to the touch and seemed made of a brown folded leaf. His son had remembered it during his sickness, regretting that he had left it behind, but consoling himself with the thought that the chrysalid inside was probably dead. He also found a torn net: a tarlatan bag on a collapsible hoop (and the muslin still smelled of summer and sun-hot grass).

Then, bending lower and lower and sobbing with his whole body, he began pulling out one by one the glass-topped drawers of the cabinet. In the dim lamplight the even files of specimens shone silk-like under the glass. Here, in this room, on that very desk, his son had spread the wings of his captures. He would first pin the carefully killed insect in the cork-bottomed groove of the setting board, between the adjustable strips of wood, and fasten down flat with pinned strips of paper the still fresh, soft wings. They had now dried long ago and been transferred to the cabinet – those spec-tacular Swallowtails, those dazzling Coppers and Blues, and the various Fritillaries, some mounted in a supine position to display the mother-of-pearl undersides. His son used to pronounce their Latin names with a moan of triumph or in an arch aside of disdain. And the moths, the moths, the first Aspen Hawk of five summers ago!

IV

The night was smoke-blue and moonlit; thin clouds were scattered about the sky but did not touch the delicate, icy moon. The trees, masses of gray frost, cast dark shadows on the drifts, which scintillated here and there with metallic sparks. In the plush-upholstered, well-heated room of the annex Ivan had placed a two-foot fir tree in a clay pot on the table, and was just attaching a candle to its cruciform tip when Sleptsov returned from the main house, chilled, red-eyed, with gray dust smears on his cheek, carrying a wooden case under his arm. Seeing the Christmas tree on the table, he asked absently: 'What's that?'

Relieving him of the case, Ivan answered in a low, mellow voice: 'There's a holiday coming up tomorrow.'

'No, take it away,' said Sleptsov with a frown, while thinking, Can this be Christmas Eve? How could I have forgotten?

Ivan gently insisted: 'It's nice and green. Let it stand for a while.'

'Please take it away,' repeated Sleptsov, and bent over the case he had brought. In it he had gathered his son's belongings – the folding butterfly net, the biscuit tin with the pear-shaped cocoon, the spreading board, the pins in their lacquered box, the blue notebook. Half of the first page had been torn out, and its remaining fragment contained part of a French dictation. There followed daily entries, names of captured butterflies, and other notes:

'Walked across the bog as far as Borovichi, . . .'

'*Raining today. Played checkers with Father, then read Goncharov's* Frigate, *a deadly bore.*'

'*Marvelous hot day. Rode my bike in the evening. A midge got in my eye. Deliberately rode by her dacha twice, but didn't see her...*'

Sleptsov raised his head, swallowed something hot and huge. Of whom was his son writing?

'*Rode my bike as usual,*' he read on. '*Our eyes nearly met. My darling, my love...*'

'This is unthinkable,' whispered Sleptsov. 'I'll never know....'

He bent over again, avidly deciphering the childish handwriting that slanted up then curved down in the margin.

'*Saw a fresh specimen of the Camberwell Beauty today. That means autumn is here. Rain in the evening. She has probably left, and we didn't even get acquainted. Farewell, my darling. I feel terribly sad....*'

'He never said anything to me....' Sleptsov tried to remember, rubbing his forehead with his palm.

On the last page there was an ink drawing: the hind view of an elephant – two thick pillars, the corners of two ears, and a tiny tail.

Sleptsov got up. He shook his head, restraining yet another onrush of hideous sobs.

'I-can't-bear-it-any-longer,' he drawled between groans, repeating even more slowly, 'I – can't – bear – it – any – longer....'

'It's Christmas tomorrow,' came the abrupt reminder, 'and I'm going to die. Of course. It's so simple. This very night...'

He pulled out a handkerchief and dried his eyes, his beard, his cheeks. Dark streaks remained on the handkerchief.

'...death,' Sleptsov said softly, as if concluding a long sentence.

The clock ticked. Frost patterns overlapped on the blue glass of the window. The open notebook shone radiantly on the table; next to it the light went through the muslin of the butterfly net, and glistened on a corner of the open tin. Sleptsov pressed his eyes shut, and had a fleeting sensation that earthly life lay before him, totally bared and comprehensible and ghastly in its sadness, humiliatingly pointless, sterile, devoid of miracles. . . .

At that instant there was a sudden snap – a thin sound like that of an overstretched rubber band breaking. Sleptsov opened his eyes. The cocoon in the biscuit tin had burst at its tip, and a black, wrinkled creature the size of a mouse was crawling up the wall above the table. It stopped, holding on to the surface with six black furry feet, and started palpitating strangely. It had emerged from the chrysalid because a man overcome with grief had transferred a tin box to his warm room, and the warmth had penetrated its taut leaf-and-silk envelope; it had awaited this moment so long, had collected its strength so tensely, and now, having broken out, it was slowly and miraculously expanding. Gradually the wrinkled tissues, the velvety fringes, unfurled; the fan-pleated veins grew firmer as they filled with air. It became a winged thing imperceptibly, as a maturing face imperceptibly becomes beautiful. And its wings – still feeble, still moist – kept growing and unfolding, and now they were developed to the limit set for them by God, and there, on the wall, instead of a little lump of life, instead of a dark mouse, was a great *Attacus* moth like those that fly, birdlike, around lamps in the Indian dusk.

And then those thick black wings, with a glazy eyespot on each and a purplish bloom dusting their hooked foretips, took a full breath under the impulse of tender, ravishing, almost human happiness.

ANN PACKER

HER FIRSTBORN

DEAN GOES TO the window and stares at the dark parking lot, half looking for Lise though she won't arrive for another ten minutes. It's after six and the lot is all but empty, just white lines glowing with new paint. He wonders what she's doing right now. Finishing a snack? Or already locking up and heading for the car? Or, no: gathering their bed pillows and *then* heading for the car. Tonight is their first childbirth class, and the flyer said to bring pillows. He imagines them piled on her backseat – flowered, lumpy, faintly scented with the deep smells of bodies asleep – and he shudders. It seems wrong somehow, a broken rule of nature: no personal bedding outside the home, please.

She pulls in right on time, her headlights sweeping the wooden fence, and he shuts down his computer and heads out to the reception area, calling goodbye to Gregor as he approaches the elevator.

'Dean, Dean, hold on.' Gregor appears in the doorway of his office with a stack of CDs in hand, an amused look on his face. 'I just want to give you a little encouragement.' *Incurgement* is how it sounds to Dean: Gregor's from West Virginia, which shows up in about a fifth of what he says.

'Thanks,' Dean says. 'It's nice to know you care.'

'I do – in a kindly, avuncular way.'

Dean laughs: Gregor is thirty-eight to his forty-one, blond and robust to his dark and stringy. Gregor is about as avuncular as Dennis the Menace.

'Come on,' Gregor says, motioning Dean closer. 'You want to be prepared, don't you? It's like anatomy class. When Jan and I went the woman had big illustrations and a pointer. She said, "This is the uterus, these are the fallopian tubes." '

'That was in Morgantown,' Dean says. 'This is Eugene, remember? There's practically a *street* named Uterus here.'

Gregor laughs, but he's looking Dean over all the same. 'Everything OK?' he asks in a carefully blended mixture of concern and nonchalance.

Dean nods.

'Sure?'

'I'm *fine*,' Dean says. 'Lise's waiting, I've got to go.'

He pounds the Down button, then doesn't want to wait for the elevator. The fire stairs are at the other end of the hall, and he takes off at a gentle jog.

'I want a full report tomorrow,' Gregor calls. 'In exchange for bearing the lion's share of our mutual burden here.'

Dean flips the bird over his shoulder, but he's grateful: he and Gregor run a small company that publishes software guides, and this is their busy season, galleys to look over, a tight production schedule to stick to. Gregor'll be here until ten or eleven tonight, easy. 'You can't have a baby in the *fall*,' he said when Dean gave him the news. He was kidding, but only just.

Outside, Lise's car is idling at the curb. Dean slides in next to her and says, 'Sorry, Gregor had to ride me a little.'

'Wimmin been birthin' babies a long time, Dean.'

'No, it was about how Mickey Mouse the class'll be.' He pulls her close for a kiss, then takes her hand from the steering wheel and kisses it, too, on the little valley between her first two knuckles. When she returns her hand to the wheel he notices a tiny oval sticker with the word 'Kegel' printed on it, right at twelve o'clock. 'Where'd you get that?'

'At my appointment today,' she says with a smile. 'I got a whole sheet of them – I'm supposed to put them all over the house as reminders.'

A Kegel is a toning exercise for pregnant women: it's like stopping your urine midflow, according to one of Lise's books. For a while, Dean found himself trying it nearly every time he peed, just to see how it felt.

'I put one over the kitchen sink,' she says, 'and one on my bedside table, but I figured that'd be enough.'

'Moderation in all things.'

'Right.'

He reaches for her belly and strokes it. 'How was the appointment?'

'Fine, except I've gained *five pounds*. I've got to pace myself.'

'Like a marathoner?'

'I've got the carbo-loading part down anyway.'

They exchange a smile: Dean's the runner in the family, although he's tapered way down since their marriage. Used to be he wouldn't miss a morning with his group, but these last two years have taught him to question pretty much everything he thought he knew about himself, like that *running* was the only path to well-being. Most mornings now he sleeps in, Lise breathing quietly beside him.

'Everything else OK?' he asks her.

'Yeah, the head's down, I'll have my internal next time probably.'

'That it?'

She doesn't reply, and when an odd, faraway expression comes over her face he's suddenly washed with tension, certain he knows what's on her mind. But then she says, 'And twenty, and that's a hundred today, and that's *all* I'm doing, damn it,' and he lets out a big breath. Kegels. That's what she was doing, just Kegels, not thinking back after all.

The class meets in a church basement, in a room with plastic chairs set up in a circle and the air of having seen a lot of twelve-step programs in its day. Dean and Lise carry their pillows in and take seats opposite the only other couple there yet, the woman tiny and auburn-haired, dwarfed by her belly. Lise's small, too, but her belly is more volleyball-size to this woman's Great Pumpkin.

The woman leans forward eagerly. 'How far along are you?'

'Thirty-three weeks,' Lise says. 'How about you?'

'The same. Looks like forty, though, huh?'

'No, you look fine.'

'I look enormous.'

Lise shrugs but doesn't disagree. She has a knack for getting along with strangers – not so much cultivating them as keeping her distance in the most amiable possible way. Dean's just the opposite, comes off as an asshole even when he's thinking there might be a friendship in the offing.

'Do you know what you're having?' the woman says.

'We decided not to find out.' Lise looks at Dean and gives his leg a pat. At the beginning, thinking it would be easier that way – easier for her – he told her that he wanted to know, but she absolutely didn't and he's grateful now. He likes to think of the baby living its secret life in there, waiting to surprise them.

'How about you?' Lise says.

The woman smiles. 'A girl. I was so nervous finding out, because I really wanted it to be a girl.' She shrugs. 'I have a friend who's pregnant with her second and she's not finding out, either. Do you have older kids?'

Dean feels his pulse quicken and turns with concern to Lise, but she just shakes her head placidly.

'I guess you wouldn't be here,' the woman says absently,

and this time Lise doesn't react. They're here for him, of course.

Gradually the room fills, and soon every seat is taken. Dean's certain he and Lise are the oldest, which shouldn't matter but somehow does. The teacher is a tall, blowsy woman with a patch of red high on each cheek. She has an easel and a stack of illustrations but, Gregor will be sorry to hear, no pointer. When the clock over the door says seven, she picks up a piece of chalk and writes three letters on a portable blackboard: 'i-n-g.'

'I'm Susan,' she says. 'Welcome to everybody, especially the moms. This class is going to hopefully get you ready for childbirth, and since that's a pretty intimate thing, I'd like us to get to know each other a little. Let's go around the room and say our names and also something you like to do.' She points at the letters on the blackboard. 'I wrote "i-n-g" because I want you to tell us something you like *do*-ing.' She turns to the woman at her left. 'Let's start with you.'

The woman blushes. 'I'm Patricia, and I guess I like gardening.' She looks at her husband, and he nods.

'Yeah, I'm Jim, and I like skiing.'

'I'm Stephanie, and I like folk dancing.'

'I'm Gary, and I like playing soccer.'

Two more people and it'll be Lise's turn. Dean leans close to her. 'Can I say that I like be-ing alone?'

She smiles and then takes his hand and places it on her belly, just in time for him to feel the baby move. 'I'm Lise,' she says a moment later. 'It's pronounced Lisa, but it's spelled L-i-s-e.' This is something she generally tells people within minutes of meeting them; it was one of the first things Dean ever heard her say. 'I like reminding myself I won't be pregnant forever.'

159

The whole class laughs, and Dean says, 'Yeah, I'm Dean, and I like the fact that that's true.'

The next person starts to talk, and it's only then that Dean realizes he didn't use an i-n-g word. I like fail-ing to follow simple instructions.

Finally it's the last couple's turn. The woman says she likes making jam, and then her husband, a big guy with a florid face and a Hawaiian shirt, says, 'She's like this, so you know one thing *I* like doing!'

The class titters, and Lise digs her elbow into Dean's side. Dean looks at the guy to see if he's kidding, but the guy just seems puffed up and proud. I like fucking? *This* is what Dean will tell Gregor about tomorrow.

In a moment Susan starts talking about fear and pain. Fear causes tension. Tension causes pain.

'Actually,' Lise says under her breath, '*contractions* cause pain.'

Susan takes up the chalk and turns to the blackboard. 'OK,' she says, 'let's go over what happens during labor.'

Halfway through the class she gives them a break. While the women line up for the bathroom, Dean climbs the stairs and goes outside to get some air. It's an early October night, still and cool, the rains a few weeks away although the air feels moist already, expectant.

After a few minutes Lise comes out to join him. For work she wears her hair pulled back, but it's down now, and the dampness has curled the shorter bits near her face. She looks pretty in the vaguely European way she looked pretty when they met, dark tendrils and dark eyes and a small, dark-red mouth. French or Italian, he thought then, and when they started talking it was all he could do not to compliment her on her excellent English.

He reaches out and fingers a lock of her hair. 'Don't they give us milk and crackers?'

'Juice and crackers. Little paper cups of apple juice and three Ritz crackers each.'

Back inside, the basement room seems overheated. All of the women are flushed. They've got something like two extra quarts of blood in their bodies, a slightly unnerving figure to Dean. Think of the pressure on their veins. How could you be the same afterward, shrunk back to your usual volume?

'Let's wind up,' Susan says a little later, 'by going around the room again and this time telling about any experience you've had with childbirth – if you've ever been with a woman during labor, or if you've actually attended a birth. And tell us your name again.'

Stricken, Dean turns to Lise, but she just smiles and keeps within herself, inside the chamber where she keeps all of that.

One woman tells about having been with a friend for the first part of her labor, another says she watched her sister give birth. None of the men has anything to say.

Lise and Dean have switched seats, so Dean has to go first this time. 'I'm still Dean,' he says. 'I have no prior experience with childbirth.'

Then it's Lise's turn, and Dean feels that the whole class has been waiting for this moment, expecting it somehow. 'I'm Lise,' she says. 'I went through childbirth myself, eight years ago.' She turns to Dean and gives him a look that's almost – *apologetic*, he finds himself thinking. She holds her eyes on his, but just as he's finally mustering a dumb smile she turns away.

'I had a little boy,' she says to the class. 'I was married to someone else then. The baby died when he was five months old.'

Dean's lips are dry, and he licks them. He doesn't know

how she can stand this – he can't himself stand the fact that she has to. He looks around the room: the women are staring at her, the men at their own hands. Susan clears her throat. 'How did he die?' she asks in a gentle voice that makes Dean think of murder.

'He died in his sleep,' Lise says, 'crib death,' and then there are no more questions, no more answers, just the sound of the clock ticking and the feel of a group of people waiting for something to be over. Dean stares into the center of the room and waits, too, moment giving way to moment until finally, mercifully, the woman next to Lise takes her turn.

In bed at home later, Dean tries to look at proofs while Lise arranges the pillows she needs for sleep. He's used to this, but he half watches anyway, thinking the pillows look different tonight, distorted somehow after their time in the bright lights of the church basement. Next week, Susan promised, they'll use them.

Lise puffs a little with the effort of getting comfortable. She's on her side with one pillow between her legs, another under her belly, and a third smaller one that she's tucking between her breasts. 'Can I get you anything?' he says, and she gives him a rueful look.

'A surrogate? I guess it's a little late for that.'

'How about a backrub?' He gets off the bed and goes around behind her, easing himself onto the mattress. He lays his hands onto the soft flannel of her nightgown and begins kneading, pressing into her muscles with the heels of his hands. There's more flesh than before, and it seems loose somehow, sliding across her back as if not quite a part of her but rather an extra layer of clothing.

'Right there,' she says, and he presses harder. 'It wasn't so bad, was it?'

'The class?' he says. 'It was OK. Susan's a bit caring.'

She laughs, but he feels tense. In her dresser, in the top drawer, there's a picture of the dead baby, and as he stares at the drawer front he can almost see it: the blond wood frame, the baby with his little topknot curl and his toothless grin, his drooly lower lip catching the reflection of the flash.

'I thought what you said...' he says. 'I thought you were amazing.'

'About Jasper?'

The name gives him a tiny shock, as always. 'Yeah.'

'It was fine.'

They are both silent, and for a while Dean just moves his hands across her back, kneading and pushing, pushing and kneading, until from her breathing he knows that she's asleep. The light's still on, but whereas before this pregnancy she was the finickiest sleeper he ever slept with, requiring perfect darkness and silence, she now falls asleep effortlessly, at will – even against her will, over books, carefully selected DVDs, sometimes even Dean's conversation.

He turns off the light, but rather than climb in next to her he goes to the window and looks outside. A misty night, starless, the rooflines of his neighborhood jagged against the lightish sky. What happened to her is just too horrible. It's unspeakable – *literally* unspeakable, in a way: when he first heard, it became for a while both all he could think of about her and also something they couldn't really talk about – *didn't* really talk about, because what was there to say? Horrible horrible horrible horrible horrible. In some true, essential way that was all that could be said.

By feel he finds shorts and his running shoes, then makes his way to the front door. It ca-thuds shut behind him and he locks it, then slips his running key into his Velcro pocket. He does stretches on the front lawn, just a quick set to take the edge off, then he sets out, first an easy trot but soon he's running all out, heaving hard, racing toward the University. His first run in how long – a week? Ten days? The dark feels like a material thing he has to penetrate. He passes the development office where Lise does graphic design, the science complex, Oregon Hall. On Agate he turns and presses even harder to get past the track – track town, he's a runner in a town of runners, out here again but alone this time, legs burning, lungs burning, sweat sliding off him in streams.

That weekend, Dean and Lise are in a Thai restaurant on Willamette when Gregor and his wife, Jan, come in. Dean hunkers in his chair, but of course Gregor spots him right away. 'Dean and Lise!' he booms from across the crowded restaurant, his arm moving over his head like a windshield wiper at top speed. 'Great! What say we join forces?'

Dean groans. After five years of working with Gregor, Dean thinks of him as a family member, but the kind with whom you don't want to be seen in public.

'It's OK,' Lise says.

The hostess leads them over, Gregor beaming, Jan just behind him with a shy look on her face, her brown hair in a new, shorter style that makes her look – there's no other word for it – matronly. Dean knows her pretty well, from his bachelor days, when once or twice a month she'd phone the office late in the afternoon to tell Gregor to bring him home for dinner, but she and Lise aren't well acquainted. The four of them have been out together only once before, back when Dean and Lise weren't married yet. Jan was pregnant then, now that Dean thinks about it. Pregnant with two kids at home. She kept getting up from the table to call the babysitter.

She sits next to Dean, leaving Gregor the chair beside Lise. He sits down and pulls forward, then gives Lise a broad smile. 'I haven't seen you in must be ten or fifteen pounds,' he says. 'Are you eating everything in sight? You're just huge.'

Lise smiles good-naturedly, but Jan gasps. '*Gregor.*' She catches Dean's eye and shakes her head apologetically. 'Ignore him,' she says to Lise. 'How are you? You look great.'

'Thanks.'

'Are you ready?'

Lise shakes her head. She tucks a strand of hair behind her ear and says, 'All we've got is a bassinet, plus some boxes of old clothes.'

Dean swallows and stares at his placemat, the tips of his ears getting hot and, no doubt, red. The old clothes are the dead baby's, and he's afraid of what will happen next. Early in his relationship with Lise, he told Gregor about what had happened to her, and though he immediately felt he'd betrayed her and swore Gregor to secrecy, he can't imagine Gregor didn't tell Jan. He's afraid to look up, afraid to see the sympathetic, probing look he's sure Jan's giving Lise.

But: 'Go shopping,' Jan says, and now Dean does look up, to find Jan smiling innocently. 'Seriously. Borrowed stuff's nice to have, but you need to get your own stuff, too. I didn't with our first, and I felt so guilty, putting him in these ratty little stretch suits. With the others I bought new stuff, and it really made a difference, really made me feel I was welcoming them right.'

'Thanks,' Lise says. 'I'll keep that in mind.'

Gregor gives Dean a defiant look, and Dean shrugs. OK, so he doubted Gregor. OK, so he was wrong.

'Do you have a stroller?' Jan says.

Lise shakes her head.

'That's where to spend some money. The expensive ones

really do last a lot longer. There's probably nothing you'll use more.'

'OK,' Lise says. 'We'll look into that.' Under the table, she presses her stockinged foot against Dean's ankle, and he brings his other leg forward and holds her foot between his calves until their food comes.

At childbirth class the following week, Susan has them all lying on the floor, heads on their bed pillows, tensing and then relaxing each muscle group in their bodies. Tense your toes. And now relax them. Tense your ankle. And now relax it. Dean's nursing a cold and lying down should feel good, but the ceiling lights bore into his eyes and he can't stop coughing.

After the break Susan shows a short movie. It features a couple straight out of the seventies – man with sideburns and a tight, striped sweater; pregnant woman with Farrah Fawcett hair and eyebrows plucked to oblivion. The film opens with them in their motel-style living room in early labor: Dean knows this because the first thing the woman does is lean back in her chair and start breathing very deliberately, as if she were following difficult instructions. Soon the couple is in their car heading for the hospital, and she's breathing harder; next they're in a hospital corridor, walking and then stopping and then walking; and finally she's on the delivery table with a doctor nearby, his gloved hands ready. Dean turns away at the moment when the crown of the baby's head first bulges out, but he forces himself to watch as it bulges again, and then the whole head appears and it's all there, born, covered with white stuff, its arms and legs curled close to its body. Near Dean one of the women in the class sobs, and through the dark he sees Lise reach into her purse for a Kleenex and pass it to her.

Leaving the class later, the woman touches Lise's arm. 'Thanks for the rescue.'

'Oh, anytime,' Lise says. 'I keep one of those little boxes of tissues in my purse.'

The woman smiles and waves, but she gives Lise a curious backward glance as she joins her husband at the door, and Dean knows she's wondering about Lise's emotional state. He understands: he used to assume Lise thought about her baby dying all the time. She's said it's not like that, but every morning she opens her top drawer and looks at his picture while she's fishing for underpants, and Dean has to fight the urge to tell her to stop. *Don't*, he wants to say. *That'll just make it worse*. Like pressing a bruise.

Out in the parking lot, Lise hands him her purse to hold while she pulls her sweater over her head. Actually it's his sweater, a baggy old shetland he's had since college, burgundy and a bit moth-eaten, and he smiles a little, remembering a line from one of her pregnancy guides.

She tilts her head to the side. 'What?'

'I was thinking of that book: "Your husband's closet is a great place to find maternity clothes, but be sure to ask first!"'

She grins. 'Like they know you better than I do. It should be called *What to Expect from an Annoying Author*. That's the same book that told me to ask myself before taking a bite of a cookie whether it was the best possible thing I could be eating for my baby. When I want a cookie I want it *because* it's a cookie, not just because it's something to eat.'

'Do you want a cookie? We could go to that café.'

She shakes her head. 'I want a quart of mocha chip ice cream, but I think I'll just have an apple at home instead.'

They make their way across the rutted parking lot, skirting puddles, walking slowly. 'She reminded me of me,' she says once they're in the car.

Dean looks at her.

'That woman.'

His throat tightens. Was Lise crying during the movie? He was next to her the whole time, wouldn't he have noticed? Shouldn't he have?

'I mean the other time,' she says. 'We saw a movie every week, and every single time I cried right when the baby was born.' She slides her car key into the ignition, then gives him a thoughtful look. 'I don't know why I didn't tonight. I kind of thought I would, although I didn't put the tissues in my purse for that very eventuality.' She smiles. 'She sure thought so, though – did you see how she looked at me? Like she wondered why I needed a *box*, but it's this little thing, look.' She fishes in her purse and pulls out a box of tissues about the size of a wallet. 'So I blow my nose a lot.'

'People have an incurable interest in what's not their business,' Dean says. 'They want to *know*.'

Lise nods and then starts the engine, pulling onto the wet street with the car tires swishing. Dean looks out the window at the porches going by – the big, wide porches of communal living, fraying easy chairs in front of plate glass windows, bicycles chained to railings. The kind of place he lived when he was new in Eugene. He had a bedroom on the third floor, half a shelf in the refrigerator. Fourteen years ago. What he remembers is the dankness of the bathroom, how his towel never really dried from one shower to the next.

At a traffic light he turns and looks at Lise's profile, her high forehead and long, narrow nose. He thinks of the woman at class tonight, her wanting to know. What he knows isn't much: that it happened during an afternoon nap, only the second time Lise went out without him; that her husband was the one at home, the one to go in after the nap had gone on much too long. Dean still remembers the night when he heard all of this, at a little Mexican restaurant out near the airport, with red-checked oilcloths covering the tables and mariachi music coming from a radio in the kitchen. She spoke evenly as she told him about the blur after the funeral, the half-year of living back to back with her husband, the two of them moving through their house like ghosts until finally she left, taking nothing but her own clothes and the baby's. Not because she hated her husband, she said, and certainly not because she blamed him: It was just that they couldn't go on. She couldn't go on.

She's lost track of him. She doesn't even know if he's still living on the West Coast. There are moments, though, like now – sitting in the dark car beside her, knowing he could ask more about it all but not wanting to press, not wanting to press on the bruise – when Dean gets a sudden intimation of the man, of a guy his own age with a permanent pain wedged in his side like a runner's stitch, and a cold fear slides through his veins.

Very early Saturday morning, Dean is woken to complete alertness by a pack of runners passing by outside, their feet slapping the road, the muted, heaving sound of their breathing checked once or twice by a low voice. Beside him Lise's deeply asleep, her dark hair a tangle, the faint, sweet scent of her hand lotion just there under the fresh-laundry smell of the sheets. He feels as wide awake as ten a.m., but he doesn't want to get up, doesn't want to go running any more than he wants to be alone in the kitchen with the gray dawn lightening outside while he makes coffee and pages through the *Register-Guard*. Up against the headboard he finds a small pillow, a stray, and he rolls over and holds it against his ear. A few months ago, a friend of Lise's from the Bay Area told him it was the early mornings rather than the interrupted

169

nights that were hardest, but he thinks that if the baby were born already, were down the hall crying right now, he wouldn't mind at all getting up. She was passing through Eugene, Lise's friend, on her way to a family reunion in Portland, her husband and three kids in tow. She was an old friend, a neighbor from Lise's old life, and her presence had an odd effect on Lise, made the color in her cheeks a bit brighter, the pitch of her voice a bit higher. Toward the end of the visit, the friend's oldest child lifted his baby brother from the floor and flew him through the air like an airplane, and Lise said, to no one in particular, 'Jasper loved that.'

When Dean wakes again it's midmorning, he can tell by the light, by how empty the bed feels next to him, as if Lise's been up for a while. Her nightgown is on a hook on the back of the bedroom door, and he wanders out and finds her dressed in her denim maternity overalls, standing in what will be the nursery, a small corner room with white walls and a square, jade green rug.

'What a sleeper,' she says when she sees him.

'I do my best.'

'Was there anything you wanted to do today? I was thinking we could go buy a rocking chair, maybe a few other things.'

An hour later, they borrow a neighbor's pickup truck and drive downtown, where they buy a rocking chair, a changing table, four hooded towels, a four-hundred-dollar stroller, a package of cloth diapers, a footstool for nursing, five flannel blankets, a car seat, a stack of pastel washcloths, a Snugli, a mobile with multicolored zoo animals hanging from it, a lambskin, and the tiniest fingernail clippers Dean has ever seen. Driving home with the big things in boxes in the truck bed behind them and shopping bags strewn at their feet, Dean is exhilarated.

After lunch he mows the front lawn, and then, because

it's something he's been meaning to do for weeks, he gathers up and takes to the supermarket several dozen empty beer bottles, which yield him for his trouble a few wrinkled dollar bills and a handful of change. Back at home he's not surprised to find Lise in the baby's room again, standing amid the morning's loot. He fetches his toolbox and assembles the changing table while she comes and goes, carrying stacks of things to and from the garage: in the distance he hears the washing machine churn and drain, and the thrum of the dryer.

As he's tightening the last screw on the footstool, she goes into the closet and reappears with a cardboard box.

'Careful, I'll do that,' he says, but she's already set it on the floor and crossed to his toolbox for a box cutter.

She slices open the edges of the box first, then pulls up the still-joined flaps and cuts them carefully, so the blade won't go through what's underneath. With a feeling of discomfort, he watches as she opens the box, and then there they are, the dead baby's clothes.

She removes a handful of little white caps and sets them aside. Next is a stack of tiny white undershirts, with shoulders that somehow remind him of the way the fly looks on Jockey underwear. Halfway across the room, he doesn't know what to do or say. He feels grossly out of place, and beyond that boorish, and beyond that paralyzed.

'Pretty basic stuff,' she says, but then her expression brightens, and she eagerly withdraws a little one-piece yellow coverall with the head of a giraffe on the front. 'Look at this,' she says, looking up at him. 'I'd forgotten about this one. We always called this the giraffe suit.'

'I can see why,' he says with an idiotic smile.

She looks at him carefully. 'What do you think about using some of this stuff?'

There's no reason not to, unless it would make her feel worse. 'Sure,' he says. 'Whatever you want.'

She brushes absently at a spot on her overalls, then sets the giraffe suit down and rubs her lower back with both hands. 'I do want us to get some new stuff,' she says, 'but I feel like – I don't know – I'd like to use some of these things, too. I mean, I saved them as Jasper outgrew them, for when he had a little brother or sister. Would it bother you?'

'Not at all.'

The doorbell rings, and he hesitates a moment, then makes his way to the front door. Outside, his neighbor's eight-year-old daughter is standing there with a small paper bag. 'Dad said you left this in the truck this morning,' she says, and Dean takes the bag and thanks her, then watches as she leaps off the porch and runs home. She goes to school just a block away: when he leaves for work each morning he sees her mother watching from the sidewalk until she's reached the schoolyard.

In the bag are the nail clippers. Dean closes the front door and returns to the nursery, not entirely surprised to find it empty. He comes back out and hesitates outside his and Lise's bedroom.

She's standing at her dresser, the top drawer open. She has the picture of the baby in one hand, something small and red-and-white striped in the other. Her head is bent, her dark hair brushing her shoulders, and Dean feels sure she's crying. He crosses the room and puts a hand on her back, and she turns. She isn't crying, but she has an air of crying about her: of just having cried or of being about to. 'Sweetie,' he says, and she looks up at him with her bottom lip clamped between her teeth.

'Do you know why he was smiling in this picture?'

Dean shakes his head.

'Because Mark had just pulled these from his feet and started tickling his toes.' She opens her hand, and the red-and-white thing unfolds into a tiny pair of socks. 'He loved having his toes tickled, he'd make this little noise, like "Arrr." I remember it so clearly.'

Dean doesn't know what to say. His throat is lumpy and he has to try a couple of times before he can swallow. At last he remembers the bag. 'Look,' he says. 'We left this in the pickup.'

She hesitates a moment, then turns and puts the picture away, pushing the drawer closed and pausing for a moment before turning back. She sets the socks on the dresser and looks inside the bag. 'Oh, the clippers,' she says. 'Good. We'll definitely need those.'

Gregor calls late Sunday night, after Lise's asleep. It's a habit Dean and he have gotten into, to catch up on things before the start of a new week. Tonight they talk for a while, but Dean's distracted, and soon Gregor's voice trails off.

'What?' Dean says.

'Go on to bed, son. Get some sleep while you can.'

'That's like telling someone to eat five dinners today because he's going to have to fast for the next week. There's only so much sleeping you can do. Go on, I was listening.'

'Nah, you weren't. Everything OK? Got the bag packed for the hospital?'

'Yes, Gregor,' Dean says wearily, although in fact Lise packed it just this afternoon. The books said to take all kinds of crazy stuff – lollipops and tennis balls, as if you were preparing to sit in the audience of *Let's Make a Deal* – but she just put in the basics.

'Don't forget your swim trunks,' Gregor says.

'What?'

'For the jacuzzi. Jan always made me get in with her so she could lean against me instead of the porcelain.'

'You're loving this,' Dean says. 'Go torment someone else, call a catalog and pick on the operator.'

'Come on,' Gregor says. 'I just want you to be prepared.'

'I am. Jesus.'

Gregor doesn't respond.

'What? I can't possibly be prepared, is that it? My life is going to change completely, I'll never have a free moment again. I know that, OK?'

Gregor laughs.

'OK, I even know that I don't really know it.'

'That's what I want to hear,' Gregor says. Then he adds, casually, 'How's Lise? Is she – '

'She's fine.'

Gregor is silent, and Dean thinks of yesterday, all the excited shopping and then the box of clothes. 'She got out his stuff,' he says, but then he stops himself. What is he doing? He doesn't want to tell Gregor this. His heart pounds, and he adds, almost against his will, 'His clothes.'

Gregor exhales. 'Jeez.' He hesitates and then says, 'Is she – I mean, are you guys –' He's silent for a moment. 'It must be scary,' he says at last, 'to think it could happen again. Is she really worried?'

'You'd think so,' Dean says, 'but she's not.' He fingers the buttons on the phone, strokes their faint concavities. Back when they first talked about getting married and having children, she told him that she saw what had happened as a one-time thing, plain bad luck – it bothered her when people expected her to fear a repeat. She said that wasn't how the world was – how she wanted to think of it, anyway.

As for him, he doesn't fear crib death, he fears ... what? Something.

He fears being afraid.

After saying goodbye to Gregor, he goes into the kitchen. It's nearly midnight but he's far too wired for sleep. He gulps a glass of orange juice, then crosses the room and opens the back door.

The backyard is small, little more than a deck and a tiny patch of grass, but it's nicely enclosed, and last spring Lise hung Italian tiles on the fence and planted lavender and rosemary in terra cotta pots. Dean sits on a wooden bench they chose together shortly after they were married, and he leans back. The night is cool, and he feels the wind stir goose bumps from his bare arms. Overhead the half-moon looks transparent. The faint scent of lavender reminds him of a trip to Provence he and Lise took two summers ago, and he finds himself remembering an evening there, in a village near Arles. Walking after coffee in a tiny café, they happened upon a kind of amateur's night at the local bullfight, and they sat and watched from rickety bleachers while boys barely old enough to shave teased and provoked bulls, then leapt to safety over the low wall of the ring. Near Dean and Lise, a small family called and cajoled to one of the boys, and when his turn in the ring was over he came and sat with them, had his head rubbed by his father and then reached to take onto his lap a little girl dressed in pink ruffles. Dean watched them openly, and when the boy looked up and met his gaze he gave Dean a look of such sweet contentment that Dean felt a rush of love not just for him but for all of them, the proud father and the fat mother, the little, overdressed girl: love and pure longing. If it did happen again, if his and Lise's baby died, too, would they survive? Would their marriage? The thing is, there's no telling. From where he sits, less than a month away from fatherhood, he sees that what they've done together acknowledges the possibility of its own undoing: that what there is to gain is exactly equal to what there is to lose.

Labor starts in the kitchen three days before Lise's due date, with a gathering of color in her face, a low moan as she bends over the counter, her weight on her forearms. In a moment she looks up and smiles, and Dean sets down the pan he's been drying and says the exact thing he hoped he wouldn't say at this moment, a line out of a bad movie: 'Is it time?'

It isn't, quite. But close to midnight, after hours with his watch in his hand, timing contractions, Dean helps her to the car and they head for the hospital, Dean trying to avoid potholes while she puffs in the seat next to him, her hands on her belly.

'Jesus,' she says, 'I better be fucking five centimeters dilated when we get there or I'm never going to make it.'

He reaches for her hand, but a moment later she moans and shakes him away. She's already told him that he's not to talk to her, touch her, or in any way get in her face while she's in hard labor. Ice chips. That was all her first husband was allowed to do, feed her ice chips.

Up ahead the hospital looms into view, and he imagines plowing right through the double front doors – the car would just about fit. The walk from the parking area takes forever, Dean standing by while Lise staggers along, bent like an old woman. Inside, a clerk takes her name and phones for a wheelchair. The orderly pushing it doesn't seem surprised when Lise refuses it, nor when, several minutes and only twenty yards later, she changes her mind.

Upstairs, minutes stretch endlessly while hours collapse upon themselves. There's a period of walking in the halls, another of standing nearby while she rests her forearms on a bar and moans. Drugs are discussed, rejected, demanded.

Then for a strange interlude Dean sits in a chair next to the bed and nearly dozes, only to be startled to alertness by a bright light aimed at his wife's crotch. All the blowing and panting, the ice chips, the dial on the fetal monitor springing up and down – it's all as he was told it would be and at the same time utterly shocking. Then suddenly Lise cries, 'Oh my God, I can't do this, I can't do this,' and the room stills to her.

'That's the wrong attitude,' the midwife says. 'You have to think you can do it.'

'I can do this, I can do this,' Lise cries; and then she does.

Lise in the rocking chair with Danny curled in her lap. Danny asleep in the very center of Dean and Lise's huge bed. Lise on her side on the couch with Danny next to her, his mouth around her nipple. Danny staring at Dean while Dean stares at Danny. Every moment feels consequential, essential to preserve somehow and yet also infinitely repeatable. Dean watches Lise watching Danny, and his eyes brim and overflow. Lise watches Dean watching her, and tears stream down her cheeks.

Dean has never been so tired in all his life. Two-fourteen in the morning, 3:45, 5:03: walking, walking. His shoulders have never felt so sore, his upper arms. Danny wants to be held. He's five days old, seven, and Dean still hasn't set foot in the office. Gregor and Jan arrive one afternoon while Lise is asleep, and answering the door with Danny in his arms, Dean hardly hears their greetings and exclamations, his only thought that at last he can go to the bathroom. They've brought gifts for Danny – a navy blue sleepsuit, a copy of *Goodnight Moon*, and three different lullaby tapes, but the thing that touches Dean is a huge dish of lasagne, good for at least four dinners. He hugs them both.

The day of Danny's two-week checkup arrives and Dean is ready with a list of questions for the doctor. The blister on Danny's upper lip, the sucking blister – could it pop and what would happen if it did? The spitting up – is it normal for there to be so much of it? The cradle cap, the hiccuping, the way one of his toes sort of curls under the one next to it...

In the living room, getting ready to go, Dean buckles a sleeping Danny into his car seat, drapes a blanket over the handle because it's misting a little outside, and turns to Lise just as she's zipping the diaper bag.

'I'll go start the car and get the heater going.'

'Good idea.' There are rings around her eyes, a small smear of what looks like mustard near the cuff of her white oxford shirt, which is actually his: since Danny's birth she's been living in his shirts – for their looseness, for how easy they are to unbutton for nursing. She follows his glance to the smear. 'Oops,' she says.

'Tough times call for tough people.'

'Still, I think I'll change. There's no one at a pediatrician's office who won't know what that is.'

She heads for the bedroom, and Dean takes the blanket off the car seat to look at Danny. He's still asleep, one round cheek resting on his shoulder: his drunken-old-man look. 'You nailed Mommy,' Dean says. 'What a thing to do.'

The doctor's office is crowded, full of small children swarming all over a colorful plastic play structure or tapping insistently on the glass of a large aquarium. Dean sets Danny's car seat in a relatively quiet corner, and he and Lise sink onto the bench next to him, each of them sighing a little as they sit down.

Lise picks up a magazine, and Dean rests idly for a moment, then stretches across her to look at Danny. He touches Danny's forehead, his cheek, his impossibly tiny fist. Danny's fingers scare Dean, how fragile they are: little matchsticks in flimsy padding.

A nurse comes into the waiting room and says, 'Daniel?,' and Lise's on her feet waiting well before Dean gets it. He lifts the car seat and follows her and the nurse back to a small examining room, where the nurse asks questions about feeding and sleep and then tells them to undress Danny. She leaves and reappears when they've got him down to his diaper, which she untapes, then she carries him to the scale, whisks the diaper out from under him, and slides the scale's weights around until she's arrived at his.

The pediatrician comes in a little later. He asks Dean, who's been holding Danny, to set him on the examining table, and then he listens to Danny's chest, rotates Danny's legs, presses his giant fingers into Danny's abdomen. Dean stands just to the side, so alert he realizes he's waiting for Danny to learn to roll over and to roll to the edge of the table: if he does this, Dean will be ready to catch him. Danny's awake now and quiet, and when the doctor finishes his examination and loops his stethoscope around his neck, he and Dean and Lise gather and stare at Danny, watch as his ocean-deep eyes move from one of them to the next.

'Can I hold him?' the doctor asks Lise, and while Dean's wondering what's odd about this, Lise nods, and the doctor lifts Danny and cradles him against his chest. 'He's a nice little bundle,' the doctor says, and all at once Dean understands that what he's feeling is the awe of ownership, amazement that permission is his and Lise's to give or refuse. Just two weeks and he's an expert on Danny, on his Dannyness, each day placing into an infinitely expandable container every new thing he knows to be true about his baby. He thinks of what he knows about the dead baby – about *Jasper* –

and it's next to nothing: he liked to be flown through the air like an airplane, he loved to have his father tickle his toes. Dean's had it all wrong: it isn't that Lise had a baby who died, but rather that she had a baby, who died. He looks at her, creases around her eyes as she smiles at Danny, and he feels a little space open up in his mind, for all she can tell him about her firstborn.

The doctor turns to Dean now, holding Danny out like an offering. 'Dad?' he says. 'Do you want him back now?'

GUY DE MAUPASSANT

SIMON'S FATHER

Translated by Ernest Boyd

NOON HAD JUST struck. The school-door opened and the youngsters streamed out tumbling over one another in their haste to get out quickly. But instead of promptly dispersing and going home to dinner as was their daily wont, they stopped a few paces off, broke up into knots and set to whispering.

The fact was that that morning Simon, the son of La Blanchotte, had, for the first time, attended school.

They had all of them in their families heard of La Blanchotte; and although in public she was welcome enough, the mothers among themselves treated her with compassion of a somewhat disdainful kind, which the children had caught without in the least knowing why.

As for Simon himself, they did not know him, for he never went abroad, and did not play around with them through the streets of the village or along the banks of the river. So they did not like him much, and it was with a certain delight, mingled with astonishment, that they gathered in groups this morning, repeating to each other this phrase pronounced by a lad of fourteen or fifteen who appeared to know all about it, so sagaciously did he wink: 'You know Simon – well, he has no father.'

La Blanchotte's son appeared in his turn upon the threshold of the school.

He was seven or eight years old, rather pale, very neat, with a timid and almost awkward manner.

He was making his way back to his mother's house when the various groups of his schoolfellows, perpetually whispering, and watching him with the mischievous and heartless eyes of children bent upon playing a nasty trick, gradually surrounded him and ended by enclosing him altogether. There he stood amongst them, surprised and embarrassed, not understanding what they were going to do to him. But the lad who had brought the news, puffed up with the success he had met with, demanded:

'What is your name?'

He answered: 'Simon.'

'Simon what?' retorted the other.

The child, altogether bewildered, repeated: 'Simon.'

The lad shouted at him: 'You must be named Simon something! That is not a name – Simon indeed!'

And he, on the brink of tears, replied for the third time: 'My name is Simon.'

The urchins began laughing. The lad triumphantly lifted up his voice: 'You can see plainly that he has no father.'

A deep silence ensued. The children were dumbfounded by this extraordinary, impossibly monstrous thing – a boy who had no father; they looked upon him as a phenomenon, an unnatural being, and they felt rising in them the hitherto inexplicable pity of their mothers for La Blanchotte. As for Simon, he had propped himself against a tree to avoid falling, and he stood there as if paralysed by an irreparable disaster. He sought to explain, but he could think of no answer for them, no way to deny this horrible charge that he had no father. At last he shouted at them quite recklessly: 'Yes, I have one.'

'Where is he?' demanded the boy.

Simon was silent, he did not know. The children shrieked, tremendously excited. These sons of the soil, more animal than human, experienced the cruel craving which makes the fowls of a farmyard destroy one of their own kind as soon as it is wounded. Simon suddenly spied a little neighbour, the son of a widow, whom he had always seen, as he himself was to be seen, quite alone with his mother.

'And no more have you,' he said, 'no more have you a father.'

'Yes,' replied the other, 'I have one.'

'Where is he?' rejoined Simon.

'He is dead,' declared the brat with superb dignity, 'he is in the cemetery, is my father.'

A murmur of approval rose amid the scapegraces, as if the fact of possessing a father dead in a cemetery made their comrade big enough to crush the other one who had no father at all. And these rogues, whose fathers were for the most part evil-doers, drunkards, thieves, and harsh with their wives, hustled each other as they pressed closer and closer to Simon as though they, the legitimate ones, would stifle in their pressure one who was beyond the law.

The lad next to Simon suddenly put his tongue out at him with a waggish air and shouted at him:

'No father! No father!'

Simon seized him by the hair with both hands and set to work to kick his legs while he bit his cheek ferociously. A tremendous struggle ensued. The two boys were separated and Simon found himself beaten, torn, bruised, rolled on the ground in the middle of the ring of applauding little vagabonds. As he arose, mechanically brushing his little blouse all covered with dust with his hand, someone shouted at him:

'Go and tell your father.'

He then felt a great sinking in his heart. They were stronger than he, they had beaten him and he had no answer to give them, for he knew it was true that he had no father. Full of pride he tried for some moments to struggle against the tears which were suffocating him. He had a choking fit, and then without cries he began to weep with great sobs which shook him incessantly. Then a ferocious joy broke out among his enemies, and, just like savages in fearful festivals, they took one another by the hand and danced in a circle about him as they repeated in refrain:

'No father! No father!'

But suddenly Simon ceased sobbing. Frenzy overtook him. There were stones under his feet; he picked them up and with all his strength hurled them at his tormentors. Two or three were struck and ran away yelling, and so formidable did he appear that the rest became panic-stricken. Cowards, like a jeering crowd in the presence of an exasperated man, they broke up and fled. Left alone, the little thing without a father set off running toward the fields, for a recollection had been awakened which nerved his soul to a great determination. He made up his mind to drown himself in the river.

He remembered, in fact, that eight days ago a poor devil who begged for his livelihood had thrown himself into the water because he was destitute. Simon had been there when they fished him out again; and the sight of the fellow, who had seemed to him so miserable and ugly, had then impressed him – his pale cheeks, his long drenched beard, and his open eyes being full of calm. The bystanders had said:

'He is dead.'

And some one had added:

'He is quite happy now.'

So Simon wished to drown himself also because he had no father, just as the wretched man did who had no money.

He reached the water and watched it flowing. Some fishes were rising briskly in the clear stream and occasionally made little leaps and caught the flies on the surface. He stopped crying in order to watch them, for their feeding interested him vastly. But, at intervals, as in the lulls of a tempest, when tremendous gusts of wind snap off trees and then die away, this thought would return to him with intense pain:

'I am about to drown myself because I have no father.'

It was very warm and lovely. The pleasant sunshine warmed the grass; the water shone like a mirror; and Simon enjoyed for some minutes the happiness of that languor which follows weeping, desirous even of falling asleep there upon the grass in the warmth of noon.

A little green frog leaped from under his feet. He endeavoured to catch it. It escaped him. He pursued it and lost it three times following. At last he caught it by one of its hind legs and began to laugh as he saw the efforts the creature made to escape. It gathered itself up on its large legs and then with a violent spring suddenly stretched them out as stiff as two bars. Its eyes stared wide open in their round, golden circle, and it beat the air with its front limbs, using them as though they were hands. It reminded him of a toy made with straight slips of wood nailed zigzag one on the other, which by a similar movement regulated the exercise of the little soldiers fastened thereon. Then he thought of his home and of his mother, and overcome by great sorrow he again began to weep. His limbs trembled; and he placed himself on his knees and said his prayers as before going to bed. But he was unable to finish them, for such hurried and violent sobs overtook him that he was completely overwhelmed. He thought no more, he no longer heeded anything around him but was wholly given up to tears.

Suddenly a heavy hand was placed upon his shoulder, and a rough voice asked him:

'What is it that causes you so much grief, my little man?'

Simon turned round. A tall workman, with a black beard and curly hair, was staring at him good-naturedly. He answered with his eyes and throat full of tears:

'They have beaten me because – I – I have no father – no father.'

'What!' said the man smiling, 'why, everybody has one.'

The child answered painfully amid his spasms of grief:

'But I – I – I have none.'

Then the workman became serious. He had recognized La Blanchotte's son, and although a recent arrival to the neighbourhood he had a vague idea of her history.

'Well,' said he, 'console yourself, my boy, and come with me home to your mother. You'll have a father.'

And so they started on the way, the big one holding the little one by the hand. The man smiled again, for he was not sorry to see this Blanchotte, who by popular report was one of the prettiest girls in the country-side, and, perhaps, he said to himself at the bottom of his heart, that a lass who had erred once might very well err again.

They arrived in front of a very neat little white house.

'There it is,' exclaimed the child, and he cried: 'Mamma.'

A woman appeared, and the workman instantly left off smiling, for he at once perceived that there was no more fooling to be done with the tall pale girl, who stood austerely at her door as though to defend from one man the threshold of that house where she had already been betrayed by another. Intimidated, his cap in his hand, he stammered out:

'See, Madame, I have brought you back your little boy, who was lost near the river.'

But Simon flung his arms about his mother's neck and told her, as he again began to cry:

'No, mamma, I wished to drown myself, because the others had beaten me – had beaten me – because I have no father.'

A painful blush covered the young woman's cheeks, and, hurt to the quick, she embraced her child passionately, while the tears coursed down her face. The man, much moved, stood there, not knowing how to get away. But Simon suddenly ran up to him and said:

'Will you be my father?'

A deep silence ensued. La Blanchotte, dumb and tortured with shame, leaned against the wall, her hands upon her heart. The child, seeing that no answer was made him, replied:

'If you do not wish it, I shall return to drown myself.'

The workman took the matter as a jest and answered laughing:

'Why, yes, I wish it, certainly.'

'What is your name,' went on the child, 'so that I may tell the others when they wish to know your name?'

'Philip,' answered the man.

Simon was silent a moment so that he might get the name well into his memory; then he stretched out his arms, quite consoled, and said:

'Well, then, Philip, you are my father.'

The workman, lifting him from the ground, kissed him hastily on both cheeks, and then strode away quickly.

When the child returned to school next day he was received with a spiteful laugh, and at the end of school, when the lad was about to begin again, Simon threw these words at his head as he would have done a stone: 'My father's name is Philip.'

Yells of delight burst out from all sides.

'Philip who? Philip what? What on earth is Philip? Where did you pick up your Philip?'

Simon answered nothing; and immovable in faith he defied them with his eye, ready to be martyred rather than fly before them. The schoolmaster came to his rescue and he returned home to his mother.

For about three months, the tall workman, Philip, frequently passed by La Blanchotte's house, and sometimes made bold to speak to her when he saw her sewing near the window. She answered him civilly, always sedately, never joking with him, nor permitting him to enter her house. Notwithstanding this, being like all men, a bit of a coxcomb, he imagined that she was often rosier than usual when she chatted with him.

But a fallen reputation is so difficult to recover, and always remains so fragile that, in spite of the shy reserve La Blanchotte maintained, they already gossiped in the neighbourhood.

As for Simon, he loved his new father very much, and walked with him nearly every evening when the day's work was done. He went regularly to school and mixed in a dignified way with his school-fellows without ever answering them back.

One day, however, the lad who had first attacked him said to him:

'You have lied. You have no father called Philip.'

'Why do you say that?' demanded Simon, much disturbed.

The youth rubbed his hands. He replied:

'Because if you had one he would be your mamma's husband.'

Simon was confused by the truth of this reasoning; nevertheless he retorted:

'He is my father all the same.'

'That may well be,' exclaimed the urchin with a sneer, 'but that is not being your father altogether.'

La Blanchotte's little one bowed his head and went off dreaming in the direction of the forge belonging to old Loizon, where Philip worked.

This forge was entombed in trees. It was very dark there,

the red glare of a formidable furnace alone lit up with great flashes five blacksmiths, who hammered upon their anvils with a terrible din. Standing enveloped in flame, they worked like demons, their eyes fixed on the red-hot iron they were pounding; and their dull ideas rising and falling with their hammers.

Simon entered without being noticed and quietly plucked his friend by the sleeve. Philip turned round. All at once the work came to a standstill and the men looked on very attentively. Then, in the midst of this unaccustomed silence, rose Simon's piping voice.

'Philip, explain to me what La Michaude's boy has just told me, that you are not altogether my father.'

'And why so?' asked the smith.

The child replied in all innocence:

'Because you are not my mamma's husband.'

No one laughed. Philip remained standing, leaning his forehead upon the back of his great hands, which held the handle of his hammer upright upon the anvil. He mused. His four companions watched him, and, like a tiny mite among these giants, Simon anxiously waited. Suddenly, one of the smiths, voicing the sentiment of all, said to Philip:

'All the same La Blanchotte is a good and honest girl, stalwart and steady in spite of her misfortune, and one who would make a worthy wife for an honest man.'

'That is true,' remarked the three others.

The smith continued:

'Is it the girl's fault if she has fallen? She had been promised marriage, and I know more than one who is much respected today and has sinned every bit as much.'

'That is true,' responded the three men in chorus.

He resumed:

'How hard she has toiled, poor thing, to educate her lad

all alone, and how much she has wept since she no longer goes out, save to church, God only knows.'

'That is also true,' said the others.

Then no more was heard save the roar of the bellows which fanned the fire of the furnace. Philip hastily bent down towards Simon:

'Go and tell your mamma that I shall come to speak to her.'

Then he pushed the child out by the shoulders. He returned to his work and in unison the five hammers again fell upon their anvils. Thus they wrought the iron until nightfall, strong, powerful, happy, like Vulcans satisfied. But as the great bell of a cathedral resounds upon feast days, above the jingling of the other bells, so Philip's hammer, dominating the noise of the others, clanged second after second with a deafening uproar. His eye on the fire, he plied his trade vigorously, erect amid the sparks.

The sky was full of stars as he knocked at La Blanchotte's door. He had his Sunday blouse on, a fresh shirt, and his beard was trimmed. The young woman showed herself upon the threshold and said in a grieved tone:

'It is not right to come this way when night has fallen, Mr Philip.'

He wished to answer, but stammered and stood confused before her.

She resumed.

'And you understand quite well that it will not do that I should be talked about any more.'

Then he said all at once:

'What does that matter to me, if you will be my wife!'

No voice replied to him, but he believed that he heard in the shadow of the room the sound of a body falling. He entered very quickly; and Simon, who had gone to his bed, distinguished the sound of a kiss and some words that his mother said very softly. Then he suddenly found himself lifted up by the hands of his friend, who, holding him at the length of his herculean arms, exclaimed to him:

'You will tell your school-fellows that your father is Philip Remy, the blacksmith, and that he will pull the ears of all who do you any harm.'

The next day, when the school was full and lessons were about to begin, little Simon stood up quite pale with trembling lips:

'My father,' said he in a clear voice, 'is Philip Remy, the blacksmith, and he has promised to box the ears of all who do me any harm.'

This time no one laughed any longer, for he was very well known, was Philip Remy, the blacksmith, and he was a father of whom they would all have been proud.

JAMES JOYCE

A LITTLE CLOUD

EIGHT YEARS BEFORE he had seen his friend off at the North Wall and wished him godspeed. Gallaher had got on. You could tell that at once by his travelled air, his well-cut tweed suit, and fearless accent. Few fellows had talents like his and fewer still could remain unspoiled by such success. Gallaher's heart was in the right place and he had deserved to win. It was something to have a friend like that.

Little Chandler's thoughts ever since lunch-time had been of his meeting with Gallaher, of Gallaher's invitation and of the great city London where Gallaher lived. He was called Little Chandler because, though he was but slightly under the average stature, he gave one the idea of being a little man. His hands were white and small, his frame was fragile, his voice was quiet and his manners were refined. He took the greatest care of his fair silken hair and moustache and used perfume discreetly on his handkerchief. The half-moons of his nails were perfect and when he smiled you caught a glimpse of a row of childish white teeth.

As he sat at his desk in the King's Inns he thought what changes those eight years had brought. The friend whom he had known under a shabby and necessitous guise had become a brilliant figure on the London Press. He turned often from his tiresome writing to gaze out of the office window. The glow of a late autumn sunset covered the grass plots and walks. It cast a shower of kindly golden dust on the untidy nurses and decrepit old men who drowsed on the benches;

it flickered upon all the moving figures – on the children who ran screaming along the gravel paths and on everyone who passed through the gardens. He watched the scene and thought of life; and (as always happened when he thought of life) he became sad. A gentle melancholy took possession of him. He felt how useless it was to struggle against fortune, this being the burden of wisdom which the ages had bequeathed to him.

He remembered the books of poetry upon his shelves at home. He had bought them in his bachelor days and many an evening, as he sat in the little room off the hall, he had been tempted to take one down from the bookshelf and read out something to his wife. But shyness had always held him back; and so the books had remained on their shelves. At times he repeated lines to himself and this consoled him.

When his hour had struck he stood up and took leave of his desk and of his fellow-clerks punctiliously. He emerged from under the feudal arch of the King's Inns, a neat modest figure, and walked swiftly down Henrietta Street. The golden sunset was waning and the air had grown sharp. A horde of grimy children populated the street. They stood or ran in the roadway or crawled up the steps before the gaping doors or squatted like mice upon the thresholds. Little Chandler gave them no thought. He picked his way deftly through all that minute vermin-like life and under the shadow of the gaunt spectral mansions in which the old nobility of Dublin had roistered. No memory of the past touched him, for his mind was full of a present joy.

He had never been in Corless's but he knew the value of the name. He knew that people went there after the theatre to eat oysters and drink liqueurs; and he had heard that the waiters there spoke French and German. Walking swiftly by at night he had seen cabs drawn up before the door and richly dressed ladies, escorted by cavaliers, alight and enter quickly. They wore noisy dresses and many wraps. Their faces were powdered and they caught up their dresses, when they touched earth, like alarmed Atalantas. He had always passed without turning his head to look. It was his habit to walk swiftly in the street even by day and whenever he found himself in the city late at night he hurried on his way apprehensively and excitedly. Sometimes, however, he courted the causes of his fear. He chose the darkest and narrowest streets and, as he walked boldly forward, the silence that was spread about his footsteps troubled him, the wandering silent figures troubled him; and at times a sound of low fugitive laughter made him tremble like a leaf.

He turned to the right towards Capel Street. Ignatius Gallaher on the London Press! Who would have thought it possible eight years before? Still, now that he reviewed the past, Little Chandler could remember many signs of future greatness in his friend. People used to say that Ignatius Gallaher was wild. Of course, he did mix with a rakish set of fellows at that time, drank freely and borrowed money on all sides. In the end he had got mixed up in some shady affair, some money transaction: at least, that was one version of his flight. But nobody denied him talent. There was always a certain ... something in Ignatius Gallaher that impressed you in spite of yourself. Even when he was out at elbows and at his wits' end for money he kept up a bold face. Little Chandler remembered (and the remembrance brought a slight flush of pride to his cheek) one of Ignatius Gallaher's sayings when he was in a tight corner:

– Half time, now, boys, he used to say light-heartedly. Where's my considering cap?

That was Ignatius Gallaher all out; and, damn it, you couldn't but admire him for it.

Little Chandler quickened his pace. For the first time in his life he felt himself superior to the people he passed. For the first time his soul revolted against the dull inelegance of Capel Street. There was no doubt about it: if you wanted to succeed you had to go away. You could do nothing in Dublin. As he crossed Grattan Bridge he looked down the river towards the lower quays and pitied the poor stunted houses. They seemed to him a band of tramps, huddled together along the river-banks, their old coats covered with dust and soot, stupefied by the panorama of sunset and waiting for the first chill of night to bid them arise, shake themselves and begone. He wondered whether he could write a poem to express his idea. Perhaps Gallaher might be able to get it into some London paper for him. Could he write something original? He was not sure what idea he wished to express but the thought that a poetic moment had touched him took life within him like an infant hope. He stepped onward bravely.

Every step brought him nearer to London, farther from his own sober inartistic life. A light began to tremble on the horizon of his mind. He was not so old – thirty-two. His temperament might be said to be just at the point of maturity. There were so many different moods and impressions that he wished to express in verse. He felt them within him. He tried to weigh his soul to see if it was a poet's soul. Melancholy was the dominant note of his temperament, he thought, but it was a melancholy tempered by recurrences of faith and resignation and simple joy. If he could give expression to it in a book of poems perhaps men would listen. He would never be popular: he saw that. He could not sway the crowd but he might appeal to a little circle of kindred minds. The English critics, perhaps, would recognize him as one of the Celtic school by reason of the melancholy tone of his poems; besides that, he would put in allusions. He began to invent sentences and phrases from the notices which his book would get. *Mr Chandler has the gift of easy and graceful verse. . . . A wistful sadness pervades these poems. . . . The Celtic note.* It was a pity his name was not more Irish-looking. Perhaps it would be better to insert his mother's name before the surname: Thomas Malone Chandler, or better still: T. Malone Chandler. He would speak to Gallaher about it.

He pursued his revery so ardently that he passed his street and had to turn back. As he came near Corless's his former agitation began to overmaster him and he halted before the door in indecision. Finally he opened the door and entered.

The light and noise of the bar held him at the doorway for a few moments. He looked about him, but his sight was confused by the shining of many red and green wine-glasses. The bar seemed to him to be full of people and he felt that the people were observing him curiously. He glanced quickly to right and left (frowning slightly to make his errand appear serious), but when his sight cleared a little he saw that nobody had turned to look at him: and there, sure enough, was Ignatius Gallaher leaning with his back against the counter and his feet planted far apart.

– Hallo, Tommy, old hero, here you are! What is it to be? What will you have? I'm taking whiskey: better stuff than we get across the water. Soda? Lithia? No mineral? I'm the same. Spoils the flavour. . . . Here, *garçon*, bring us two halves of malt whiskey, like a good fellow. . . . Well, and how have you been pulling along since I saw you last? Dear God, how old we're getting! Do you see any signs of ageing in me – eh, what? A little grey and thin on the top – what?

Ignatius Gallaher took off his hat and displayed a large closely cropped head. His face was heavy, pale and clean-shaven. His eyes, which were of bluish slate-colour, relieved his unhealthy pallor and shone out plainly above the vivid orange tie he wore. Between these rival features the lips appeared very long and shapeless and colourless. He bent his head and felt with two sympathetic fingers the thin hair at the crown. Little Chandler shook his head as a denial. Ignatius Gallaher put on his hat again.

– It pulls you down, he said, Press life. Always hurry and scurry, looking for copy and sometimes not finding it: and then, always to have something new in your stuff. Damn proofs and printers, I say, for a few days. I'm deuced glad, I can tell you, to get back to the old country. Does a fellow good, a bit of a holiday. I feel a ton better since I landed again in dear dirty Dublin. . . . Here you are, Tommy. Water? Say when.

Little Chandler allowed his whiskey to be very much diluted.

– You don't know what's good for you, my boy, said Ignatius Gallaher. I drink mine neat.

– I drink very little as a rule, said Little Chandler modestly. An odd half-one or so when I meet any of the old crowd: that's all.

– Ah, well, said Ignatius Gallaher, cheerfully, here's to us and to old times and old acquaintance.

They clinked glasses and drank the toast.

– I met some of the old gang today, said Ignatius Gallaher. O'Hara seems to be in a bad way. What's he doing?

– Nothing, said Little Chandler. He's gone to the dogs.

– But Hogan has a good sit, hasn't he?

– Yes; he's in the Land Commission.

– I met him one night in London and he seemed to be very flush. . . . Poor O'Hara! Booze, I suppose?

– Other things, too, said Little Chandler shortly.

Ignatius Gallaher laughed.

– Tommy, he said, I see you haven't changed an atom.

You're the very same serious person that used to lecture me on Sunday mornings when I had a sore head and a fur on my tongue. You'd want to knock about a bit in the world. Have you never been anywhere, even for a trip?

– I've been to the Isle of Man, said Little Chandler.

Ignatius Gallaher laughed.

– The Isle of Man! he said. Go to London or Paris: Paris, for choice. That'd do you good.

– Have you seen Paris?

– I should think I have! I've knocked about there a little.

– And is it really so beautiful as they say? asked Little Chandler.

He sipped a little of his drink while Ignatius Gallaher finished his boldly.

– Beautiful? said Ignatius Gallaher, pausing on the word and on the flavour of his drink. It's not so beautiful, you know. Of course, it is beautiful. . . . But it's the life of Paris; that's the thing. Ah, there's no city like Paris for gaiety, movement, excitement. . . .

Little Chandler finished his whiskey and, after some trouble, succeeded in catching the barman's eye. He ordered the same again.

– I've been to the Moulin Rouge, Ignatius Gallaher continued when the barman had removed their glasses, and I've been to all the Bohemian cafés. Hot stuff! Not for a pious chap like you, Tommy.

Little Chandler said nothing until the barman returned with the two glasses: then he touched his friend's glass lightly and reciprocated the former toast. He was beginning to feel somewhat disillusioned. Gallaher's accent and way of expressing himself did not please him. There was something vulgar in his friend which he had not observed before. But perhaps it was only the result of living in London amid the bustle and competition of the Press. The old personal charm was still there under this new gaudy manner. And, after all, Gallaher had lived, he had seen the world. Little Chandler looked at his friend enviously.

– Everything in Paris is gay, said Ignatius Gallaher. They believe in enjoying life – and don't you think they're right? If you want to enjoy yourself properly you must go to Paris. And, mind you, they've a great feeling for the Irish there. When they heard I was from Ireland they were ready to eat me, man.

Little Chandler took four or five sips from his glass.

– Tell me, he said, is it true that Paris is so . . . immoral as they say?

Ignatius Gallaher made a catholic gesture with his right arm.

– Every place is immoral, he said. Of course you do find spicy bits in Paris. Go to one of the students' balls, for instance. That's lively, if you like, when the *cocottes* begin to let themselves loose. You know what they are, I suppose?

– I've heard of them, said Little Chandler.

Ignatius Gallaher drank off his whiskey and shook his head.

– Ah, he said, you may say what you like. There's no woman like the Parisienne – for style, for go.

– Then it is an immoral city, said Little Chandler, with timid insistence – I mean, compared with London or Dublin?

– London! said Ignatius Gallaher. It's six of one and half-a-dozen of the other. You ask Hogan, my boy. I showed him a bit about London when he was over there. He'd open your eye. . . . I say, Tommy, don't make punch of that whiskey: liquor up.

– No, really. . . .

– O, come on, another one won't do you any harm. What is it? The same again, I suppose?

– Well . . . all right.

– *François*, the same again. . . . Will you smoke, Tommy?

Ignatius Gallaher produced his cigar-case. The two friends lit their cigars and puffed at them in silence until their drinks were served.

– I'll tell you my opinion, said Ignatius Gallaher, emerging after some time from the clouds of smoke in which he had taken refuge, it's a rum world. Talk of immorality! I've heard of cases – what am I saying? – I've known them: cases of . . . immorality. . . .

Ignatius Gallaher puffed thoughtfully at his cigar and then, in a calm historian's tone, he proceeded to sketch for his friend some pictures of the corruption which was rife abroad. He summarized the vices of many capitals and seemed inclined to award the palm to Berlin. Some things he could not vouch for (his friends had told him), but of others he had had personal experience. He spared neither rank nor caste. He revealed many of the secrets of religious houses on the Continent and described some of the practices which were fashionable in high society and ended by telling, with details, a story about an English duchess – a story which he knew to be true. Little Chandler was astonished.

– Ah, well, said Ignatius Gallaher, here we are in old jog-along Dublin where nothing is known of such things.

– How dull you must find it, said Little Chandler, after all the other places you've seen!

– Well, said Ignatius Gallaher, it's a relaxation to come over here, you know. And, after all, it's the old country, as they say, isn't it? You can't help having a certain feeling for it. That's human nature. . . . But tell me something about yourself. Hogan told me you had . . . tasted the joys of connubial bliss. Two years ago, wasn't it?

Little Chandler blushed and smiled.

– Yes, he said. I was married last May twelve months.

– I hope it's not too late in the day to offer my best wishes, said Ignatius Gallaher. I didn't know your address or I'd have done so at the time.

He extended his hand, which Little Chandler took.

– Well, Tommy, he said, I wish you and yours every joy in life, old chap, and tons of money, and may you never die till I shoot you. And that's the wish of a sincere friend, an old friend. You know that?

– I know that, said Little Chandler.

– Any youngsters? said Ignatius Gallaher.

Little Chandler blushed again.

– We have one child, he said.

– Son or daughter?

– A little boy.

Ignatius Gallaher slapped his friend sonorously on the back.

– Bravo, he said, I wouldn't doubt you, Tommy.

Little Chandler smiled, looked confusedly at his glass and bit his lower lip with three childishly white front teeth.

– I hope you'll spend an evening with us, he said, before you go back. My wife will be delighted to meet you. We can have a little music and –

– Thanks awfully, old chap, said Ignatius Gallaher, I'm sorry we didn't meet earlier. But I must leave tomorrow night.

– Tonight, perhaps . . . ?

– I'm awfully sorry, old man. You see I'm over here with another fellow, clever young chap he is too, and we arranged to go to a little card-party. Only for that . . .

– O, in that case. . . .

206

– But who knows? said Ignatius Gallaher considerately. Next year I may take a little skip over here now that I've broken the ice. It's only a pleasure deferred.

– Very well, said Little Chandler, the next time you come we must have an evening together. That's agreed now, isn't it?

– Yes, that's agreed, said Ignatius Gallaher. Next year if I come, *parole d'honneur.*

– And to clinch the bargain, said Little Chandler, we'll just have one more now.

Ignatius Gallaher took out a large gold watch and looked at it.

– Is it to be the last? he said. Because you know, I have an a.p.

– O, yes, positively, said Little Chandler.

– Very well, then, said Ignatius Gallaher, let us have another one as a *deoc an doruis* – that's good vernacular for a small whiskey, I believe.

Little Chandler ordered the drinks. The blush which had risen to his face a few moments before was establishing itself. A trifle made him blush at any time: and now he felt warm and excited. Three small whiskeys had gone to his head and Gallaher's strong cigar had confused his mind, for he was a delicate and abstinent person. The adventure of meeting Gallaher after eight years, of finding himself with Gallaher in Corless's surrounded by lights and noise, of listening to Gallaher's stories and of sharing for a brief space Gallaher's vagrant and triumphant life, upset the equipoise of his sensitive nature. He felt acutely the contrast between his own life and his friend's, and it seemed to him unjust. Gallaher was his inferior in birth and education. He was sure that he could do something better than his friend had ever done, or could ever do, something higher than mere tawdry journalism if he only got the chance. What was it that stood in his way?

His unfortunate timidity! He wished to vindicate himself in some way, to assert his manhood. He saw behind Gallaher's refusal of his invitation. Gallaher was only patronizing him by his friendliness just as he was patronizing Ireland by his visit.

The barman brought their drinks. Little Chandler pushed one glass towards his friend and took up the other boldly.

– Who knows? he said, as they lifted their glasses. When you come next year I may have the pleasure of wishing long life and happiness to Mr and Mrs Ignatius Gallaher.

Ignatius Gallaher in the act of drinking closed one eye expressively over the rim of his glass. When he had drunk he smacked his lips decisively, set down his glass and said:

– No blooming fear of that, my boy. I'm going to have my fling first and see a bit of life and the world before I put my head in the sack – if I ever do.

– Some day you will, said Little Chandler calmly.

Ignatius Gallaher turned his orange tie and slate-blue eyes full upon his friend.

– You think so? he said.

– You'll put your head in the sack, repeated Little Chandler stoutly, like everyone else if you can find the girl.

He had slightly emphasized his tone and he was aware that he had betrayed himself; but, though the colour had heightened in his cheek, he did not flinch from his friend's gaze. Ignatius Gallaher watched him for a few moments and then said:

– If ever it occurs, you may bet your bottom dollar there'll be no mooning and spooning about it. I mean to marry money. She'll have a good fat account at the bank or she won't do for me.

Little Chandler shook his head.

– Why, man alive, said Ignatius Gallaher, vehemently, do you know what it is? I've only to say the word and tomorrow

I can have the woman and the cash. You don't believe it? Well, I know it. There are hundreds – what am I saying? – thousands of rich Germans and Jews, rotten with money, that'd only be too glad. . . . You wait a while, my boy. See if I don't play my cards properly. When I go about a thing I mean business, I tell you. You just wait.

He tossed his glass to his mouth, finished his drink and laughed loudly. Then he looked thoughtfully before him and said in a calmer tone:

– But I'm in no hurry. They can wait. I don't fancy tying myself up to one woman, you know.

He imitated with his mouth the act of tasting and made a wry face.

– Must get a bit stale, I should think, he said.

Little Chandler sat in the room off the hall, holding a child in his arms. To save money they kept no servant but Annie's young sister Monica came for an hour or so in the morning and an hour or so in the evening to help. But Monica had gone home long ago. It was a quarter to nine. Little Chandler had come home late for tea and, moreover, he had forgotten to bring Annie home the parcel of coffee from Bewley's. Of course she was in a bad humour and gave him short answers. She said she would do without any tea but when it came near the time at which the shop at the corner closed she decided to go out herself for a quarter of a pound of tea and two pounds of sugar. She put the sleeping child deftly in his arms and said:

– Here. Don't waken him.

A little lamp with a white china shade stood upon the table and its light fell over a photograph which was enclosed in a frame of crumpled horn. It was Annie's photograph. Little Chandler looked at it, pausing at the thin tight lips. She wore the pale blue summer blouse which he had brought her home as a present one Saturday. It had cost him ten and eleven-pence; but what an agony of nervousness it had cost him! How he had suffered that day, waiting at the shop door until the shop was empty, standing at the counter and trying to appear at his ease while the girl piled ladies' blouses before him, paying at the desk and forgetting to take up the odd penny of his change, being called back by the cashier, and, finally, striving to hide his blushes as he left the shop by examining the parcel to see if it was securely tied. When he brought the blouse home Annie kissed him and said it was very pretty and stylish; but when she heard the price she threw the blouse on the table and said it was a regular swindle to charge ten and elevenpence for that. At first she wanted to take it back but when she tried it on she was delighted with it, especially with the make of the sleeves, and kissed him and said he was very good to think of her.

Hm! . . .

He looked coldly into the eyes of the photograph and they answered coldly. Certainly they were pretty and the face itself was pretty. But he found something mean in it. Why was it so unconscious and lady-like? The composure of the eyes irritated him. They repelled him and defied him: there was no passion in them, no rapture. He thought of what Gallaher had said about rich Jewesses. Those dark Oriental eyes, he thought, how full they are of passion, of voluptuous longing! . . . Why had he married the eyes in the photograph?

He caught himself up at the question and glanced nervously round the room. He found something mean in the pretty furniture which he had bought for his house on the hire system. Annie had chosen it herself and it reminded him of her. It too was prim and pretty. A dull resentment against his life awoke within him. Could he not escape from his little house? Was it too late for him to try to live bravely like Gallaher? Could he go to London? There was the furniture still to be paid for. If he could only write a book and get it published, that might open the way for him.

A volume of Byron's poems lay before him on the table. He opened it cautiously with his left hand lest he should waken the child and began to read the first poem in the book:

> Hushed are the winds and still the evening gloom,
>   Not e'en a Zephyr wanders through the grove,
> Whilst I return to view my Margaret's tomb
> And scatter flowers on the dust I love.

He paused. He felt the rhythm of the verse about him in the room. How melancholy it was! Could he, too, write like that, express the melancholy of his soul in verse? There were so many things he wanted to describe: his sensation of a few hours before on Grattan Bridge, for example. If he could get back again into that mood. . . .

The child awoke and began to cry. He turned from the page and tried to hush it: but it would not be hushed. He began to rock it to and fro in his arms but its wailing cry grew keener. He rocked it faster while his eyes began to read the second stanza:

> Within this narrow cell reclines her clay,
>   That clay where once . . .

It was useless. He couldn't read. He couldn't do anything. The wailing of the child pierced the drum of his ear. It was useless, useless! He was a prisoner for life. His arms trembled with anger and suddenly bending to the child's face he shouted:

– Stop!

The child stopped for an instant, had a spasm of fright

and began to scream. He jumped up from his chair and walked hastily up and down the room with the child in his arms. It began to sob piteously, losing its breath for four or five seconds, and then bursting out anew. The thin walls of the room echoed the sound. He tried to soothe it but it sobbed more convulsively. He looked at the contracted and quivering face of the child and began to be alarmed. He counted seven sobs without a break between them and caught the child to his breast in fright. If it died! . . .

The door was burst open and a young woman ran in, panting.

– What is it? What is it? she cried.

The child, hearing its mother's voice, broke out into a paroxysm of sobbing.

– It's nothing, Annie . . . it's nothing. . . . He began to cry . . .

She flung her parcels on the floor and snatched the child from him.

– What have you done to him? she cried, glaring into his face.

Little Chandler sustained for one moment the gaze of her eyes and his heart closed together as he met the hatred in them. He began to stammer:

– It's nothing. . . . He . . . he began to cry. . . . I couldn't . . . I didn't do anything. . . . What?

Giving no heed to him she began to walk up and down the room, clasping the child tightly in her arms and murmuring:

– My little man! My little mannie! Was 'ou frightened, love? . . . There now, love! There now! . . . Lambabaun! Mamma's little lamb of the world! . . . There now!

Little Chandler felt his cheeks suffused with shame and he stood back out of the lamplight. He listened while the paroxysm of the child's sobbing grew less and less; and tears of remorse started to his eyes.

GRACE PALEY

ANXIETY

THE YOUNG FATHERS are waiting outside the school. What curly heads! Such graceful brown mustaches. They're sitting on their haunches eating pizza and exchanging information. They're waiting for the 3 p.m. bell. It's springtime, the season of first looking out the window. I have a window box of greenhouse marigolds. The young fathers can be seen through the ferny leaves.

The bell rings. The children fall out of school, tumbling through the open door. One of the fathers sees his child. A small girl. Is she Chinese? A little. Up u-u-p, he says, and hoists her to his shoulders. U-u-p, says the second father, and hoists his little boy. The little boy sits on top of his father's head for a couple of seconds before sliding to his shoulders. Very funny, says the father.

They start off down the street, right under and past my window. The two children are still laughing. They try to whisper a secret. The fathers haven't finished their conversation. The frailer father is uncomfortable; his little girl wiggles too much.

Stop it this minute, he says.

Oink oink, says the little girl.

What'd you say?

Oink oink, she says.

The young father says What! three times. Then he seizes the child, raises her high above his head, and sets her hard on her feet.

What'd I do so bad, she says, rubbing her ankle.

Just hold my hand, screams the frail and angry father.

I lean far out the window. Stop! Stop! I cry.

The young father turns, shading his eyes, but sees. What? he says. His friend says, Hey? Who's that? He probably thinks I'm a family friend, a teacher maybe.

Who're you? he says.

I move the pots of marigold aside. Then I'm able to lean on my elbow way out into unshadowed visibility. Once, not too long ago, the tenements were speckled with women like me in every third window up to the fifth story, calling the children from play to receive orders and instruction. This memory enables me to say strictly, Young man, I am an older person who feels free because of that to ask questions and give advice.

Oh? he says, laughs with a little embarrassment, says to his friend, Shoot if you will that old gray head. But he's joking, I know, because he has established himself, legs apart, hands behind his back, his neck arched to see and hear me out.

How old are you? I call. About thirty or so?

Thirty-three.

First I want to say you're about a generation ahead of your father in your attitude and behavior toward your child.

Really? Well? Anything else, ma'am.

Son, I said, leaning another two, three dangerous inches toward him. Son, I must tell you that madmen intend to destroy this beautifully made planet. That the murder of our children by these men has got to become a terror and a sorrow to you, and starting now, it had better interfere with any daily pleasure.

Speech speech, he called.

I waited a minute, but he continued to look up. So, I said,

216

I can tell by your general appearance and loping walk that you agree with me.

I do, he said, winking at his friend; but turning a serious face to mine, he said again, Yes, yes, I do.

Well then, why did you become so angry at that little girl whose future is like a film which suddenly cuts to white. Why did you nearly slam this little doomed person to the ground in your uncontrollable anger.

Let's not go too far, said the young father. She *was* jumping around on my poor back and hollering oink oink.

When were you angriest – when she wiggled and jumped or when she said oink?

He scratched his wonderful head of dark well-cut hair. I guess when she said oink.

Have you ever said oink oink? Think carefully. Years ago, perhaps?

No. Well maybe. Maybe.

Whom did you refer to in this way?

He laughed. He called to his friend, Hey Ken, this old person's got something. The cops. In a demonstration. Oink oink, he said, remembering, laughing.

The little girl smiled and said, Oink oink.

Shut up, he said.

What do you deduce from this?

That I was angry at Rosie because she was dealing with me as though I was a figure of authority, and it's not my thing, never has been, never will be.

I could see his happiness, his nice grin, as he remembered this.

So, I continued, since those children are such lovely examples of what may well be the last generation of humankind, why don't you start all over again, right from the school door, as though none of this had ever happened.

Thank you, said the young father. Thank you. It would be nice to be a horse, he said, grabbing little Rosie's hand. Come on Rosie, let's go. I don't have all day.

U-up, says the first father. U-up, says the second.

Giddap, shout the children, and the fathers yell neigh neigh, as horses do. The children kick their fathers' horse-chests, screaming giddap giddap, and they gallop wildly westward.

I lean way out to cry once more, Be careful! Stop! But they've gone too far. Oh, anyone would love to be a fierce fast horse carrying a beloved beautiful rider, but they are galloping toward one of the most dangerous street corners in the world. And they may live beyond that trisection across other dangerous avenues.

So I must shut the window after patting the April-cooled marigolds with their rusty smell of summer. Then I sit in the nice light and wonder how to make sure that they gallop safely home through the airy scary dreams of scientists and the bulky dreams of automakers. I wish I could see just how they sit down at their kitchen tables for a healthy snack (orange juice or milk and cookies) before going out into the new spring afternoon to play.

FRANZ KAFKA

THE JUDGMENT

Translated by Willa and Edwin Muir

IT WAS A SUNDAY morning in the very height of spring. Georg Bendemann, a young merchant, was sitting in his own room on the first floor of one of a long row of small, ramshackle houses stretching beside the river which were scarcely distinguishable from each other in height and coloring. He had just finished a letter to an old friend of his who was now living abroad, had put it into its envelope in a slow and dreamy fashion, and with his elbows propped on the writing table was gazing out of the window at the river, the bridge, and the hills on the farther bank with their tender green.

He was thinking about his friend, who had actually run away to Russia some years before, being dissatisfied with his prospects at home. Now he was carrying on a business in St Petersburg, which had flourished to begin with but had long been going downhill, as he always complained on his increasingly rare visits. So he was wearing himself out to no purpose in a foreign country, the unfamiliar full beard he wore did not quite conceal the face Georg had known so well since childhood, and his skin was growing so yellow as to indicate some latent disease. By his own account he had no regular connection with the colony of his fellow countrymen out there and almost no social intercourse with Russian families, so that he was resigning himself to becoming a permanent bachelor.

What could one write to such a man, who had obviously run off the rails, a man one could be sorry for but could not help. Should one advise him to come home, to transplant himself and take up his old friendships again – there was nothing to hinder him – and in general to rely on the help of his friends? But that was as good as telling him, and the more kindly the more offensively, that all his efforts hitherto had miscarried, that he should finally give up, come back home, and be gaped at by everyone as a returned prodigal, that only his friends knew what was what and that he himself was just a big child who should do what his successful and home-keeping friends prescribed. And was it certain, besides, that all the pain one would have to inflict on him would achieve its object? Perhaps it would not even be possible to get him to come home at all – he said himself that he was now out of touch with commerce in his native country – and then he would still be left an alien in a foreign land embittered by his friends' advice and more than ever estranged from them. But if he did follow their advice and then didn't fit in at home – not out of malice, of course, but through force of circumstances – couldn't get on with his friends or without them, felt humiliated, couldn't be said to have either friends or a country of his own any longer, wouldn't it have been better for him to stay abroad just as he was? Taking all this into account, how could one be sure that he would make a success of life at home?

For such reasons, supposing one wanted to keep up correspondence with him, one could not send him any real news such as could frankly be told to the most distant acquaintance. It was more than three years since his last visit, and for this he offered the lame excuse that the political situation in Russia was too uncertain, which apparently would not permit even the briefest absence of a small businessman while it allowed hundreds of thousands of Russians to travel peacefully abroad. But during these three years Georg's own position in life had changed a lot. Two years ago his mother had died, since when he and his father had shared the household together, and his friend had of course been informed of that and had expressed his sympathy in a letter phrased so dryly that the grief caused by such an event, one had to conclude, could not be realized in a distant country. Since that time, however, Georg had applied himself with greater determination to the business as well as to everything else.

Perhaps during his mother's lifetime his father's insistence on having everything his own way in the business had hindered him from developing any real activity of his own, perhaps since her death his father had become less aggressive, although he was still active in the business, perhaps it was mostly due to an accidental run of good fortune – which was very probable indeed – but at any rate during those two years the business had developed in a most unexpected way, the staff had had to be doubled, the turnover was five times as great; no doubt about it, further progress lay just ahead.

But Georg's friend had no inkling of this improvement. In earlier years, perhaps for the last time in that letter of condolence, he had tried to persuade Georg to emigrate to Russia and had enlarged upon the prospects of success for precisely Georg's branch of trade. The figures quoted were microscopic by comparison with the range of Georg's present operations. Yet he shrank from letting his friend know about his business success, and if he were to do it now retrospectively that certainly would look peculiar.

So Georg confined himself to giving his friend unimportant items of gossip such as rise at random in the memory when one is idly thinking things over on a quiet Sunday. All he desired was to leave undisturbed the idea of the home town which his friend must have built up to his own content during the long interval. And so it happened to Georg that three times in three fairly widely separated letters he had told his friend about the engagement of an unimportant man to an equally unimportant girl, until indeed, quite contrary to his intentions, his friend began to show some interest in this notable event.

Yet Georg preferred to write about things like these rather than to confess that he himself had got engaged a month ago to a Fräulein Frieda Brandenfeld, a girl from a well-to-do family. He often discussed this friend of his with his fiancée and the peculiar relationship that had developed between them in their correspondence. 'So he won't be coming to our wedding,' said she, 'and yet I have a right to get to know all your friends.' 'I don't want to trouble him,' answered Georg, 'don't misunderstand me, he would probably come, at least I think so, but he would feel that his hand had been forced and he would be hurt, perhaps he would envy me and certainly he'd be discontented and without being able to do anything about his discontent he'd have to go away again alone. Alone – do you know what that means?' 'Yes, but may he not hear about our wedding in some other fashion?' 'I can't prevent that, of course, but it's unlikely, considering the way he lives.' 'Since your friends are like that, Georg, you shouldn't ever have got engaged at all.' 'Well, we're both to blame for that; but I wouldn't have it any other way now.' And when, breathing quickly under his kisses, she still brought out: 'All the same, I do feel upset,' he thought it could not really involve him in trouble were he to send the news to his friend. 'That's the kind of man I am and he'll just have to take me as I am,' he said to himself, 'I can't cut myself to another pattern that might make a more suitable friend for him.'

And in fact he did inform his friend, in the long letter he

had been writing that Sunday morning, about his engagement, with these words: 'I have saved my best news to the end. I have got engaged to a Fräulein Frieda Brandenfeld, a girl from a well-to-do family, who only came to live here a long time after you went away, so that you're hardly likely to know her. There will be time to tell you more about her later, for today let me just say that I am very happy and as between you and me the only difference in our relationship is that instead of a quite ordinary kind of friend you will now have in me a happy friend. Besides that, you will acquire in my fiancée, who sends her warm greetings and will soon write you herself, a genuine friend of the opposite sex, which is not without importance to a bachelor. I know that there are many reasons why you can't come to see us, but would not my wedding be precisely the right occasion for giving all obstacles the go-by? Still, however that may be, do just as seems good to you without regarding any interests but your own.'

With this letter in his hand Georg had been sitting a long time at the writing table, his face turned toward the window. He had barely acknowledged, with an absent smile, a greeting waved to him from the street by a passing acquaintance.

At last he put the letter in his pocket and went out of his room across a small lobby into his father's room, which he had not entered for months. There was in fact no need for him to enter it, since he saw his father daily at business and they took their midday meal together at an eating house; in the evening, it was true, each did as he pleased, yet even then, unless Georg – as mostly happened – went out with friends or, more recently, visited his fiancée, they always sat for a while, each with his newspaper, in their common sitting room.

It surprised Georg how dark his father's room was even on this sunny morning. So it was overshadowed as much as that by the high wall on the other side of the narrow courtyard. His father was sitting by the window in a corner hung with various mementoes of Georg's dead mother, reading a newspaper which he held to one side before his eyes in an attempt to overcome a defect of vision. On the table stood the remains of his breakfast, not much of which seemed to have been eaten.

'Ah, Georg,' said his father, rising at once to meet him. His heavy dressing gown swung open as he walked and the skirts of it fluttered around him. – 'My father is still a giant of a man,' said Georg to himself.

'It's unbearably dark here,' he said aloud.

'Yes, it's dark enough,' answered his father.

'And you've shut the window, too?'

'I prefer it like that.'

'Well, it's quite warm outside,' said Georg, as if continuing his previous remark, and sat down.

His father cleared away the breakfast dishes and set them on a chest.

'I really only wanted to tell you,' went on Georg, who had been vacantly following the old man's movements, 'that I am now sending the news of my engagement to St Petersburg.' He drew the letter a little way from his pocket and let it drop back again.

'To St Petersburg?' asked his father.

'To my friend there,' said Georg, trying to meet his father's eye. – In business hours he's quite different, he was thinking, how solidly he sits here with his arms crossed.

'Oh yes. To your friend,' said his father, with peculiar emphasis.

'Well, you know, Father, that I wanted not to tell him about my engagement at first. Out of consideration for him, that was the only reason. You know yourself he's a difficult

226

man. I said to myself that someone else might tell him about my engagement, although he's such a solitary creature that that was hardly likely – I couldn't prevent that – but I wasn't ever going to tell him myself.'

'And now you've changed your mind?' asked his father, laying his enormous newspaper on the window sill and on top of it his spectacles, which he covered with one hand.

'Yes, I've been thinking it over. If he's a good friend of mine, I said to myself, my being happily engaged should make him happy too. And so I wouldn't put off telling him any longer. But before I posted the letter I wanted to let you know.'

'Georg,' said his father, lengthening his toothless mouth, 'listen to me! You've come to me about this business, to talk it over with me. No doubt that does you honor. But it's nothing, it's worse than nothing, if you don't tell me the whole truth. I don't want to stir up matters that shouldn't be mentioned here. Since the death of our dear mother certain things have been done that aren't right. Maybe the time will come for mentioning them, and maybe sooner than we think. There's many a thing in the business I'm not aware of, maybe it's not done behind my back – I'm not going to say that it's done behind my back – I'm not equal to things any longer, my memory's failing, I haven't an eye for so many things any longer. That's the course of nature in the first place, and in the second place the death of our dear mother hit me harder than it did you. – But since we're talking about it, about this letter, I beg you, Georg, don't deceive me. It's a trivial affair, it's hardly worth mentioning, so don't deceive me. Do you really have this friend in St Petersburg?'

Georg rose in embarrassment. 'Never mind my friends. A thousand friends wouldn't make up to me for my father. Do you know what I think? You're not taking enough care of yourself. But old age must be taken care of. I can't do without you in the business, you know that very well, but if the business is going to undermine your health, I'm ready to close it down tomorrow forever. And that won't do. We'll have to make a change in your way of living. But a radical change. You sit here in the dark, and in the sitting room you would have plenty of light. You just take a bite of breakfast instead of properly keeping up your strength. You sit by a closed window, and the air would be so good for you. No, Father! I'll get the doctor to come, and we'll follow his orders. We'll change your room, you can move into the front room and I'll move in here. You won't notice the change, all your things will be moved with you. But there's time for all that later, I'll put you to bed now for a little, I'm sure you need to rest. Come, I'll help you to take off your things, you'll see I can do it. Or if you would rather go into the front room at once, you can lie down in my bed for the present. That would be the most sensible thing.'

Georg stood close beside his father, who had let his head with its unkempt white hair sink on his chest.

'Georg,' said his father in a low voice, without moving.

Georg knelt down at once beside his father, in the old man's weary face he saw the pupils, overlarge, fixedly looking at him from the corners of the eyes.

'You have no friend in St Petersburg. You've always been a leg-puller and you haven't even shrunk from pulling my leg. How could you have a friend out there! I can't believe it.'

'Just think back a bit, Father,' said Georg, lifting his father from the chair and slipping off his dressing gown as he stood feebly enough, 'it'll soon be three years since my friend came to see us last. I remember that you used not to like him very much. At least twice I kept you from seeing him, although he was actually sitting with me in my room. I could quite

228

well understand your dislike of him, my friend has his peculiarities. But then, later, you got on with him very well. I was proud because you listened to him and nodded and asked him questions. If you think back you're bound to remember. He used to tell us the most incredible stories of the Russian Revolution. For instance, when he was on a business trip to Kiev and ran into a riot, and saw a priest on a balcony who cut a broad cross in blood on the palm of his hand and held the hand up and appealed to the mob. You've told that story yourself once or twice since.'

Meanwhile Georg had succeeded in lowering his father down again and carefully taking off the woolen drawers he wore over his linen underpants and his socks. The not particularly clean appearance of his underwear made him reproach himself for having been neglectful. It should have certainly been his duty to see that his father had clean changes of underwear. He had not yet explicitly discussed with his bride-to-be what arrangements should be made for his father in the future, for they had both of them silently taken it for granted that the old man would go on living alone in the old house. But now he made a quick, firm decision to take him into his own future establishment. It almost looked, on closer inspection, as if the care he meant to lavish there on his father might come too late.

He carried his father to bed in his arms. It gave him a dreadful feeling to notice that while he took the few steps toward the bed the old man on his breast was playing with his watch chain. He could not lay him down on the bed for a moment, so firmly did he hang on to the watch chain.

But as soon as he was laid in bed, all seemed well. He covered himself up and even drew the blankets farther than usual over his shoulders. He looked up at Georg with a not unfriendly eye.

'You begin to remember my friend, don't you?' asked Georg, giving him an encouraging nod.

'Am I well covered up now?' asked his father, as if he were not able to see whether his feet were properly tucked in or not.

'So you find it snug in bed already,' said Georg, and tucked the blankets more closely around him.

'Am I well covered up?' asked the father once more, seeming to be strangely intent upon the answer.

'Don't worry, you're well covered up.'

'No!' cried his father, cutting short the answer, threw the blankets off with a strength that sent them all flying in a moment and sprang erect in bed. Only one hand lightly touched the ceiling to steady him.

'You wanted to cover me up, I know, my young sprig, but I'm far from being covered up yet. And even if this is the last strength I have, it's enough for you, too much for you. Of course I know your friend. He would have been a son after my own heart. That's why you've been playing him false all these years. Why else? Do you think I haven't been sorry for him? And that's why you had to lock yourself up in your office – the Chief is busy, mustn't be disturbed – just so that you could write your lying little letters to Russia. But thank goodness a father doesn't need to be taught how to see through his son. And now that you thought you'd got him down, so far down that you could set your bottom on him and sit on him and he wouldn't move, then my fine son makes up his mind to get married!'

Georg stared at the bogey conjured up by his father. His friend in St Petersburg, whom his father suddenly knew too well, touched his imagination as never before. Lost in the vastness of Russia he saw him. At the door of an empty, plundered warehouse he saw him. Among the wreckage of his showcases, the slashed remnants of his wares, the falling gas brackets, he was just standing up. Why did he have to go so far away!

'But attend to me!' cried his father, and Georg, almost distracted, ran toward the bed to take everything in, yet came to a stop halfway.

'Because she lifted up her skirts,' his father began to flute, 'because she lifted her skirts like this, the nasty creature,' and mimicking her he lifted his shirt so high that one could see the scar on his thigh from his war wound, 'because she lifted her skirts like this and this you made up to her, and in order to make free with her undisturbed you have disgraced your mother's memory, betrayed your friend, and stuck your father into bed so that he can't move. But he can move, or can't he?'

And he stood up quite unsupported and kicked his legs out. His insight made him radiant.

Georg shrank into a corner, as far away from his father as possible. A long time ago he had firmly made up his mind to watch closely every least movement so that he should not be surprised by any indirect attack, a pounce from behind or above. At this moment he recalled this long-forgotten resolve and forgot it again, like a man drawing a short thread through the eye of a needle.

'But your friend hasn't been betrayed after all!' cried his father, emphasizing the point with stabs of his forefinger. 'I've been representing him here on the spot.'

'You comedian!' Georg could not resist the retort, realized at once the harm done and, his eyes starting in his head, bit his tongue back, only too late, till the pain made his knees give.

'Yes, of course I've been playing a comedy! A comedy! That's a good expression! What other comfort was left to a poor old widower? Tell me – and while you're answering me be you still my living son – what else was left to me, in my back room, plagued by a disloyal staff, old to the marrow of my bones? And my son strutting through the world, finishing off deals that I had prepared for him, bursting with triumphant glee, and stalking away from his father with the closed face of a respectable businessman! Do you think I didn't love you, I, from whom you are sprung?'

Now he'll lean forward, thought Georg, what if he topples and smashes himself! These words went hissing through his mind.

His father leaned forward but did not topple. Since Georg did not come any nearer, as he had expected, he straightened himself again.

'Stay where you are, I don't need you! You think you have strength enough to come over here and that you're only hanging back of your own accord. Don't be too sure! I am still much the stronger of us two. All by myself I might have had to give way, but your mother has given me so much of her strength that I've established a fine connection with your friend and I have your customers here in my pocket!'

'He has pockets even in his shirt!' said Georg to himself, and believed that with this remark he could make him an impossible figure for all the world. Only for a moment did he think so, since he kept on forgetting everything.

'Just take your bride on your arm and try getting in my way! I'll sweep her from your very side, you don't know how!'

Georg made a grimace of disbelief. His father only nodded, confirming the truth of his words, toward Georg's corner.

'How you amused me today, coming to ask me if you should tell your friend about your engagement. He knows it already, you stupid boy, he knows it all! I've been writing to him, for you forgot to take my writing things away from me. That's why he hasn't been here for years, he knows everything a hundred times better than you do yourself, in his left hand he crumples your letters unopened while in his right hand he holds up my letters to read through!'

In his enthusiasm he waved his arm over his head. 'He knows everything a thousand times better!' he cried.

'Ten thousand times!' said Georg, to make fun of his father, but in his very mouth the words turned into deadly earnest.

'For years I've been waiting for you to come with some such question! Do you think I concern myself with anything else? Do you think I read my newspapers? Look!' and he threw Georg a newspaper sheet which he had somehow taken to bed with him. An old newspaper, with a name entirely unknown to Georg.

'How long a time you've taken to grow up! Your mother had to die, she couldn't see the happy day, your friend is going to pieces in Russia, even three years ago he was yellow enough to be thrown away, and as for me, you see what condition I'm in. You have eyes in your head for that!'

'So you've been lying in wait for me!' cried Georg.

His father said pityingly, in an offhand manner: 'I suppose you wanted to say that sooner. But now it doesn't matter.' And in a louder voice: 'So now you know what else there was in the world besides yourself, till now you've known only about yourself! An innocent child, yes, that you were, truly, but still more truly have you been a devilish human being! – And therefore take note: I sentence you now to death by drowning!'

Georg felt himself urged from the room, the crash with which his father fell on the bed behind him was still in his ears as he fled. On the staircase, which he rushed down as if its steps were an inclined plane, he ran into his charwoman on her way up to do the morning cleaning of the room. 'Jesus!' she cried, and covered her face with her apron, but he was already gone. Out of the front door he rushed, across the roadway, driven toward the water. Already he was grasping at the railings as a starving man clutches food. He swung himself over, like the distinguished gymnast he had once been in his youth, to his parents' pride. With weakening grip he was still holding on when he spied between the railings a motor-bus coming which would easily cover the noise of his fall, called in a low voice: 'Dear parents, I have always loved you, all the same,' and let himself drop.

At this moment an unending stream of traffic was just going over the bridge.

KATHERINE MANSFIELD

THE DAUGHTERS
OF THE LATE
COLONEL

I

THE WEEK AFTER was one of the busiest weeks of their lives. Even when they went to bed it was only their bodies that lay down and rested; their minds went on, thinking things out, talking things over, wondering, deciding, trying to remember where . . .

Constantia lay like a statue, her hands by her sides, her feet just overlapping each other, the sheet up to her chin. She stared at the ceiling.

'Do you think father would mind if we gave his top-hat to the porter?'

'The porter?' snapped Josephine. 'Why ever the porter? What a very extraordinary idea!'

'Because,' said Constantia slowly, 'he must often have to go to funerals. And I noticed at – at the cemetery that he only had a bowler.' She paused. 'I thought then how very much he'd appreciate a top-hat. We ought to give him a present, too. He was always very nice to father.'

'But,' cried Josephine, flouncing on her pillow and staring across the dark at Constantia, 'father's head!' And suddenly, for one awful moment, she nearly giggled. Not, of course, that she felt in the least like giggling. It must have been habit. Years ago, when they had stayed awake at night talking, their beds had simply heaved. And now the porter's head, disappearing, popped out, like a candle, under father's hat. . . . The giggle mounted, mounted; she clenched her hands; she fought it down; she frowned fiercely at the dark and said 'Remember' terribly sternly.

'We can decide tomorrow,' she said.

Constantia had noticed nothing; she sighed.

'Do you think we ought to have our dressing-gowns dyed as well?'

'Black?' almost shrieked Josephine.

'Well, what else?' said Constantia. 'I was thinking – it doesn't seem quite sincere, in a way, to wear black out of doors and when we're fully dressed, and then when we're at home—'

'But nobody sees us,' said Josephine. She gave the bed-clothes such a twitch that both her feet became uncovered and she had to creep up the pillows to get them well under again.

'Kate does,' said Constantia. 'And the postman very well might.'

Josephine thought of her dark-red slippers, which matched her dressing-gown, and of Constantia's favourite indefinite green ones which went with hers. Black! Two black dressing-gowns and two pairs of black woolly slippers, creeping off to the bathroom like black cats.

'I don't think it's absolutely necessary,' said she.

Silence. Then Constantia said, 'We shall have to post the papers with the notice in them tomorrow to catch the Ceylon mail. . . . How many letters have we had up till now?'

'Twenty-three.'

Josephine had replied to them all, and twenty-three times when she came to 'We miss our dear father so much' she had broken down and had to use her handkerchief, and on some of them even to soak up a very light-blue tear with an edge of blotting-paper. Strange! She couldn't have put it on – but twenty-three times. Even now, though, when she said over to herself sadly 'We miss our dear father *so* much,' she could have cried if she'd wanted to.

'Have you got enough stamps?' came from Constantia.

'Oh, how can I tell?' said Josephine crossly. 'What's the good of asking me that now?'

'I was just wondering,' said Constantia mildly.

Silence again. There came a little rustle, a scurry, a hop.

'A mouse,' said Constantia.

'It can't be a mouse because there aren't any crumbs,' said Josephine.

'But it doesn't know there aren't,' said Constantia.

A spasm of pity squeezed her heart. Poor little thing! She wished she'd left a tiny piece of biscuit on the dressing-table. It was awful to think of it not finding anything. What would it do?

'I can't think how they manage to live at all,' she said slowly.

'Who?' demanded Josephine.

And Constantia said more loudly than she meant to, 'Mice.'

Josephine was furious. 'Oh, what nonsense, Con!' she said. 'What have mice got to do with it? You're asleep.'

'I don't think I am,' said Constantia. She shut her eyes to make sure. She was.

Josephine arched her spine, pulled up her knees, folded her arms so that her fists came under her ears, and pressed her cheek hard against the pillow.

II

Another thing which complicated matters was they had Nurse Andrews staying on with them that week. It was their own fault; they had asked her. It was Josephine's idea. On the morning – well, on the last morning, when the doctor had gone, Josephine had said to Constantia, 'Don't you think it would be rather nice if we asked Nurse Andrews to stay on for a week as our guest?'

'Very nice,' said Constantia.

'I thought,' went on Josephine quickly, 'I should just say this afternoon, after I've paid her, "My sister and I would be very pleased, after all you've done for us, Nurse Andrews, if you would stay on for a week as our guest." I'd have to put that in about being our guest in case—'

'Oh, but she could hardly expect to be paid!' cried Constantia.

'One never knows,' said Josephine sagely.

Nurse Andrews had, of course, jumped at the idea. But it was a bother. It meant they had to have regular sit-down meals at the proper times, whereas if they'd been alone they could just have asked Kate if she wouldn't have minded bringing them a tray wherever they were. And meal-times now that the strain was over were rather a trial.

Nurse Andrews was simply fearful about butter. Really they couldn't help feeling that about butter, at least, she took advantage of their kindness. And she had that maddening habit of asking for just an inch more bread to finish what she had on her plate, and then, at the last mouthful, absent-mindedly – of course it wasn't absent-mindedly – taking another helping. Josephine got very red when this happened, and she fastened her small, bead-like eyes on the tablecloth as if she saw a minute strange insect creeping through the web of it. But Constantia's long, pale face lengthened and set, and she gazed away – away – far over the desert, to where that line of camels unwound like a thread of wool. . . .

'When I was with Lady Tukes,' said Nurse Andrews, 'she had such a dainty little contrayvance for the buttah. It was a silvah Cupid balanced on the – on the bordah of a glass dish, holding a tayny fork. And when you wanted some buttah you simply pressed his foot and he bent down and speared you a piece. It was quite a gayme.'

Josephine could hardly bear that. But 'I think those things are very extravagant' was all she said.

'But whey?' asked Nurse Andrews, beaming through her eyeglasses. 'No one, surely, would take more buttah than one wanted – would one?'

'Ring, Con,' cried Josephine. She couldn't trust herself to reply.

And proud young Kate, the enchanted princess, came in to see what the old tabbies wanted now. She snatched away their plates of mock something or other and slapped down a white, terrified blancmange.

'Jam, please, Kate,' said Josephine kindly.

Kate knelt and burst open the sideboard, lifted the lid of the jam-pot, saw it was empty, put it on the table, and stalked off.

'I'm afraid,' said Nurse Andrews a moment later, 'there isn't any.'

'Oh, what a bother!' said Josephine. She bit her lip. 'What had we better do?'

Constantia looked dubious. 'We can't disturb Kate again,' she said softly.

Nurse Andrews waited, smiling at them both. Her eyes wandered, spying at everything behind her eyeglasses. Constantia in despair went back to her camels. Josephine frowned heavily – concentrated. If it hadn't been for this idiotic woman she and Con would, of course, have eaten their blancmange without. Suddenly the idea came.

'I know,' she said. 'Marmalade. There's some marmalade in the sideboard. Get it, Con.'

'I hope,' laughed Nurse Andrews – and her laugh was like a spoon tinkling against a medicine-glass – 'I hope it's not very bittah marmalayde.'

III

But, after all, it was not long now, and then she'd be gone for good. And there was no getting over the fact that she had been very kind to father. She had nursed him day and night at the end. Indeed, both Constantia and Josephine felt privately she had rather overdone the not leaving him at the very last. For when they had gone in to say goodbye Nurse Andrews had sat beside his bed the whole time, holding his wrist and pretending to look at her watch. It couldn't have been necessary. It was so tactless, too. Supposing father had wanted to say something – something private to them. Not that he had. Oh, far from it! He lay there, purple, a dark, angry purple in the face, and never even looked at them when they came in. Then, as they were standing there, wondering what to do, he had suddenly opened one eye. Oh, what a difference it would have made, what a difference to their memory of him, how much easier to tell people about it, if he had only opened both! But no – one eye only. It glared at them a moment and then ... went out.

IV

It had made it very awkward for them when Mr Farolles, of St John's, called the same afternoon.

'The end was quite peaceful, I trust?' were the first words

he said as he glided towards them through the dark drawing-room.

'Quite,' said Josephine faintly. They both hung their heads. Both of them felt certain that eye wasn't at all a peaceful eye.

'Won't you sit down?' said Josephine.

'Thank you, Miss Pinner,' said Mr Farolles gratefully. He folded his coat-tails and began to lower himself into father's armchair, but just as he touched it he almost sprang up and slid into the next chair instead.

He coughed. Josephine clasped her hands; Constantia looked vague.

'I want you to feel, Miss Pinner,' said Mr Farolles, 'and you, Miss Constantia, that I'm trying to be helpful. I want to be helpful to you both, if you will let me. These are the times,' said Mr Farolles, very simply and earnestly, 'when God means us to be helpful to one another.'

'Thank you very much, Mr Farolles,' said Josephine and Constantia.

'Not at all,' said Mr Farolles gently. He drew his kid gloves through his fingers and leaned forward. 'And if either of you would like a little Communion, either or both of you, here *and* now, you have only to tell me. A little Communion is often very help – a great comfort,' he added tenderly.

But the idea of a little Communion terrified them. What! In the drawing-room by themselves – with no – no altar or anything! The piano would be much too high, thought Constantia, and Mr Farolles could not possibly lean over it with the chalice. And Kate would be sure to come bursting in and interrupt them, thought Josephine. And supposing the bell rang in the middle? It might be somebody important – about their mourning. Would they get up reverently and go out, or would they have to wait . . . in torture?

'Perhaps you will send round a note by your good Kate if you would care for it later,' said Mr Farolles.

'Oh yes, thank you very much!' they both said.

Mr Farolles got up and took his black straw hat from the round table.

'And about the funeral,' he said softly. 'I may arrange that – as your dear father's old friend and yours, Miss Pinner – and Miss Constantia?'

Josephine and Constantia got up too.

'I should like it to be quite simple,' said Josephine firmly, 'and not too expensive. At the same time, I should like—'

'A good one that will last,' thought dreamy Constantia, as if Josephine were buying a nightgown. But, of course, Josephine didn't say that. 'One suitable to our father's position.' She was very nervous.

'I'll run round to our good friend Mr Knight,' said Mr Farolles soothingly. 'I will ask him to come and see you. I am sure you will find him very helpful indeed.'

V

Well, at any rate, all that part of it was over, though neither of them could possibly believe that father was never coming back. Josephine had had a moment of absolute terror at the cemetery, while the coffin was lowered, to think that she and Constantia had done this thing without asking his permission. What would father say when he found out? For he was bound to find out sooner or later. He always did. 'Buried. You two girls had me *buried*!' She heard his stick thumping. Oh, what would they say? What possible excuse could they make? It sounded such an appallingly heartless thing to do. Such a wicked advantage to take of a person because he happened to be helpless at the moment. The other people seemed to treat it all as a matter of course. They were strangers; they couldn't be expected to understand that father was the very last person for such a thing to happen to. No, the entire blame for it all would fall on her and Constantia. And the expense, she thought, stepping into the tight-buttoned cab. When she had to show him the bills. What would he say then?

She heard him absolutely roaring. 'And do you expect me to pay for this gimcrack excursion of yours?'

'Oh,' groaned poor Josephine aloud, 'we shouldn't have done it, Con!'

And Constantia, pale as a lemon in all that blackness, said in a frightened whisper, 'Done what, Jug?'

'Let them bu-bury father like that,' said Josephine, breaking down and crying into her new, queer-smelling mourning handkerchief.

'But what else could we have done?' asked Constantia wonderingly. 'We couldn't have kept him, Jug – we couldn't have kept him unburied. At any rate, not in a flat that size.'

Josephine blew her nose; the cab was dreadfully stuffy.

'I don't know,' she said forlornly. 'It is all so dreadful. I feel we ought to have tried to, just for a time at least. To make perfectly sure. One thing's certain' – and her tears sprang out again – 'father will never forgive us for this – never!'

VI

Father would never forgive them. That was what they felt more than ever when, two mornings later, they went into his room to go through his things. They had discussed it quite calmly. It was even down on Josephine's list of things to be done. *Go through father's things and settle about them.* But that was a very different matter from saying after breakfast:

'Well, are you ready, Con?'

'Yes, Jug – when you are.'

'Then I think we'd better get it over.'

It was dark in the hall. It had been a rule for years never to disturb father in the morning, whatever happened. And now they were going to open the door without knocking even. . . . Constantia's eyes were enormous at the idea; Josephine felt weak in the knees.

'You – you go first,' she gasped, pushing Constantia.

But Constantia said, as she always had said on those occasions, 'No, Jug, that's not fair. You're eldest.'

Josephine was just going to say – what at other times she wouldn't have owned to for the world – what she kept for her very last weapon, 'But you're tallest,' when they noticed that the kitchen door was open, and there stood Kate. . . .

'Very stiff,' said Josephine, grasping the door-handle and doing her best to turn it. As if anything ever deceived Kate!

It couldn't be helped. That girl was . . . Then the door was shut behind them, but – but they weren't in father's room at all. They might have suddenly walked through the wall by mistake into a different flat altogether. Was the door just behind them? They were too frightened to look. Josephine knew that if it was it was holding itself tight shut; Constantia felt that, like the doors in dreams, it hadn't any handle at all. It was the coldness which made it so awful. Or the whiteness – which? Everything was covered. The blinds were down, a cloth hung over the mirror, a sheet hid the bed; a huge fan of white paper filled the fire-place. Constantia timidly put out her hand; she almost expected a snowflake to fall. Josephine felt a queer tingling in her nose, as if her nose was freezing. Then a cab klop-klopped over the cobbles below, and the quiet seemed to shake into little pieces.

'I had better pull up a blind,' said Josephine bravely.

'Yes, it might be a good idea,' whispered Constantia.

They only gave the blind a touch, but it flew up and the cord flew after, rolling round the blind-stick, and the little tassel tapped as if trying to get free. That was too much for Constantia.

'Don't you think – don't you think we might put it off for another day?' she whispered.

'Why?' snapped Josephine, feeling, as usual, much better now that she knew for certain that Constantia was terrified. 'It's got to be done. But I do wish you wouldn't whisper, Con.'

'I didn't know I was whispering,' whispered Constantia.

'And why do you keep on staring at the bed?' said Josephine, raising her voice almost defiantly. 'There's nothing *on* the bed.'

'Oh, Jug, don't say so!' said poor Connie. 'At any rate, not so loudly.'

Josephine felt herself that she had gone too far. She took a wide swerve over to the chest of drawers, put out her hand, but quickly drew it back again.

'Connie!' she gasped, and she wheeled round and leaned with her back against the chest of drawers.

'Oh, Jug – what?'

Josephine could only glare. She had the most extraordinary feeling that she had just escaped something simply awful. But how could she explain to Constantia that father was in the chest of drawers? He was in the top drawer with his handkerchiefs and neckties, or in the next with his shirts and pyjamas, or in the lowest of all with his suits. He was watching there, hidden away – just behind the door-handle – ready to spring.

She pulled a funny old-fashioned face at Constantia, just as she used to in the old days when she was going to cry.

'I can't open,' she nearly wailed.

'No, don't, Jug,' whispered Constantia earnestly. 'It's much better not to. Don't let's open anything. At any rate, not for a long time.'

'But – but it seems so weak,' said Josephine, breaking down.

'But why not be weak for once, Jug?' argued Constantia, whispering quite fiercely. 'If it is weak.' And her pale stare flew from the locked writing-table – so safe – to the huge glittering wardrobe, and she began to breathe in a queer, panting way. 'Why shouldn't we be weak for once in our lives, Jug? It's quite excusable. Let's be weak – be weak, Jug. It's much nicer to be weak than to be strong.'

And then she did one of those amazingly bold things that she'd done about twice before in their lives: she marched over to the wardrobe, turned the key, and took it out of the lock. Took it out of the lock and held it up to Josephine, showing Josephine by her extraordinary smile that she knew what she'd done – she'd risked deliberately father being in there among his overcoats.

If the huge wardrobe had lurched forward, had crashed down on Constantia, Josephine wouldn't have been surprised. On the contrary, she would have thought it the only suitable thing to happen. But nothing happened. Only the room seemed quieter than ever, and bigger flakes of cold air fell on Josephine's shoulders and knees. She began to shiver.

'Come, Jug,' said Constantia, still with that awful callous smile; and Josephine followed just as she had that last time, when Constantia had pushed Benny into the round pond.

But the strain told on them when they were back in the dining-room. They sat down, very shaky, and looked at each other.

'I don't feel I can settle to anything,' said Josephine, 'until I've had something. Do you think we could ask Kate for two cups of hot water?'

'I really don't see why we shouldn't,' said Constantia carefully. She was quite normal again. 'I won't ring. I'll go to the kitchen door and ask her.'

'Yes, do,' said Josephine, sinking down into a chair. 'Tell her, just two cups, Con, nothing else – on a tray.'

'She needn't even put the jug on, need she?' said Constantia, as though Kate might very well complain if the jug had been there.

'Oh no, certainly not! The jug's not at all necessary. She can pour it direct out of the kettle,' cried Josephine, feeling that would be a labour-saving indeed.

Their cold lips quivered at the greenish brims. Josephine curved her small red hands round the cup; Constantia sat up and blew on the wavy steam, making it flutter from one side to the other.

'Speaking of Benny,' said Josephine.

And though Benny hadn't been mentioned Constantia immediately looked as though he had.

'He'll expect us to send him something of father's, of course. But it's so difficult to know what to send to Ceylon.'

'You mean things get unstuck so on the voyage,' murmured Constantia.

'No, lost,' said Josephine sharply. 'You know there's no post. Only runners.'

Both paused to watch a black man in white linen drawers

249

running through the pale fields for dear life, with a large brown-paper parcel in his hands. Josephine's black man was tiny; he scurried along glistening like an ant. But there was something blind and tireless about Constantia's tall, thin fellow, which made him, she decided, a very unpleasant person indeed. . . . On the veranda, dressed all in white and wearing a cork helmet, stood Benny. His right hand shook up and down, as father's did when he was impatient. And behind him, not in the least interested, sat Hilda, the unknown sister-in-law. She swung in a cane rocker and flicked over the leaves of the *Tatler*.

'I think his watch would be the most suitable present,' said Josephine.

Constantia looked up; she seemed surprised.

'Oh, would you trust a gold watch to a native?'

'But, of course, I'd disguise it,' said Josephine. 'No one would know it was a watch.' She liked the idea of having to make a parcel such a curious shape that no one could possibly guess what it was. She even thought for a moment of hiding the watch in a narrow cardboard corset-box that she'd kept by her for a long time, waiting for it to come in for something. It was such beautiful, firm cardboard. But, no, it wouldn't be appropriate for this occasion. It had lettering on it: *Medium Women's 28. Extra Firm Busks*. It would be almost too much of a surprise for Benny to open that and find father's watch inside.

'And, of course, it isn't as though it would be going – ticking, I mean,' said Constantia, who was still thinking of the native love of jewellery. 'At least,' she added, 'it would be very strange if after all that time it was.'

Josephine made no reply. She had flown off on one of her tangents. She had suddenly thought of Cyril. Wasn't it more usual for the only grandson to have the watch? And then dear Cyril was so appreciative and a gold watch meant so much to a young man. Benny, in all probability, had quite got out of the habit of watches; men so seldom wore waistcoats in those hot climates. Whereas Cyril in London wore them from year's end to year's end. And it would be so nice for her and Constantia, when he came to tea, to know it was there. 'I see you've got on grandfather's watch, Cyril.' It would be somehow so satisfactory.

Dear boy! What a blow his sweet, sympathetic little note had been! Of course they quite understood; but it was most unfortunate.

'It would have been such a point, having him,' said Josephine.

'And he would have enjoyed it so,' said Constantia, not thinking what she was saying.

However, as soon as he got back he was coming to tea with his aunties. Cyril to tea was one of their rare treats.

'Now, Cyril, you mustn't be frightened of our cakes. Your Auntie Con and I bought them at Buszard's this morning. We know what a man's appetite is. So don't be ashamed of making a good tea.'

Josephine cut recklessly into the rich dark cake that stood for her winter gloves or the soling and heeling of Constantia's only respectable shoes. But Cyril was most unmanlike in appetite.

'I say, Aunt Josephine, I simply can't. I've only just had lunch, you know.'

'Oh, Cyril, that can't be true! It's after four,' cried

Josephine. Constantia sat with her knife poised over the chocolate-roll.

'It is, all the same,' said Cyril. 'I had to meet a man at Victoria, and he kept me hanging about till … there was only time to get lunch and to come on here. And he gave me – phew' – Cyril put his hand to his forehead – 'a terrific blow-out,' he said.

It was disappointing – today of all days. But still he couldn't be expected to know.

'But you'll have a meringue, won't you, Cyril?' said Aunt Josephine. 'These meringues were bought specially for you. Your dear father was so fond of them. We were sure you are, too.'

'I *am*, Aunt Josephine,' cried Cyril ardently. 'Do you mind if I take half to begin with?'

'Not at all, dear boy; but we mustn't let you off with that.'

'Is your dear father still so fond of meringues?' asked Auntie Con gently. She winced faintly as she broke through the shell of hers.

'Well, I don't quite know, Auntie Con,' said Cyril breezily.

At that they both looked up.

'Don't know?' almost snapped Josephine. 'Don't know a thing like that about your own father, Cyril?'

'Surely,' said Auntie Con softly.

Cyril tried to laugh it off. 'Oh, well,' he said, 'it's such a long time since—' He faltered. He stopped. Their faces were too much for him.

'Even *so*,' said Josephine.

And Auntie Con looked.

Cyril put down his teacup. 'Wait a bit,' he cried. 'Wait a bit, Aunt Josephine. What am I thinking of?'

He looked up. They were beginning to brighten. Cyril slapped his knee.

'Of course,' he said, 'it was meringues. How could I have forgotten? Yes, Aunt Josephine, you're perfectly right. Father's most frightfully keen on meringues.'

They didn't only beam. Aunt Josephine went scarlet with pleasure; Auntie Con gave a deep, deep sigh.

'And now, Cyril, you must come and see father,' said Josephine. 'He knows you were coming today.'

'Right,' said Cyril, very firmly and heartily. He got up from his chair; suddenly he glanced at the clock.

'I say, Auntie Con, isn't your clock a bit slow? I've got to meet a man at – at Paddington just after five. I'm afraid I shan't be able to stay very long with grandfather.'

'Oh, he won't expect you to stay *very* long!' said Aunt Josephine.

Constantia was still gazing at the clock. She couldn't make up her mind if it was fast or slow. It was one or the other, she felt almost certain of that. At any rate, it had been.

Cyril still lingered. 'Aren't you coming along, Auntie Con?'

'Of course,' said Josephine, 'we shall all go. Come on, Con.'

IX

They knocked at the door, and Cyril followed his aunts into grandfather's hot, sweetish room.

'Come on,' said Grandfather Pinner. 'Don't hang about. What is it? What've you been up to?'

He was sitting in front of a roaring fire, clasping his stick. He had a thick rug over his knees. On his lap there lay a beautiful pale yellow silk handkerchief.

'It's Cyril, father,' said Josephine shyly. And she took Cyril's hand and led him forward.

'Good afternoon, grandfather,' said Cyril, trying to take

his hand out of Aunt Josephine's. Grandfather Pinner shot his eyes at Cyril in the way he was famous for. Where was Auntie Con? She stood on the other side of Aunt Josephine; her long arms hung down in front of her; her hands were clasped. She never took her eyes off grandfather.

'Well,' said Grandfather Pinner, beginning to thump, 'what have you got to tell me?'

What had he, what had he got to tell him? Cyril felt himself smiling like a perfect imbecile. The room was stifling, too.

But Aunt Josephine came to his rescue. She cried brightly, 'Cyril says his father is still very fond of meringues, father dear.'

'Eh?' said Grandfather Pinner, curving his hand like a purple meringue-shell over one ear.

Josephine repeated, 'Cyril says his father is still very fond of meringues.'

'Can't hear,' said old Colonel Pinner. And he waved Josephine away with his stick, then pointed with his stick to Cyril. 'Tell me what she's trying to say,' he said.

(My God!) 'Must I?' said Cyril, blushing and staring at Aunt Josephine.

'Do, dear,' she smiled. 'It will please him so much.'

'Come on, out with it!' cried Colonel Pinner testily, beginning to thump again.

And Cyril leaned forward and yelled, 'Father's still very fond of meringues.'

At that Grandfather Pinner jumped as though he had been shot.

'Don't shout!' he cried. 'What's the matter with the boy? *Meringues!* What about 'em?'

'Oh, Aunt Josephine, must we go on?' groaned Cyril desperately.

'It's quite all right, dear boy,' said Aunt Josephine, as though he and she were at the dentist's together. 'He'll understand in a minute.' And she whispered to Cyril, 'He's getting a bit deaf; you know.' Then she leaned forward and really bawled at Grandfather Pinner, 'Cyril only wanted to tell you, father dear, that *his* father is still very fond of meringues.'

Colonel Pinner heard that time, heard and brooded, looking Cyril up and down.

'What an esstrordinary thing!' said old Grandfather Pinner. 'What an esstrordinary thing to come all this way here to tell me!'

And Cyril felt it *was*.

'Yes, I shall send Cyril the watch,' said Josephine.

'That would be very nice,' said Constantia. 'I seem to remember last time he came there was some little trouble about the time.'

X

They were interrupted by Kate bursting through the door in her usual fashion, as though she had discovered some secret panel in the wall.

'Fried or boiled?' asked the bold voice.

Fried or boiled? Josephine and Constantia were quite bewildered for the moment. They could hardly take it in.

'Fried or boiled what, Kate?' asked Josephine, trying to begin to concentrate.

Kate gave a loud sniff. 'Fish.'

'Well, why didn't you say so immediately?' Josephine reproached her gently. 'How could you expect us to understand, Kate? There are a great many things in this world, you know, which are fried or boiled.' And after such a display of courage she said quite brightly to Constantia, 'Which do you prefer, Con?'

'I think it might be nice to have it fried,' said Constantia. 'On the other hand, of course, boiled fish is very nice. I think I prefer both equally well ... Unless you ... In that case –'

'I shall fry it,' said Kate, and she bounced back, leaving their door open and slamming the door of her kitchen.

Josephine gazed at Constantia; she raised her pale eyebrows until they rippled away into her pale hair. She got up. She said in a very lofty, imposing way, 'Do you mind following me into the drawing-room, Constantia? I've something of great importance to discuss with you.'

For it was always to the drawing-room they retired when they wanted to talk over Kate.

Josephine closed the door meaningly. 'Sit down, Constantia,' she said, still very grand. She might have been receiving Constantia for the first time. And Con looked round vaguely for a chair, as though she felt indeed quite a stranger.

'Now the question is,' said Josephine, bending forward, 'whether we shall keep her or not.'

'That is the question,' agreed Constantia.

'And this time,' said Josephine firmly, 'we must come to a definite decision.'

Constantia looked for a moment as though she might begin going over all the other times, but she pulled herself together and said, 'Yes, Jug.'

'You see, Con,' explained Josephine, 'everything is so changed now.' Constantia looked up quickly. 'I mean,' went on Josephine, 'we're not dependent on Kate as we were.' And she blushed faintly. 'There's not father to cook for.'

'That is perfectly true,' agreed Constantia. 'Father certainly doesn't want any cooking now whatever else—'

Josephine broke in sharply, 'You're not sleepy, are you, Con?'

'Sleepy, Jug?' Constantia was wide-eyed.

'Well, concentrate more,' said Josephine sharply, and she returned to the subject. 'What it comes to is, if we did' – and this she barely breathed, glancing at the door – 'give Kate notice' – she raised her voice again – 'we could manage our own food.'

'Why not?' cried Constantia. She couldn't help smiling. The idea was so exciting. She clasped her hands. 'What should we live on, Jug?'

'Oh, eggs in various forms!' said Jug, lofty again. 'And, besides, there are all the cooked foods.'

'But I've always heard,' said Constantia, 'they are considered so very expensive.'

'Not if one buys them in moderation,' said Josephine. But she tore herself away from this fascinating bypath and dragged Constantia after her.

'What we've got to decide now, however, is whether we really do trust Kate or not.'

Constantia leaned back. Her flat little laugh flew from her lips.

'Isn't it curious, Jug,' said she, 'that just on this one subject I've never been able to quite make up my mind?'

XI

She never had. The whole difficulty was to prove anything. How did one prove things, how could one? Suppose Kate had stood in front of her and deliberately made a face. Mightn't she very well have been in pain? Wasn't it impossible, at any rate, to ask Kate if she was making a face at her?

If Kate answered 'No' – and, of course, she would say 'No' – what a position! How undignified! Then, again, Constantia suspected, she was almost certain that Kate went to her chest of drawers when she and Josephine were out, not to take things but to spy. Many times she had come back to find her amethyst cross in the most unlikely places, under her lace ties or on top of her evening Bertha. More than once she had laid a trap for Kate. She had arranged things in a special order and then called Josephine to witness.

'You see, Jug?'

'Quite, Con.'

'Now we shall be able to tell.'

But, oh dear, when she did go to look, she was as far off from a proof as ever! If anything was displaced, it might so very well have happened as she closed the drawer; a jolt might have done it so easily.

'You come, Jug, and decide. I really can't. It's too difficult.'

But after a pause and a long glare Josephine would sigh, 'Now you've put the doubt into my mind, Con, I'm sure I can't tell myself.'

'Well, we can't postpone it again,' said Josephine. 'If we postpone it this time—'

XII

But at that moment in the street below a barrel-organ struck up. Josephine and Constantia sprang to their feet together.

'Run, Con,' said Josephine. 'Run quickly. There's sixpence on the—'

Then they remembered. It didn't matter. They would never have to stop the organ-grinder again. Never again would she and Constantia be told to make that monkey take his noise somewhere else. Never would sound that loud, strange bellow when father thought they were not hurrying enough. The organ-grinder might play there all day and the stick would not thump.

It never will thump again,
It never will thump again,

played the barrel-organ.

What was Constantia thinking? She had such a strange smile; she looked different. She couldn't be going to cry.

'Jug, Jug,' said Constantia softly, pressing her hands together. 'Do you know what day it is? It's Saturday. It's a week today, a whole week.'

A week since father died,
A week since father died,

cried the barrel-organ. And Josephine, too, forgot to be practical and sensible; she smiled faintly, strangely. On the Indian carpet there fell a square of sunlight, pale red; it came and went and came – and stayed, deepened – until it shone almost golden.

'The sun's out,' said Josephine, as though it really mattered.

A perfect fountain of bubbling notes shook from the barrel-organ, round, bright notes, carelessly scattered.

Constantia lifted her big, cold hands as if to catch them, and then her hands fell again. She walked over to the mantelpiece to her favourite Buddha. And the stone and gilt image, whose smile always gave her such a queer feeling, almost a pain and yet a pleasant pain, seemed today to be more than smiling. He knew something; he had a secret. 'I know something that you don't know,' said her Buddha. Oh, what was

259

it, what could it be? And yet she had always felt there was . . . something.

The sunlight pressed through the windows, thieved its way in, flashed its light over the furniture and the photographs. Josephine watched it. When it came to mother's photograph, the enlargement over the piano, it lingered as though puzzled to find so little remained of mother, except the ear-rings shaped like tiny pagodas and a black feather boa. Why did the photographs of dead people always fade so? wondered Josephine. As soon as a person was dead their photograph died too. But, of course, this one of mother was very old. It was thirty-five years old. Josephine remembered standing on a chair and pointing out that feather boa to Constantia and telling her that it was a snake that had killed their mother in Ceylon. . . . Would everything have been different if mother hadn't died? She didn't see why. Aunt Florence had lived with them until they had left school, and they had moved three times and had their yearly holiday and . . . and there'd been changes of servants, of course.

Some little sparrows, young sparrows they sounded, chirped on the window-ledge. *Yeep – eyeep – yeep*. But Josephine felt they were not sparrows, not on the window-ledge. It was inside her, that queer little crying noise. *Yeep – eyeep – yeep*. Ah, what was it crying, so weak and forlorn?

If mother had lived, might they have married? But there had been nobody for them to marry. There had been father's Anglo-Indian friends before he quarrelled with them. But after that she and Constantia never met a single man except clergymen. How did one meet men? Or even if they'd met them, how could they have got to know men well enough to be more than strangers? One read of people having adventures, being followed, and so on. But nobody had ever followed Constantia and her. Oh yes, there had been one year at Eastbourne a mysterious man at their boarding-house who had put a note on the jug of hot water outside their bedroom door! But by the time Connie had found it the steam had made the writing too faint to read; they couldn't even make out to which of them it was addressed. And he had left next day. And that was all. The rest had been looking after father and at the same time keeping out of father's way. But now? But now? The thieving sun touched Josephine gently. She lifted her face. She was drawn over to the window by gentle beams. . . .

Until the barrel-organ stopped playing Constantia stayed before the Buddha, wondering, but not as usual, not vaguely. This time her wonder was like longing. She remembered the times she had come in here, crept out of bed in her nightgown when the moon was full, and lain on the floor with her arms outstretched, as though she was crucified. Why? The big, pale moon had made her do it. The horrible dancing figures on the carved screen had leered at her and she hadn't minded. She remembered too how, whenever they were at the seaside, she had gone off by herself and got as close to the sea as she could, and sung something, something she had made up, while she gazed all over that restless water. There had been this other life, running out, bringing things home in bags, getting things on approval, discussing them with Jug, and taking them back to get more things on approval, and arranging father's trays and trying not to annoy father. But it all seemed to have happened in a kind of tunnel. It wasn't real. It was only when she came out of the tunnel into the moonlight or by the sea or into a thunderstorm that she really felt herself. What did it mean? What was it she was always wanting? What did it all lead to? Now? Now?

She turned away from the Buddha with one of her vague gestures. She went over to where Josephine was standing.

She wanted to say something to Josephine, something frightfully important, about – about the future and what . . .

'Don't you think perhaps—' she began.

But Josephine interrupted her. 'I was wondering if now—' she murmured. They stopped; they waited for each other.

'Go on, Con,' said Josephine.

'No, no, Jug; after you,' said Constantia.

'No, say what you were going to say. You began,' said Josephine.

'I . . . I'd rather hear what you were going to say first,' said Constantia.

'Don't be absurd, Con.'

'Really, Jug.'

'Connie!'

'Oh, *Jug*!'

A pause. Then Constantia said faintly, 'I can't say what I was going to say, Jug, because I've forgotten what it was . . . that I was going to say.'

Josephine was silent for a moment. She stared at a big cloud where the sun had been. Then she replied shortly, 'I've forgotten too.'

HELEN SIMPSON

SORRY?

'SORRY?' SAID PATRICK. 'I didn't quite catch that.'

'SOUP OF THE DAY IS WILD MUSHROOM,' bellowed the waiter.

'No need to shout,' said Patrick, putting his hand to his troublesome ear.

The new gadget screeched in protest.

'They take a bit of getting used to,' grimaced Matthew Herring, the deaf chap he'd been fixed up with for a morale-boosting lunch.

'You don't say,' he replied.

Some weeks ago Patrick had woken up to find he had gone deaf in his right ear – not just a bit deaf but profoundly deaf. There was nothing to be done, it seemed. It had probably been caused by a tiny flake of matter dislodged by wear-and-tear change in the vertebrae, the doctor had said, shrugging. He had turned his head on his pillow, in all likeli-hood; sometimes that was all it took. This neck movement would have shifted a minuscule scrap of detritus into the river of blood running towards the brain, a fragment that must have finished by blocking the very narrowest bit of the entire arterial system, the ultrafine pipe leading to the inner ear. Bad luck.

'I don't hear perfectly,' said Matthew Herring now. 'It's not magic, a digital hearing aid, it doesn't turn your hearing into perfect hearing.'

'Mine's not working properly yet,' said Patrick. 'I've got an appointment after lunch to get it seen to.'

'Mind you, it's better than the old one,' continued Matthew comfortably. 'You used to be able to hear me wherever I went with the analog one – it used to go before me, screeching like a steam train.'

He chuckled at the memory.

Patrick did not smile at this cosy reference to engine whistles. He had been astonished at the storm of head noise that had arrived with deafness, the whistles and screeches over a powerful cloud of hissing just like the noise from his wife Elizabeth's old pressure cooker. His brain was generating sound to compensate for the loss of hearing, he had been told. Apparently that was part and parcel of the deafness, as well as dizzy episodes. Ha! Thanks to the vertigo that had sent him arse over tip several times since the start of all this, he was having to stay with his daughter Rachel for a while.

'Two girls,' he said tersely in answer to a question from his tedious lunch companion. He and Elizabeth had wished for boys, but there you were. Rachel was the only one so far to have provided him with grandchildren. The other daughter, Ruth, had decamped to Australia some time ago. Who knew what she was up to but she was still out there so presumably she had managed to make a go of it, something she had signally failed to do in England.

'I used to love music,' Matthew Herring was saying, undaunted. 'But it's not the same now that I'm so deaf. Now it tires me out; in fact, I don't listen any more. I deliberately avoid it. The loss of it is a grief, I must admit.'

'Oh well, music means nothing to me,' said Patrick. 'Never has. So I shan't miss *that*.'

He wasn't about to confide in Matthew Herring, but of all his symptoms it had been the auditory hallucinations produced by the hearing aid that had been the most disturbing for him. The low violent stream of nonsense issuing from

266

the general direction of his firstborn had become insupportable in the last week, and he had had to turn the damned thing off.

At his after-lunch appointment with the audiologist, he found himself curiously unable to describe the hallucinatory problem.

'I seem to be picking up extra noise,' he said eventually. 'It's difficult to describe.'

'Sounds go into your hearing aid, where they are processed electronically,' she intoned, 'then played back to you over a tiny loudspeaker.'

'Yes, I know that,' he snapped. 'I am aware of that, thank you. What I'm asking is, might one of the various settings you programmed be capable of, er, amplifying sounds that would normally remain unheard?'

'Let's see, shall we,' she said, still talking to him as though he were a child or a half-wit. 'I wonder whether you've been picking up extra stuff on the Loop.'

'The Loop?'

'It works a bit like Wi-Fi,' she said. 'Electromagnetic fields. If you're in an area that's on the Loop, you can pick up on it with your hearing aid when you turn on the T-setting.'

'The T-setting?'

'That little extra bit of doohickey there,' she said, pointing at it. 'I didn't mention it before; I didn't want to confuse you while you were getting used to the basics. You must have turned it on by mistake, from what you're saying.'

'But what *sort* of extra sounds does it pick up?' he persisted.

Rachel's lips had not been moving during that initial weird diatribe a week ago, he was sure of it, nor during the battery of bitter little remarks he'd had to endure since then.

'Well, it can be quite embarrassing,' the audiologist said, laughing merrily. 'Walls don't block the magnetic waves from a Loop signal, so you might well be able to listen in on confidential conversations if neighbouring rooms are also on it.'

'Hmm,' he said, 'I'm not sure that quite explains this particular problem. But I suppose it might have something to do with it.'

'Look, I've turned off the T-setting,' she said. 'If you want to test what it does, simply turn it on again and see what happens.'

'Or hear,' he said. 'Hear what happens.'

'You're right!' she declared, with more merry laughter.

He really couldn't see what was so amusing, and said so.

Back at Rachel's, he made his way to the armchair in the little bay window and whiled away the minutes until six o'clock by rereading the *Telegraph*. The trouble with this house was that its interior walls had been knocked down, so you were all in it hugger-mugger together. He could not himself see the advantage of being forced to witness every domestic detail. Frankly, it was bedlam, with the spin cycle going and Rachel's twins screeching and Rachel washing her hands at the kitchen sink yet again like Lady Macbeth. Now she was doing that thing she did with the brown paper bag, blowing into it and goggling her eyes, which seemed to amuse the twins at least.

Small children were undoubtedly tiresome, but the way she indulged hers made them ten times worse. Like so many of her generation she seemed to be making a huge song and dance about the whole business. She was ridiculous with them, ludicrously over-indulgent and lacking in any sort of authority. It was when he had commented on this in passing that the auditory hallucinations had begun.

'I don't want to do to them what you did to me, you old beast,' the voice had growled, guttural and shocking, although her lips had not been moving. 'I don't want to hand on the misery, I don't want that horrible Larkin poem to be true.' He had glared at her, amazed, and yet it had been quite obvious that she was blissfully unaware of what he had heard. Or thought he had heard.

He must have been hearing things.

Now he held up his wrist and tapped his watch at her. She waved back at him, giving one last puff into the paper bag before scurrying to the fridge for the ice and lemon. As he watched her prepare his first drink of the evening, he decided to test out the audiologist's theory.

'Sit with me,' he ordered, taking the clinking glass.

'I'd love to, Dad, but the twins . . . ,' she said.

'Nonsense,' he said. 'Look at them, you can see them from here – they're all right for now.'

She perched on the arm of the chair opposite his and started twisting a strand of her lank brown hair.

'Tell me about your day,' he commanded.

'My day?' she said. 'Are you sure? Nothing very much happened. I took the twins to playgroup, then we went round the supermarket.'

'Keep talking,' he said, fiddling with his hearing aid. 'I want to test this gadget out.'

'. . . then I had to stand in line at the post office, and I wasn't very popular with the double stroller,' she droned on.

He flicked the switch to the T-setting.

'. . . never good enough for you, you old beast, you never had any time for me, you never listened to anything I said,' came the low growling voice he remembered from before. 'You cold old beast, Ruth says you're emotionally autistic, definitely somewhere on the autistic spectrum anyway, that's why she went to the other side of the world but she says she still can't get away from it there, your lack of interest, you blanked us, you blotted us out, you don't even know the names of your grandchildren let alone their birthdays...'

He flicked the switch back.

'...after their nap, then I put the washing on and peeled some potatoes for tonight's dinner while they watched CBeebies,' she continued in her toneless everyday voice.

'That's enough for now, thanks,' he said crisply. He took a big gulp of his drink, and then another. 'Scarlett and, er, Mia. You'd better see what they're up to.'

'Are you OK, Dad?'

'Fine,' he snapped. 'You go off and do whatever it is you want to do.' He closed his eyes. He needed Elizabeth now. She'd taken no nonsense from the girls. He had left them to her, which was the way she'd wanted it. All this hysteria! Elizabeth had known how to deal with them.

He sensed he was in for another bad night, and he was right. He lay rigid as a stone knight on a tomb, claustrophobic in his partially closed-down head and its frantic brain noise. The deafer he got, the louder it became; that was how it was, that was the deal. He grimaced at the future, his other ear gone, reduced to the company of Matthew Herring and his like, a shoal of old boys mouthing at each other.

The thing was, he had been the breadwinner. Children needed their mothers. It was true he hadn't been very interested in them, but then, frankly, they hadn't been very interesting. Was he supposed to pretend? Neither of them had amounted to much. And, he had had his own life to get on with.

He'd seen the way they were with their children these days – 'Oh that's wonderful darling! You *are* clever' and 'Love you!' at the end of every exchange, with the young fathers behaving like old women, cooing and planting big sloppy kisses on their babies as if they were in a Disney film. The whole culture had gone soft, it gave him the creeps; opening up to your feminine side! He shuddered in his pyjamas.

Elizabeth was dead. That was what he really couldn't bear.

The noise inside his head was going wild, crackles and screeching and pressure-cooker hisses; he needed to distract his brain with – what had the doctor called it? – 'sound enrichment'. Give it some competition, fight fire with fire; that was the idea. Fiddling with the radio's tuning wheel in the dark, he swore viciously and wondered why it was you could never find the World Service when you needed it. He wanted talk but there was only music, which would have to do. Nothing but a meaningless racket to him, though at least it was a different *sort* of racket; that was the theory.

No, that was no better. If anything, it was worse.

Wasn't the hearing aid supposed to help cancel tinnitus? So the doctor had suggested. Maybe the T-setting would come into its own in this sort of situation. He turned on the tiny gadget, made the necessary adjustments, and poked it into his ear.

It was like blood returning to a dead leg, but in his head and chest. What an extraordinary sensation! It was completely new to him. Music was stealing hotly, pleasurably through his veins for the first time in his life, unspeakably delicious. He heard himself moan aloud. The waves of sound were announcing bliss and at the same time they brought cruel pain. He'd done his best, hadn't he? He didn't know what the girls expected from him. He'd given them full financial support until they were eighteen, which was more than many fathers could say. What was it exactly that he was supposed not to have done?

Lifting him on a dark upsurge into the night, the music also felled him with inklings of what he did not know and had not known, intimations of things lovely beyond imagination which would never now be his as death was next. A tear crept down his face.

He hadn't cried since he was a baby. Appalling! At this rate he'd be wetting himself. When his mother had died, he and his sisters had been called into the front room and given a handkerchief each and told to go to their bedrooms until teatime. Under the carpet. Into thin air.

The music was so astonishingly beautiful, that was the trouble. Waves of entrancing sound were threatening to breach the sea wall. Now he was coughing dry sobs.

This was not on. Frankly, he preferred any combination of troublesome symptoms to getting in this state. He fumbled with the hearing aid and at last managed to turn the damned thing *off*. Half-unhinged, he tottered to the bathroom and ran a basin of water over it, submerged the beastly little gadget, drowned it. Then he fished it out and flushed it down the lavatory. Best place for it.

No more funny business, he vowed. That was that. From now on he would put up and shut up, he swore it on Elizabeth's grave. Back in bed, he once again lowered his head onto the pillow.

Straightaway the infernal noise factory started up; he was staggering along beat by beat in a heavy shower of noise and howling.

'It's not real,' he whispered to himself in the dark. 'Compensatory brain activity, that's what this is.'

Inside his skull all hell had broken loose. He had never heard anything like it.

D. H. LAWRENCE

THE CHRISTENING

THE MISTRESS OF the British School stepped down from her school gate, and instead of turning to the left as usual, she turned to the right. Two women who were hastening home to scramble their husband's dinners together – it was five minutes to four – stopped to look at her. They stood gazing after her for a moment; then they glanced at each other with a woman's little grimace.

To be sure, the retreating figure was ridiculous: small and thin, with a black straw hat, and a rusty cashmere dress hanging full all round the skirt. For so small and frail and rusty a creature to sail with slow, deliberate stride was also absurd. Hilda Rowbotham was less than thirty, so it was not years that set the measure of her pace; she had heart disease. Keeping her face, that was small with sickness, but not uncomely, firmly lifted and fronting ahead, the young woman sailed on past the market-place, like a black swan of mournful, disreputable plumage.

She turned into Berryman's, the baker's. The shop displayed bread and cakes, sacks of flour and oatmeal, flitches of bacon, hams, lard and sausages. The combination of scents was not unpleasing. Hilda Rowbotham stood for some minutes nervously tapping and pushing a large knife that lay on the counter, and looking at the tall, glittering brass scales. At last a morose man with sandy whiskers came down the step from the house-place.

'What is it?' he asked, not apologizing for his delay.

'Will you give me six-pennyworth of assorted cakes and pastries – and put in some macaroons, please?' she asked, in remarkably rapid and nervous speech. Her lips fluttered like two leaves in a wind, and her words crowded and rushed like a flock of sheep at a gate.

'We've got no macaroons,' said the man churlishly.

He had evidently caught that word. He stood waiting.

'Then I can't have any, Mr Berryman. Now I do feel disappointed. I like those macaroons, you know, and it's not often I treat myself. One gets so tired of trying to spoil oneself, don't you think? It's less profitable even than trying to spoil somebody else.' She laughed a quick little nervous laugh, putting her hand to her face.

'Then what'll you have?' asked the man, without the ghost of an answering smile. He evidently had not followed, so he looked more glum than ever.

'Oh, anything you've got,' replied the schoolmistress, flushing slightly. The man moved slowly about, dropping the cakes from various dishes one by one into a paper bag.

'How's that sister o' yours getting on?' he asked, as if he were talking to the flour scoop.

'Whom do you mean?' snapped the schoolmistress.

'The youngest,' answered the stooping, pale-faced man, with a note of sarcasm.

'Emma! Oh, she's very well, thank you!' The schoolmistress was very red, but she spoke with sharp, ironical defiance. The man grunted. Then he handed her the bag and watched her out of the shop without bidding her 'Good afternoon'.

She had the whole length of the main street to traverse, a half-mile of slow-stepping torture, with shame flushing over her neck. But she carried her white bag with an appearance of steadfast unconcern. When she turned into the field she seemed to droop a little. The wide valley opened out from her, with the far woods withdrawing into twilight, and away in the centre the great pit streaming its white smoke and chuffing as the men were being turned up. A full, rose-coloured moon, like a flamingo flying low under the far, dusky east, drew out of the mist. It was beautiful, and it made her irritable sadness soften, diffuse.

Across the field, and she was at home. It was a new, substantial cottage, built with unstinted hand, such a house as an old miner could build himself out of his savings. In the rather small kitchen a woman of dark, saturnine complexion sat nursing a baby in a long white gown; a young woman of heavy, brutal cast stood at the table, cutting bread and butter. She had a downcast, humble mien that sat unnaturally on her, and was strangely irritating. She did not look round when her sister entered. Hilda put down the bag of cakes and left the room, not having spoken to Emma, nor to the baby, not to Mrs Carlin, who had come in to help for the afternoon.

Almost immediately the father entered from the yard with a dustpan full of coals. He was a large man, but he was going to pieces. As he passed through, he gripped the door with his free hand to steady himself, but turning, he lurched and swayed. He began putting the coals on the fire, piece by piece. One lump fell from his hand and smashed on the white hearth. Emma Rowbotham looked round, and began in a rough, loud voice of anger: 'Look at you!' Then she consciously moderated her tones. 'I'll sweep it up in a minute – don't you bother; you'll only be going head first into the fire.'

Her father bent down nevertheless to clear up the mess he had made, saying, articulating his words loosely and slavering in his speech:

'The lousy bit of a thing, it slipped between my fingers like a fish.'

As he spoke he went tilting towards the fire. The dark-browed woman cried out: he put his hand on the hot stove to save himself. Emma swung round and dragged him off.

'Didn't I tell you!' she cried roughly. 'Now, have you burnt yourself?'

She held tight hold of the big man, and pushed him into his chair.

'What's the matter?' cried a sharp voice from the other room. The speaker appeared, a hard well-favoured woman of twenty-eight. 'Emma, don't speak like that to father.' Then, in a tone not so cold, but just as sharp: 'Now father, what have you been doing?'

Emma withdrew to her table sullenly.

'It's nöwt,' said the old man, vainly protesting. 'It's nöwt, at a'. Get on wi' what you're doin'.'

'I'm afraid 'e's burnt 'is 'and,' said the black-browed woman, speaking of him with a kind of hard pity, as if he were a cumbersome child. Bertha took the old man's hand and looked at it, making a quick tut-tutting noise of impatience.

'Emma, get that zinc ointment – and some white rag,' she commanded sharply. The younger sister put down her loaf with the knife in it, and went. To a sensitive observer, this obedience was more intolerable than the most hateful discord. The dark woman bent over the baby and made silent, gentle movements of motherliness to it. The little one smiled and moved on her lap. It continued to move and twist.

'I believe this child's hungry,' she said. 'How long is it since he had anything?'

'Just afore dinner,' said Emma dully.

'Good gracious!' exclaimed Bertha. 'You needn't starve the child now you've got it. Once every two hours it ought to be fed, as I've told you; and now it's three. Take him, poor little mite – I'll cut the bread.' She bent and looked at the bonny baby. She could not help herself: she smiled, and pressed its cheek with her finger, and nodded to it, making little noises. Then she turned and took the loaf from her sister. The woman rose and gave the child to its mother. Emma bent over the little sucking mite. She hated it when she looked at it, and saw it as a symbol, but when she felt it, her love was like fire in her blood.

'I should think 'e canna be comin',' said the father uneasily, looking up at the clock.

'Nonsense, father – the clock's fast! It's but half-past four! Don't fidget!' Bertha continued to cut the bread and butter.

'Open a tin of pears,' she said to the woman, in a much milder tone. Then she went into the next room. As soon as she was gone, the old man said again: 'I should ha'e thought he'd 'a' been 'ere by now, if he means comin'.'

Emma, engrossed, did not answer. The father had ceased to consider her, since she had become humbled.

''E'll come – 'e'll come!' assured the stranger.

A few minutes later Bertha hurried into the kitchen, taking off her apron. The dog barked furiously. She opened the door, commanded the dog to silence, and said: 'He will be quiet now, Mr Kendal.'

'Thank you,' said a sonorous voice, and there was the sound of a bicycle being propped against a wall. A clergyman entered, a big-boned, thin, ugly man of nervous manner. He went straight to the father.

'Ah – how are you?' he asked musically, peering down on the great frame of the miner, ruined by locomotor ataxy.

His voice was full of gentleness, but he seemed as if he could not see distinctly, could not get things clear.

'Have you hurt your hand?' he said comfortingly, seeing the white rag.

279

'It wor nöwt but a pestered bit o' coal as dropped, an' I put my hand on th' hub. I thought tha worna commin'.'

The familiar 'tha', and the reproach, were unconscious retaliation on the old man's part. The minister smiled, half wistfully, half indulgently. He was full of vague tenderness. Then he turned to the young mother, who flushed sullenly because her dishonoured breast was uncovered.

'How are *you*?' he asked, very softly and gently, as if she were ill and he were mindful of her.

'I'm all right,' she replied, awkwardly taking his hand without rising, hiding her face and the anger that rose in her.

'Yes – yes' – he peered down at the baby, which sucked with distended mouth upon the firm breast. 'Yes, yes.' He seemed lost in a dim musing.

Coming to, he shook hands unseeingly with the woman.

Presently they all went into the next room, the minister hesitating to help his crippled old deacon.

'I can go by myself thank yer,' testily replied the father.

Soon all were seated. Everybody was separated in feeling and isolated at table. High tea was spread in the middle kitchen, a large, ugly room kept for special occasions.

Hilda appeared last, and the clumsy, raw-boned clergyman rose to meet her. He was afraid of this family, the well-to-do old collier, and the brutal, self-willed children. But Hilda was queen among them. She was the clever one, and had been to college. She felt responsible for the keeping up of a high standard of conduct in all the members of the family. There *was* a difference between the Rowbothams and the common collier folk. Woodbine Cottage was a superior house to most – and was built in pride by the old man. She, Hilda, was a college-trained schoolmistress; she meant to keep up the prestige of her house in spite of blows.

She had put on a dress of green voile for this special

occasion. But she was very thin; her neck protruded painfully. The clergyman, however, greeted her almost with reverence, and, with some assumption of dignity, she sat down before the tray. At the far end of the table sat the broken, massive frame of her father. Next to him was the youngest daughter, nursing the restless baby. The minister sat between Hilda and Bertha, hulking his bony frame uncomfortably.

There was a great spread on the table, of tinned fruits and tinned salmon, ham and cakes. Miss Rowbotham kept a keen eye on everything: she felt the importance of the occasion. The young mother who had given rise to all this solemnity ate in sulky discomfort, snatching sullen little smiles at her child, smiles which came, in spite of her, when she felt its little limbs stirring vigorously on her lap. Bertha, sharp and abrupt, was chiefly concerned with the baby. She scorned her sister, and treated her like dirt. But the infant was a streak of light to her. Miss Rowbotham concerned herself with the function and the conversation. Her hands fluttered; she talked in little volleys, exceedingly nervous. Towards the end of the meal, there came a pause. The old man wiped his mouth with his red handkerchief, then, his blue eyes going fixed and staring, he began to speak, in a loose, slobbering fashion, charging his words at the clergyman.

'Well, mester – we'n axed you to come her ter christen this childt, an' you'n come, an' I'm sure we're very thankful. I can't see lettin' the poor blessed childt miss baptizing, an' they aren't for goin' to church wi't –' He seemed to lapse into a muse. 'So,' he resumed, 'we've axed you to come here to do the job. I'm not sayin' as it's not 'ard on us, it is. I'm breakin' up, an' mother's gone. I don't like leavin' a girl o'mine in a situation like 'ers is, but what the Lord's done, He's done, an' it's no matter murmuring. . . . There's one thing to be thankful

281

for, an' we *are* thankful for it: they never need know the want of bread.'

Miss Rowbotham, the lady of the family, sat very stiff and pained during this discourse. She was sensitive to so many things that she was bewildered. She felt her young sister's shame, then a kind of swift protecting love for the baby, a feeling that included the mother; she was at a loss before her father's religious sentiment, and she felt and resented bitterly the mark upon the family, against which the common folk could lift their fingers. Still she winced from the sound of her father's words. It was a painful ordeal.

'It is hard for you,' began the clergyman in his soft, lingering unworldly voice. 'It is hard for you today, but the Lord gives comfort in His time. A man child is born unto us, therefore let us rejoice and be glad. If sin has entered in among us, let us purify our hearts before the Lord...'

He went on with his discourse. The young mother lifted the whimpering infant, till its face was hid in her loose hair. She was hurt, and a little glowering anger shone in her face. But nevertheless her fingers clasped the body of the child beautifully. She was stupefied with anger against this emotion let loose on her account.

Miss Bertha rose and went to the little kitchen, returning with water in a china bowl. She placed it there among the tea-things.

'Well, we're all ready,' said the old man, and the clergyman began to read the service. Miss Bertha was godmother, the two men godfathers. The old man sat with bent head. The scene became impressive. At last Miss Bertha took the child and put it in the arms of the clergyman. He, big and ugly, shone with a kind of unreal love. He had never mixed with life, and women were all unliving, Biblical things to him. When he asked for the name, the old man lifted his head fiercely. 'Joseph William, after me,' he said, almost out of breath.

'Joseph William, I baptize thee . . .' resounded the strange full, chanting voice of the clergyman. The baby was quite still.

'Let us pray!' It came with relief to them all. They knelt before their chairs, all but the young mother, who bent and hid herself over her baby. The clergyman began his hesitating, struggling prayer.

Just then heavy footsteps were heard coming up the path, ceasing at the window. The young mother, glancing up, saw her brother, black in his pit dirt, grinning in through the panes. His red mouth curved in a sneer; his fair hair shone above his blackened skin. He caught the eye of his sister and grinned. Then his black face disappeared. He had gone on into the kitchen. The girl with the child sat still and anger filled her heart. She herself hated now the praying clergyman and the whole emotional business; she hated her brother bitterly. In anger and bondage she sat and listened.

Suddenly her father began to pray. His familiar, loud, rambling voice made her shut herself up and become even insentient. Folks said his mind was weakening. She believed it to be true, and kept herself always disconnected from him.

'We ask Thee, Lord,' the old man cried, 'to look after this childt. Fatherless he is. But what does the earthly father matter before Thee? The childt is Thine, he is Thy childt. Lord, what father has a man but Thee? Lord, when a man says he is a father, he is wrong from the first word. For Thou art the Father, Lord. Lord, take away from us the conceit that our children are ours. Lord, Thou art Father of this childt as is fatherless here. O God, Thou bring him up. For I have stood between Thee and my children; I've had *my* way with them, Lord; I've stood between Thee and my children; I've cut 'em off from Thee because they were mine. And they've grown twisted, because of me. Who is their father, Lord, but Thee? But I put myself in the way, they've been plants under a stone, because of me. Lord, if it hadn't been for me, they might ha' been trees in the sunshine. Let me own it, Lord, I've done 'em mischief. It could ha' been better if they'd never known no father. No man is a father, Lord: only Thou art. They can never grow beyond Thee, but I hampered them. Lift 'em up again, and undo what I've done to my children. And let this young childt be like a willow tree beside the waters, with no father but Thee, O God. Aye an' I wish it had been so with my children, that they'd had no father but Thee. For I've been like a stone upon them, and they rise up and curse me in their wickedness. But let me go, an' lift Thou them up, Lord . . .'

The minister, unaware of the feelings of a father, knelt in trouble, hearing without understanding the special language of fatherhood. Miss Rowbotham alone felt and understood a little. Her heart began to flutter; she was in pain. The two younger daughters kneeled unhearing, stiffened and impervious. Bertha was thinking of the baby; and the younger mother thought of the father of her child, whom she hated. There was a clatter in the scullery. There the youngest son made as much noise as he could, pouring out the water for his wash, muttering in deep anger:

'Blortin', slaverin' old fool!'

And while the praying of his father continued, his heart was burning with rage. On the table was a paper bag. He picked it up and read, 'John Berryman – Bread, Pastries, etc'. Then he grinned with a grimace. The father of the baby was baker's man at Berryman's. The prayer went on in the middle kitchen. Laurie Rowbotham gathered together the mouth of the bag, inflated it, and burst it with his fist. There was a loud report. He grinned to himself. But he writhed at the same time with shame and fear of his father.

The father broke off from his prayer; the party shuffled to their feet. The young mother went into the scullery.

'What art doin', fool?' she said.

The collier youth tipped the baby under the chin, singing:

> 'Pat-a-cake, pat-a-cake, baker's man,
> Bake me a cake as fast as you can. . . .'

The mother snatched the child away. 'Shut thy mouth,' she said, the colour coming into her cheek.

> 'Prick it and stick it and mark it with P,
> And put it i' th' oven for baby an' me. . . .'

He grinned, showing a grimy, and jeering and unpleasant red mouth and white teeth.

'I s'll gi'e thee a dab ower th' mouth,' said the mother of the baby grimly. He began to sing again, and she struck out at him.

'Now what's to do?' said the father, staggering in.

The youth began to sing again. His sister stood sullen and furious.

'Why, does *that* upset you?' asked the eldest Miss Rowbotham, sharply, of Emma the mother. 'Good gracious, it hasn't improved your temper.'

Miss Bertha came in, and took the bonny baby.

The father sat big and unheeding in his chair, his eyes vacant, his physique wrecked. He let them do as they would, he fell to pieces. And yet some power, involuntary, like a curse, remained in him. The very ruin of him was like a lodestone that held them in its control. The wreck of him still dominated the house, in his dissolution even he compelled their being. They had never lived; his life, his will had always

285

been upon them and contained them. They were only half-individuals.

The day after the christening he staggered in at the door-way declaring, in a loud voice, with joy in life still: 'The daisies light up the earth, they clap their hands in multitudes, in praise of the morning.' And his daughters shrank, sullen.

EDITH WHARTON

HIS FATHER'S SON

I

AFTER HIS WIFE'S death Mason Grew took the moment-
ous step of selling out his business and moving from Wingfield, Connecticut, to Brooklyn.

For years he had secretly nursed the hope of such a change,
but had never dared to suggest it to Mrs Grew, a woman of
immutable habits. Mr Grew himself was attached to Wingfield, where he had grown up, prospered, and become what
the local press described as 'prominent.' He was attached to
his brick house with sandstone trimmings and a cast-iron
area-railing neatly sanded to match; to the similar row of
houses across the street, with 'trolley' wires forming a kind of
aerial pathway between, and to the vista closed by the sandstone steeple of the church which he and his wife had always
attended, and where their only child had been baptised.

It was hard to snap all these threads of association, yet
still harder, now that he was alone, to live so far from his
boy. Ronald Grew was practicing law in New York, and
there was no more chance of his returning to live at Wingfield than of a river's flowing inland from the sea. Therefore
to be near him his father must move; and it was character-
istic of Mr Grew, and of the situation generally, that the
translation, when it took place, was to Brooklyn, and not to
New York.

'Why you bury yourself in that hole I can't think,' had
been Ronald's comment; and Mr Grew simply replied that

rents were lower in Brooklyn, and that he had heard of a house there that would suit him. In reality he had said to himself – being the only recipient of his own confidences – that if he went to New York he might be on the boy's mind; whereas, if he lived in Brooklyn, Ronald would always have a good excuse for not popping over to see him every other day. The sociological isolation of Brooklyn, combined with its geographical nearness, presented in fact the precise conditions that Mr Grew sought. He wanted to be near enough to New York to go there often, to feel under his feet the same pavement that Ronald trod, to sit now and then in the same theaters, and find on his breakfast-table the journals which, with increasing frequency, inserted Ronald's name in the sacred bounds of the society column. It had always been a trial to Mr Grew to have to wait twenty-four hours to read that 'among those present was Mr Ronald Grew.' Now he had it with his coffee, and left it on the breakfast-table to the perusal of a 'hired girl' cosmopolitan enough to do it justice. In such ways Brooklyn attested the advantages of its nearness to New York, while remaining, as regards Ronald's duty to his father, as remote and inaccessible as Wingfield.

It was not that Ronald shirked his filial obligations, but rather because of his heavy sense of them, that Mr Grew so persistently sought to minimize and lighten them. It was he who insisted, to Ronald, on the immense difficulty of getting from New York to Brooklyn.

'Any way you look at it, it makes a big hole in the day; and there's not much use in the ragged rim left. You say you're dining out next Sunday? Then I forbid you to come over here to lunch. Do you understand me, sir? You disobey at the risk of your father's malediction! Where did you say you were dining? With the Waltham Bankshires again? Why, that's the second time in three weeks, ain't it? Big blow-out, I suppose?

Gold plate and orchids – opera singers in afterward? Well, you'd be in a nice box if there was a fog on the river, and you got hung up half-way over. That'd be a handsome return for the attention Mrs Bankshire has shown you – singling out a whipper-snapper like you twice in three weeks! (What's the daughter's name – Daisy?) No, *sir* – don't you come fooling round here next Sunday, or I'll set the dogs on you. And you wouldn't find me in anyhow, come to think of it. I'm lunching out myself, as it happens – yes, sir, *lunching out*. Is there anything especially comic in my lunching out? I don't often do it, you say? Well, that's no reason why I never should. Who with? Why, with – with old Dr Bleaker: Dr Eliphalet Bleaker. No, you wouldn't know about him – he's only an old friend of your mother's and mine.'

Gradually Ronald's insistence became less difficult to overcome. With his customary sweetness and tact (as Mr Grew put it) he began to 'take the hint,' to give in to 'the old gentleman's' growing desire for solitude.

'I'm set in my ways, Ronny, that's about the size of it; I like to go tick-ticking along like a clock. I always did. And when you come bouncing in I never feel sure there's enough for dinner – or that I haven't sent Maria out for the evening. And I don't want the neighbors to see me opening my own door to my son. That's the kind of cringing snob I am. Don't give me away, will you? I want 'em to think I keep four or five powdered flunkeys in the hall day and night – same as the lobby of one of those Fifth Avenue hotels. And if you pop over when you're not expected, how am I going to keep up the bluff?'

Ronald yielded after the proper amount of resistance – his intuitive sense, in every social transaction, of the proper amount of force to be expended, was one of the qualities his father most admired in him. Mr Grew's perceptions in this line were probably more acute than his son suspected. The souls of short thick-set men, with chubby features, mutton-chop whiskers, and pale eyes peering between folds of fat like almond kernels in half-split shells – souls thus encased do not reveal themselves to the casual scrutiny as delicate emotional instruments. But in spite of the disguise in which he walked Mr Grew vibrated exquisitely in response to every imagina-tive appeal; and his son Ronald was always stimulating and feeding his imagination.

Ronald in fact constituted Mr Grew's one escape from the element of mediocrity which had always hemmed him in. To a man so enamored of beauty, and so little qualified to add to its sum total, it was a wonderful privilege to have bestowed on the world such a being. Ronald's resemblance to Mr Grew's early conception of what he himself would have liked to look might have put new life into the dis-credited theory of pre-natal influences. At any rate, if the young man owed his beauty, his distinction and his winning manner to the dreams of one of his parents, it was certainly to those of Mr Grew, who, while outwardly devoting his life to the manufacture and dissemination of Grew's Secure Suspender Buckle, moved in an enchanted inward world peopled with all the figures of romance. In this company Mr Grew cut as brilliant a figure as any of its noble phantoms; and to see his vision of himself projected on the outer world in the shape of a brilliant popular conquering son, seemed, in retrospect, to give to it a belated reality. There were even moments when, forgetting his face, Mr Grew said to himself that if he'd had 'half a chance' he might have done as well as Ronald; but this only fortified his resolve that Ronald should do infinitely better.

Ronald's ability to do well almost equaled his gift of look-ing well. Mr Grew constantly affirmed to himself that the boy was 'not a genius'; but, barring this slight deficiency, he had almost every gift that a parent could wish. Even at Harvard he had managed to be several desirable things at once – writing poetry in the college magazine, playing delightfully 'by ear,' acquitting himself creditably of his studies, and yet holding his own in the sporting set that formed, as it were, the gateway of the temple of Society. Mr Grew's idealism did not preclude the frank desire that his son should pass through that gateway; but the wish was not prompted by material considerations. It was Mr Grew's notion that, in the rough and hurrying current of a new civilization, the little pools of leisure and enjoyment must nurture delicate growths, material graces as well as moral refinements, likely to be uprooted and swept away by the rush of the main torrent. He based his theory on the fact that he had liked the few 'society' people he had met – had found their manners simpler, their voices more agreeable, their views more consonant with his own, than those of the leading citizens of Wingfield. But then he had met very few.

Ronald's sympathies needed no urging in the same direction. He took naturally, dauntlessly, to all the high and exceptional things about which his father's imagination had so long ineffectually hovered – from the start he *was* what Mr Grew had dreamed of being. And so precise, so detailed, was Mr Grew's vision of his own imaginary career, that as Ronald grew up, and began to travel in a widening orbit, his father had an almost uncanny sense of the extent to which that career was enacting itself before him. At Harvard, Ronald had done exactly what the hypothetical Mason Grew would have done, had not his actual self, at the same age, been working his way up in old Slagden's button factory – the institution which was later to acquire fame, and even notoriety, as the birthplace of Grew's Secure Suspender

Buckle. Afterward, at a period when the actual Grew had passed from the factory to the bookkeeper's desk, his invisible double had been reading law at Columbia – precisely again what Ronald did! But it was when the young man left the paths laid out for him by the parental hand, and cast himself boldly on the world, that his adventures began to bear the most astonishing resemblance to those of the unrealized Mason Grew. It was in New York that the scene of this hypothetical being's first exploits had always been laid; and it was in New York that Ronald was to achieve his first triumph. There was nothing small or timid about Mr Grew's imagination; it had never stopped at anything between Wingfield and the metropolis. And the real Ronald had the same cosmic vision as his parent. He brushed aside with a contemptuous laugh his mother's entreaty that he should stay at Wingfield and continue the dynasty of the Grew Suspender Buckle. Mr Grew knew that in reality Ronald winced at the Buckle, loathed it, blushed for his connection with it. Yet it was the Buckle that had seen him through Groton, Harvard and the Law School, and had permitted him to enter the office of a distinguished corporation lawyer, instead of being enslaved to some sordid business with quick returns. The Buckle had been Ronald's fairy godmother – yet his father did not blame him for abhorring and disowning it. Mr Grew himself often bitterly regretted having attached his own name to the instrument of his material success, though, at the time, his doing so had been the natural expression of his romanticism. When he invented the Buckle, and took out his patent, he and his wife both felt that to bestow their name on it was like naming a battle-ship or a peak of the Andes.

Mrs Grew had never learned to know better; but Mr Grew had discovered his error before Ronald was out of school. He read it first in a black eye of his boy's. Ronald's symmetry had been marred by the insolent fist of a fourth former whom he had chastised for alluding to his father as 'Old Buckles'; and when Mr Grew heard the epithet he understood in a flash that the Buckle was a thing to blush for. It was too late then to dissociate his name from it, or to efface from the hoardings of the entire continent the picture of two gentlemen, one contorting himself in the abject effort to repair a broken brace, while the careless ease of the other's attitude proclaimed his trust in the Secure Suspender Buckle. These records were indelible, but Ronald could at least be spared all direct connection with them; and that day Mr Grew decided that the boy should not return to Wingfield.

'You'll see,' he had said to Mrs Grew, 'he'll take right hold in New York. Ronald's got my knack for taking hold,' he added, throwing out his chest.

'But the way you took hold was in business,' objected Mrs Grew, who was large and literal.

Mr Grew's chest collapsed, and he became suddenly conscious of his comic face in its rim of sandy whisker. 'That's not the only way,' he said, with a touch of wistfulness which escaped his wife's analysis.

'Well, of course you could have written beautifully,' she rejoined with admiring eyes.

'*Written*? Me!' Mr Grew became sardonic.

'Why, those letters – weren't *they* beautiful, I'd like to know?'

The couple exchanged a glance, innocently allusive and amused on the wife's part, and charged with a sudden tragic significance on the husband's.

'Well, I've got to be going along to the office now,' he merely said, dragging himself out of his chair.

* * *

This had happened while Ronald was still at school; and now Mrs Grew slept in the Wingfield cemetery, under a life-size theological virtue of her own choosing, and Mr Grew's prognostications as to Ronald's ability to 'take right hold' in New York were being more and more brilliantly fulfilled.

II

Ronald obeyed his father's injunction not to come to luncheon on the day of the Bankshires' dinner; but in the middle of the following week Mr Grew was surprised by a telegram from his son.

'Want to see you important matter. Expect me tomorrow afternoon.'

Mr Grew received the telegram after breakfast. To peruse it he had lifted his eye from a paragraph of the morning paper describing a fancy-dress dinner which the Hamilton Gliddens' had given the night before for the house-warming of their new Fifth Avenue palace.

'Among the couples who afterward danced in the Poets' Quadrille were Miss Daisy Bankshire, looking more than usually lovely as Laura, and Mr Ronald Grew as the young Petrarch.'

Petrarch and Laura! Well – if *anything* meant anything, Mr Grew supposed he knew what that meant. For weeks past he had noticed how constantly the names of the young people were coupled in the society notes he so insatiably devoured. Even the soulless reporter was getting into the habit of uniting them in his lists. And this Laura and Petrarch business was almost an announcement...

Mr Grew dropped the telegram, wiped his eye-glasses and re-read the paragraph. 'Miss Daisy Bankshire ... more than usually lovely . . .' Yes; she *was* lovely. He had often seen her photograph in the papers – seen her represented in every attitude of the mundane game: fondling her prize bulldog, taking a fence on her thoroughbred, dancing a *gavotte*, all patches and plumes, or fingering a guitar, all tulle and lilies; and once he had caught a glimpse of her at the theater. Hearing that Ronald was going to a fashionable first-night with the Bankshires, Mr Grew had for once overcome his repugnance to following his son's movements, and had secured for himself, under the shadow of the balcony, a stall whence he could observe the Bankshire box without fear of detection. Ronald had never known of his father's presence; and for three blessed hours Mr Grew had watched his boy's handsome dark head bent above the fair hair and averted shoulder that were all he could catch of Miss Bankshire's beauties.

He recalled the vision now; and with it came, as usual, its ghostly double: the vision of his young self bending above such a shoulder and such shining hair. Needless to say that the real Mason Grew had never found himself in so enviable a situation. The late Mrs Grew had no more resembled Miss Daisy Bankshire than he had looked like the happy victorious Ronald. And the mystery was that from their dull faces, their dull endearments, the miracle of Ronald should have sprung. It was almost – fantastically – as if the boy had been a changeling, child of a Latmian night, whom the divine companion of Mr Grew's early reveries had secretly laid in the cradle of the Wingfield bedroom while Mr and Mrs Grew slept the sleep of conjugal indifference.

The young Mason Grew had not at first accepted this astral episode as the complete canceling of his claims on romance. He too had grasped at the high-hung glory; and, with his tendency to reach too far when he reached at all, had singled out the prettiest girl in Wingfield. When he recalled his stammered confession of love his face still tingled under her cool bright stare. His audacity had struck her dumb; and when she recovered her voice it was to fling a taunt at him.

'Don't be too discouraged, you know – have you ever thought of trying Addie Wicks?'

All Wingfield would have understood the gibe: Addie Wicks was the dullest girl in town. And a year later he had married Addie Wicks . . .

He looked up from the perusal of Ronald's telegram with this memory in his mind. Now at last his dream was coming true! His boy would taste of the joys that had mocked his thwarted youth and his dull middle-age. And it was fitting that they should be realized in Ronald's destiny. Ronald was made to take happiness boldly by the hand and lead it home like a bride. He had the carriage, the confidence, the high faith in his fortune, that compel the willful stars. And, thanks to the Buckle, he would also have the background of material elegance that became his conquering person. Since Mr Grew had retired from business his investments had prospered, and he had been saving up his income for just such a purpose. His own wants were few: he had brought the Wingfield furniture to Brooklyn, and his sitting-room was a replica of that in which the long years of his married life had been spent. Even the florid carpet on which Ronald's first footsteps had been taken was carefully matched when it became too threadbare. And on the marble center-table, with its beaded cover and bunch of dyed pampas grass, lay the illustrated Longfellow and the copy of Ingersoll's lectures which represented literature to Mr Grew when he had led home his bride. In the light of Ronald's romance, Mr Grew found himself re-living, with mingled pain and tenderness, all the

298

poor prosaic incidents of his own personal history. Curiously enough, with this new splendor on them they began to emit a faint ray of their own. His wife's armchair, in its usual place by the fire, recalled her placid unperceiving presence, seated opposite to him during the long drowsy years; and he felt her kindness, her equanimity, where formerly he had only ached at her obtuseness. And from the chair he glanced up at the discolored photograph on the wall above, with a withered laurel wreath suspended on a corner of the frame. The photograph represented a young man with a poetic necktie and untrammeled hair, leaning against a Gothic chair-back, a roll of music in his hand; and beneath was scrawled a bar of Chopin, with the words: *'Adieu, Adèle.'*

The portrait was that of the great pianist, Fortuné Dolbrowski; and its presence on the wall of Mr Grew's sitting-room commemorated the only exquisite hour of his life save that of Ronald's birth. It was some time before the latter event, a few months only after Mr Grew's marriage, that he had taken his wife to New York to hear the great Dolbrowski. Their evening had been magically beautiful, and even Addie, roused from her usual inexpressiveness, had waked into a momentary semblance of life. 'I never – I never –' she gasped out when they had regained their hotel bedroom, and sat staring back entranced at the evening's vision. Her large face was pink and tremulous, and she sat with her hands on her knees, forgetting to roll up her bonnet strings and prepare her curl-papers.

'I'd like to *write* him just how I felt – I wisht I knew how!' she burst out in a final effervescence of emotion.

Her husband lifted his head and looked at her.

'Would you? I feel that way too,' he said with a sheepish laugh. And they continued to stare at each other through a transfiguring mist of sound.

The scene rose before Mr Grew as he gazed up at the pianist's photograph. 'Well, I owe her that anyhow – poor Addie!' he said, with a smile at the inconsequences of fate. With Ronald's telegram in his hand he was in a mood to count his mercies.

III

'A clear twenty-five thousand a year: that's what you can tell 'em with my compliments,' said Mr Grew, glancing complacently across the center-table at his boy.

It struck him that Ronald's gift for looking his part in life had never so completely expressed itself. Other young men, at such a moment, would have been red, damp, tight about the collar; but Ronald's cheek was a shade paler, and the contrast made his dark eyes more expressive.

'A clear twenty-five thousand; yes, sir – that's what I always meant you to have.'

Mr Grew leaned carelessly back, his hands thrust in his pockets, as though to divert attention from the agitation of his features. He had often pictured himself rolling out that phrase to Ronald, and now that it was on his lips he could not control their tremor.

Ronald listened in silence, lifting a hand to his slight mustache, as though he, too, wished to hide some involuntary betrayal of emotion. At first Mr Grew took his silence for an expression of gratified surprise; but as it prolonged itself it became less easy to interpret.

'I – see here, my boy; did you expect more? Isn't it enough?' Mr Grew cleared his throat. 'Do *they* expect more?' he asked nervously. He was hardly able to face the pain of inflicting a disappointment on Ronald at the very moment when he had counted on putting the final touch to his bliss.

Ronald moved uneasily in his chair and his eyes wandered upward to the laurel-wreathed photograph of the pianist.

'*Is* it the money, Ronald? Speak out, my boy. We'll see, we'll look round – I'll manage somehow.'

'No, no,' the young man interrupted, abruptly raising his hand as though to check his father.

Mr Grew recovered his cheerfulness. 'Well, what's the trouble then, if *she's* willing?'

Ronald shifted his position again and finally rose from his seat and wandered across the room.

'Father,' he said, coming back, 'there's something I've got to tell you. I can't take your money.'

Mr Grew sat speechless a moment, staring blankly at his son; then he emitted a laugh. 'My money? What are you talking about? What's this about my money? Why, it ain't *mine*, Ronny; it's all yours – every cent of it!'

The young man met his tender look with a gesture of tragic refusal.

'No, no, it's not mine – not even in the sense you mean. Not in any sense. Can't you understand my feeling so?'

'Feeling so? I don't know how you're feeling. I don't know what you're talking about. Are you too proud to touch any money you haven't earned? Is that what you're trying to tell me?'

'No. It's not that. You must know –'

Mr Grew flushed to the rim of his bristling whiskers. 'Know? Know *what*? Can't you speak out?'

Ronald hesitated, and the two faced each other for a long strained moment, during which Mr Grew's congested countenance grew gradually pale again.

'What's the meaning of this? Is it because you've done

301

something . . . something you're ashamed of . . . ashamed to tell me?' he gasped; and walking around the table he laid his hand gently on his son's shoulder. 'There's nothing you can't tell me, my boy.'

'It's not that. Why do you make it so hard for me?' Ronald broke out with passion. 'You must have known this was sure to happen sooner or later.'

'Happen? What was sure to hap—?' Mr Grew's question wavered on his lip and passed into a tremulous laugh. 'Is it something *I've* done that you don't approve of? Is it – is it *the Buckle* you're ashamed of, Ronald Grew?'

Ronald laughed too, impatiently. 'The Buckle? No, I'm not ashamed of the Buckle; not any more than you are,' he returned with a flush. 'But I'm ashamed of all I owe to it – all I owe to you – when – when –' He broke off and took a few distracted steps across the room. 'You might make this easier for me,' he protested, turning back to his father.

'Make what easier? I know less and less what you're driving at,' Mr Grew groaned.

Ronald's walk had once more brought him beneath the photograph on the wall. He lifted his head for a moment and looked at it; then he looked again at Mr Grew.

'Do you suppose I haven't always known?'

'Known –?'

'Even before you gave me those letters at the time of my mother's death – even before that, I suspected. I don't know how it began . . . perhaps from little things you let drop . . . you and she . . . and resemblances that I couldn't help seeing . . . in myself . . . How on earth could you suppose I *shouldn't guess*? I always thought you gave me the letters as a way of telling me –'

Mr Grew rose slowly from his chair. 'The letters? Do you mean Dolbrowski's letters?'

Ronald nodded with white lips. 'You must remember giving them to me the day after the funeral.'

Mr Grew nodded back. 'Of course. I wanted you to have everything your mother valued.'

'Well – how could I help knowing after that?'

'Knowing *what*?' Mr Grew stood staring helplessly at his son. Suddenly his look caught at a clue that seemed to confront it with a deeper difficulty. 'You thought – you thought those letters ... Dolbrowski's letters ... you thought they meant ...'

'Oh, it wasn't only the letters. There were so many other signs. My love of music – my – all my feelings about life ... and art ... And when you gave me the letters I thought you must mean me to know.'

Mr Grew had grown quiet. His lips were firm, and his small eyes looked out steadily from their creased lids.

'To know that you were Fortuné Dolbrowski's son?'

Ronald made a mute sign of assent.

'I see. And what did you intend to do?'

'I meant to wait till I could earn my living, and then repay you ... as far as I can ever repay you ... for what you'd spent on me ... But now that there's a chance of my marrying ... and that your generosity overwhelms me ... I'm obliged to speak.'

'I see,' said Mr Grew again. He let himself down into his chair, looking steadily and not unkindly at the young man. 'Sit down too, Ronald. Let's talk.'

Ronald made a protesting movement. 'Is anything to be gained by it? You can't change me – change what I feel. The reading of those letters transformed my whole life – I was a boy till then: they made a man of me. From that moment I understood myself.' He paused, and then looked up at Mr Grew's face. 'Don't imagine that I don't appreciate your

303

kindness – your extraordinary generosity. But I can't go through life in disguise. And I want you to know that I have not won Daisy under false pretenses –'

Mr Grew started up with the first expletive Ronald had ever heard on his lips.

'You damned young fool, you, you haven't *told* her –?'

Ronald raised his head with pride. 'Oh, you don't know her, sir! She thinks no worse of me for knowing my secret. She is above and beyond all such conventional prejudices. She's *proud* of my parentage –' he straightened his slim young shoulders – 'as I'm proud of it . . . yes, sir, proud of it . . .'

Mr Grew sank back into his seat with a dry laugh. 'Well, you ought to be. You come of good stock. And you're your father's son, every inch of you!' He laughed again, as though the humor of the situation grew on him with its closer contemplation.

'Yes, I've always felt that,' Ronald murmured, gravely.

'Your father's son, and no mistake.' Mr Grew leaned forward. 'You're the son of as big a fool as yourself. And here he sits, Ronald Grew!'

The young man's color deepened to crimson; but his reply was checked by Mr Grew's decisive gesture. 'Here he sits, with all your young nonsense still alive in him. Don't you begin to see the likeness? If you don't I'll tell you the story of those letters.'

Ronald stared. 'What do you mean? Don't they tell their own story?'

'I supposed they did when I gave them to you; but you've given it a twist that needs straightening out.' Mr Grew squared his elbows on the table, and looked at the young man across the gift-books and dyed pampas grass. 'I wrote all the letters that Dolbrowski answered.'

Ronald gave back his look in frowning perplexity. '*You*

304

wrote them? I don't understand. His letters are all addressed to my mother.'

'Yes. And he thought he was corresponding with her.'

'But my mother – what did she think?'

Mr Grew hesitated, puckering his thick lids. 'Well, I guess she kinder thought it was a joke. Your mother didn't think about things much.'

Ronald continued to bend a puzzled frown on the question. 'I don't understand,' he reiterated.

Mr Grew cleared his throat with a nervous laugh. 'Well, I don't know as you ever will – *quite*. But this is the way it came about. I had a toughish time of it when I was young. Oh, I don't mean so much the fight I had to put up to make my way – there was always plenty of fight in me. But inside of myself it was kinder lonesome. And the outside didn't attract callers.' He laughed again, with an apologetic gesture toward his broad blinking face. 'When I went round with the other young fellows I was always the forlorn hope – the one that had to eat the drumsticks and dance with the left-overs. As sure as there was a blighter at a picnic I had to swing her, and feed her, and drive her home. And all the time I was mad after all the things you've got – poetry and music and all the joy-forever business. So there were the pair of us – my face and my imagination – chained together, and fighting, and hating each other like poison.

'Then your mother came along and took pity on me. It sets up a gawky fellow to find a girl who ain't ashamed to be seen walking with him Sundays. And I was grateful to your mother, and we got along first-rate. Only I couldn't say things to her – and she couldn't answer. Well – one day, a few months after we were married, Dolbrowski came to New York, and the whole place went wild about him. I'd never heard any good music, but I'd always had an inkling of what

305

it must be like, though I couldn't tell you to this day how I knew. Well, your mother read about him in the papers too, and she thought it'd be the swagger thing to go to New York and hear him play – so we went . . . I'll never forget that evening. Your mother wasn't easily stirred up – she never seemed to need to let off steam. But that night she seemed to understand the way I felt. And when we got back to the hotel she said to me: "I'd like to tell him how I feel. I'd like to sit right down and write to him."

' "Would you?" I said. "So would I."

'There was paper and pens there before us, and I pulled a sheet toward me, and began to write. "Is this what you'd like to say to him?" I asked her when the letter was done. And she got pink and said: "I don't understand it, but it's lovely." And she copied it out and signed her name to it, and sent it.'

Mr Grew paused, and Ronald sat silent, with lowered eyes.

'That's how it began; and that's where I thought it would end. But it didn't, because Dolbrowski answered. His first letter was dated January 10, 1872. I guess you'll find I'm correct. Well, I went back to hear him again, and I wrote him after the performance, and he answered again. And after that we kept it up for six months. Your mother always copied the letters and signed them. She seemed to think it was a kinder joke, and she was proud of his answering my letters. But she never went back to New York to hear him, though I saved up enough to give her the treat again. She was too lazy, and she let me go without her. I heard him three times in New York; and in the spring he came to Wingfield and played once at the Academy. Your mother was sick and couldn't go; so I went alone. After the performance I meant to get one of the directors to take me in to see him; but when the time came, I just went back home and wrote to him instead. And the month after, before he went back to Europe, he sent your mother a last little note, and that picture hanging up there...'

Mr Grew paused again, and both men lifted their eyes to the photograph.

'Is that all?' Ronald slowly asked.

'That's all – every bit of it,' said Mr Grew.

'And my mother – my mother never even spoke to Dolbrowski?'

'Never. She never even saw him but that once in New York at his concert.'

The blood crept again to Ronald's face. 'Are you sure of that, sir?' he asked in a trembling voice.

'Sure as I am that I'm sitting here. Why, she was too lazy to look at his letters after the first novelty wore off. She copied the answers just to humor me – but she always said she couldn't understand what we wrote.'

'But how could you go on with such a correspondence? It's incredible!'

Mr Grew looked at his son thoughtfully. 'I suppose it is, to you. You've only had to put out your hand and get the things I was starving for – music, and good talk, and ideas. Those letters gave me all that. You've read them, and you know that Dolbrowski was not only a great musician but a great man. There was nothing beautiful he didn't see, nothing fine he didn't feel. For six months I breathed his air, and I've lived on it ever since. Do you begin to understand a little now?'

'Yes – a little. But why write in my mother's name? Why make it appear like a sentimental correspondence?'

Mr Grew reddened to his bald temples. 'Why, I tell you it began that way, as a kinder joke. And when I saw that the first letter pleased and interested him, I was afraid to tell him – *I couldn't* tell him. Do you suppose he'd gone on writing if he'd ever seen me, Ronny?'

Ronald suddenly looked at him with new eyes. 'But he must have thought your letters very beautiful – to go on as he did,' he broke out.

'Well – I did my best,' said Mr Grew modestly.

Ronald pursued his idea. 'Where *are* all your letters, I wonder? Weren't they returned to you at his death?'

Mr Grew laughed. 'Lord, no. I guess he had trunks and trunks full of better ones. I guess Queens and Empresses wrote to him.'

'I should have liked to see your letters,' the young man insisted.

'Well, they weren't bad,' said Mr Grew drily. 'But I'll tell you one thing, Ronny,' he added. Ronald raised his head with a quick glance, and Mr Grew continued: 'I'll tell you where the best of those letters is – it's in *you*. If it hadn't been for that one look at life I couldn't have made you what you are. Oh, I know you've done a good deal of your own making – but I've been there behind you all the time. And you'll never know the work I've spared you and the time I've saved you. Fortuné Dolbrowski helped me do that. I never saw things in little again after I'd looked at 'em with him. And I tried to give you the big view from the start ... So that's what became of my letters.'

Mr Grew paused, and for a long time Ronald sat motionless, his elbows on the table, his face dropped on his hands.

Suddenly Mr Grew's touch fell on his shoulder.

'Look at here, Ronald Grew – do you want me to tell you how you're feeling at this minute? Just a mite let down, after all, at the idea that you ain't the romantic figure you'd got to think yourself ... Well, that's natural enough, too; but I'll tell you what it proves. It proves you're my son right enough, if any more proof was needed. For it's just the kind of fool nonsense I used to feel at your age – and if there's anybody here to laugh at it's myself, and not you. And you can laugh at me just as much as you like . . .'

JIM SHEPARD

THE MORTALITY
OF PARENTS

IT'S 1970. HE'S THE glue that holds us together, the UN van pelted with rocks and bottles, the pro wrestling ref floored by the occasional dropkick but always gamely back on his feet and working to keep the eye-gouging to a minimum. Morning in and morning out, my father's up and has the coffee made and is reasonably ready for whatever we're about to, in our misery and impatience and bell-jar self-absorption, dish out.

Ours is not one of those families in which the tensions are played out in intricately subterranean gestures. My brother has thrown me across the living room so that my back impacted the wall above the sofa. To more fully demonstrate his dissatisfaction with the general drift of our family life, in our presence he's upended the dining room table, fully set, a massive Shaker cherry rectangle with big, cross-beamed legs. My mother has slung a just-filled humidifier across the length of the kitchen. The water reservoir's rubber-sealed cap ricocheted off the ceiling. I've been known to run full bore at the walls, all shoulders and elbows, the hero in a movie breaking down doors where no doors are evident. Our plaster is patched with football-sized ovals. The trim is scissored with scuff marks. Homicidal or suicidal exasperation is the norm.

As *Life* magazine reminds us every so often, it's a time of great uncertainty.

In each case, our attempts at self-expression are diverted

313

by Shep into channels at least eventually more acceptable to the neighbors. He reasons, he pleads, he cajoles, he throws people around. The fact that we're still standing is incontrovertible evidence that he gets results.

I've put the leg of a serving table through the speaker on our console television from across the room during a football game. My mother has snapped an *oar* – a kid's oar from a plastic boat, but an oar nonetheless – around a cross-beam support in the basement when I ducked and wove while she was trying to apply a two-handed lesson. My brother has cleared our driveway from his second-story window with his turntable when the thing still made vocalists sound vaguely quaaluded after a third straight trip to the repair shop.

So there it is, the big broad granite slab perpendicular to our slippery little slope, dug in at the bottom of an increasingly steep drop: *What's going to happen when Shep dies?* We're going to go head-on smash into it sometime soon – he's fifty-nine and not the healthiest guy in the world in 1970 – and none of us, including him, are anywhere in the neighborhood of being prepared. So what *is* going to happen? At all of fourteen years old I manage to think about it incessantly without enlightening myself on the matter. I don't know. I don't know because I don't want to know. In our family, we're either screaming or breaking things or cleaning up. Who has time for hypotheticals?

Everyone calls him Shep. He's been Shep since the Dawn of Time. I apparently started calling him Shep when I was three, amusing visiting relatives and friends. My mother only became Ida when I was thirteen or so. He has his faults – for the sake of everyone concerned, in social situations, we don't get my mother started on his faults – but in 1970, for the fourteen years I've been alive and the ten I've been sentient, he's been for me the epitome of good – good being defined as patient and/or generous in his dispensation of care. Nowhere in my world do I know anyone as doggedly resourceful in his desire to do what he can for others.

Though my mother, when she overhears relatives marveling at how often her husband thinks of others, works to make clear that by 'others,' we all mean his two sons, me being one. By 1970 she's long been of the opinion that she gets a raw deal when it comes to conflicts with her sons, and as far as her sons are concerned, she's right; Shep's mode with her is an only slightly amended version of a position he's taken from the very beginning: *They're* just kids, but *you* should know better.

Our lives are divided into ongoing topics of contention. What do we fight about? Everything. My father has gone on record as believing we could fuck up a wet dream. Some subjects seem to roll out the ordnance more reliably than others, though. In ascending order of seriousness:

Number one: music. My mother inclines toward Jimmy Roselli and Lou Monte: singers so Italian they embarrass even other Italian singers. My father favors Nelson Eddy and Earl Wrightson: booming-voiced guys who sound as though they only sing in Mountie uniforms. Passing the stereo, they turn each other's music down, or off. My brother and I crack each other up regularly by making fun of both *oeuvres*. He favors vandalizing my mother's scungilli favorites – *Please, Mr Columbus, turn-a da ship aroun'*. I get a bang out of replicating on car rides that basso-pretentious sound my father so enjoys: *Give me ten men that are stout-hearted men . . .*

Music generates the most benign of our free-for-alls. My father gives as good as he gets when it comes to heaping abuse on what he hears. He's caustic on the subject of Janis Joplin. He periodically suggests a saliva test for Joe Cocker. He refers to Jimi Hendrix only as 'that banshee.' But when he can make out the lyrics, and they're witty – as in the case of the Kinks or Randy Newman – every so often, from down below in the living room, our stuff can get a laugh.

Number two: drinking. Shep puts it away like he has a hollow leg, and the volume annoys my mother mostly because of the insulation it seems to provide. Maybe because he brushed by alcoholism so closely himself, and certainly because he's had so many good friends who've taken that easy slide into the pool (the best man at his wedding died of cirrhosis of the liver), his comedy is particularly blunt on the subject. Which, for Shep, is saying something. 'She was a jug artist,' he'll say. 'He was always facedown in the sauce somewhere.'

For spiff events, my mother drinks whiskey sours. When she thinks she's getting a cold, she may take the occasional shot of four-dollar brandy or rye. Her favorite drink is Thunderbird: wine of choice for winos, screw-topped and so cheap that it seems a bargain even to her. It smells so awful that I begin making fun of it when my age is still in the single digits. It tastes like something from a crankcase. 'It's good enough for me,' my mother always says in response.

Which brings us to number three: money. Money dictates our children-of-the-Depression parents' mantra, the bottom-line creed by which they live: *It's good enough for me.* Restaurants with linen napkins are too fancy, a big car or a new car is more than we need, vacations somewhere other than a dank knotty-pine cabin on Lake Champlain would be very nice if money meant absolutely nothing to us and was pouring in at an unprecedented rate. In Beloit, Wisconsin, years later, traveling on my own, I come across a marketing strategy apparently designed for my parents: a billboard that reads *Miller: Because Budweiser Is Just Too Darned Expensive.*

All expenses and all bills for whatever amount irk Ida. All charges of whatever size seem fair to Shep. Ida's expression will darken after having opened an electric bill of seventeen cents, while Shep's face will remain unperturbed watching a cashier ring up a wiffle bat for $21.95. Without waiting for birthdays or holidays, Shep spreads his money around like Diamond Jim Brady. He could spend twenty dollars on a trip to the dump. He buys the boys smallish things – four-dollar models, five-dollar albums – that the boys have agitated for, while Ida does her best to save, hating her role as the bad cop who always gets to suggest that the boys can wait. We're encouraged to hide gifts when arriving back home, but Ida checks all incoming packages like a customs agent. Fights follow. We sit up in our rooms enjoying our new whatevers while in the arena below the insults escalate in volume. Sometimes we go downstairs for a drink in the middle of it all. Nobody asks, but privately, we take Shep's side, while intuiting guiltily that Ida's probably right.

Then there are the topics that cause much more serious fights.

The Length of the Boys' Hair.

The Dean Martin Celebrity Roasts.

My brother's refusal to go to school.

Relatives.

My brother in general.

Me.

By 1970 my brother and I have put in a staggering thirty-one combined years with Shep and Ida in our household, and time with Shep and Ida in our household is the analog to spending time with Henny Youngman and Anna Magnani in Beirut. My brother and I don't have a lot of advanced training in this area, but even we can sense that as far as our parents' emotional lives go, there are compatibility and empathy issues that are not being properly addressed. Certain goals that are not being well met.

All of this would have sailed along with its own kind of stability – the way events sailed along from Shiloh to Antietam to Fredericksburg in 1862 – but in August of 1970 my father had the first of his three heart attacks.

As far as my mother was concerned, his heart had always been the problem. His heart was too big, his heart was too good, his heart was the problem. His heart was evidently listening.

By the time I'm fourteen and my brother's seventeen, in 1970, we've provided my father with a string of unprecedented opportunities to confirm his status with relatives and friends as the biggest worrier they've ever known. At my brother's suggestion, I've taken a wagon down the steepest paved hill in a five-hundred-mile radius and landed on my face. We've both been caught jumping off the roof of our neighbors' house in an attempt to conceal that we'd been poking around the ground floor uninvited. Our summer fad of pelting passing cars with jawbreaker-sized rocks has backfired badly.

My father's response to our mulish and heroic refusal to acquire common sense is a darkly comic and highly obscene mixture of epithets and despairing interrogation that's often metrically pleasing – *What goes through your fucking head? Your brains stuck up your ass?* – and we can see, in the aftermath of one of our catastrophic exercises of free will, the physical toll it takes on him: for days afterward, he's exhausted, tentative in his steps, fractionally hesitant when lowering himself into a recliner. He's too old for this. He ages, while we watch.

Of course, in some ways he brings it on himself. We act up, he acts out. *He loves us, he loves us*, we think when the shouting subsides. We go to bed pleased, and entertained, besides.

Shep, don't get excited, Ida says, while he throws Tom Collins glasses against the side of the garage. At times like that – when the boys have shown yet again that they have the collective reasoning power of a squirrel – Ida placates, and assumes a long-view perspective, as if to suggest that we'll all chuckle over such shenanigans a few years down the road.

But Shep is a long way from Big Picture serenity. On the day of his first heart attack, he's in a chaise lounge in the backyard, recovering from the revelation that my brother and I have been running around the summer streets at three and four in the morning, potting streetlights with our BB gun, naked. The police have delivered this revelation in the middle of the night after having picked us up. We're without explanation as far as the naked part goes. Our MO is to leave our clothes on one corner or another and retrieve them on the way home.

The heart attack arrives long after the verbal abuse has subsided and all is relatively calm. My brother and I have gone to the beach. My mother is in the kitchen browning meat for a sauce.

All morning long, as far as Shep's concerned, he doesn't feel exactly right. Ida lends a sympathetic ear but her capacity for alarm is muffled by her sense of his slight hypochondria. A burning, parenthesis-shaped pain spreads beneath his sternum. Anxiety builds up, conjuring all sorts of scenarios. He resists jumping to conclusions.

When he leans forward, the pain lances upward to the base of his throat. This is cause for concern. He has trouble breathing. He calls Ida. The grease from the beef is making a racket in the bottom of the pan and he has to call her again.

He works at Avco Lycoming Industries, marketing helicopter engines, and so just as a basic business strategy always affects a formality with strangers whom he considers to be better educated. He tells the Emergency Room intern that he's 'experiencing chest difficulties.'

Blood is taken, an EKG is hooked up, and medication is fed into him intravenously before we get word down at the beach. Ida thinks to call a neighbor, who trots the five blocks to tell us, and then is nice enough to drive us to the hospital to boot. It's the same guy who found us on his roof.

When we come into the room, Ida's sitting there holding his hand, and he's chatting with the intern. He's saying, 'Once you know it *is* your heart, there's a certain anxiety that takes over, and that affects the whole goddamn thing too, you know –' and then we interrupt. We take turns bending over and putting our hands behind his shoulders, the quasi hug for the bedridden.

He lies there for a while while we ask various questions and joke. Ida's eyes mist up every so often. My brother asks how he's feeling and he answers, 'Not so good. I had a heart attack.'

After his diagnosis, he's given stuff to stabilize his arrhythmia. In 1970 heart medicine is turning a corner from the Tertiary to the Quaternary, and tests are not as sophisticated as they are today. Certain predilections, certain hidden weaknesses, are missed. After a few days of observation, the little plastic bracelet is snipped off his wrist and he's sent home with medication. After a prudent interval, stress tests are administered. The problem of arterial blockage is addressed.

But Shep's heart, that big shaky flatbed trundling us down the hill, is not all right. It goes on about its business quietly, while we go on about ours. But its business involves preparing to blow up on Shep two more times.

As a family we resolve, with a minimum of discussion, to take it easy. No more battling of the sort that would only add to his strain. Israel and the Palestinians agree to be good. The Protestants and the Catholics decide to just Try Peace in Northern Ireland.

Because we love him so much and because we cannot do without him, our resolution holds up for a month and a half. Opportunities for strife come and go daily, unpursued. In the den one evening after four hours of uneventful television watching, Shep expresses his gratitude. It's not the kind of thing that comes easily to him, and his family is genuinely touched.

In early October the party comes to an end. My brother is sent home from the shitty public high school he attends for having let his hair get too long – shoulder-length, in the back – and I come home from the same educational sink-hole two hours later in an equally black mood. My brother accuses me, even before I set a foot into my room, of having played his Elvin Bishop album. His tone is not interrogatory. I offer to let him kiss my ass. He throws me down the stairs.

This time Shep is in the hospital for four days longer than we expect. His face, when we visit, is gray. He talks hoarsely, when he talks at all. The intravenous seems to be pulling stuff out of him rather than putting stuff in. The three of us – Ida, my brother, and myself – are frozen with fear.

Between visits, our personal grooming habits decay. Our meals are cold cereal or tuna forked from the can at the kitchen table, our expressions ashen.

We were all raised Catholic. My mother prays. When my brother and I watch movies late into the night, she's audible in her bedroom next to the den, her smoker's voice quavering through the rosary. When I finally go to bed – school is temporarily out, as far as we're concerned, for the duration of the crisis – I open negotiations with God. Even at fourteen I feel the need to explain my previous lack of interest, and I do so by proposing that it be viewed not so much as hypocrisy as a desire not to bother Him over every petty little thing.

When I'm at my most honest, my formulations all express the same terror: *I can't live without him. I can't live without him. I can't live without him.*

Has God listened? Is He affected? In that early morning delirium before sleep, I'm oddly confident. Shep always did. Shep always was.

A specialist is consulted. It turns out that he doesn't like the look of things. We start bringing as gifts hefty biographies instead of magazines. Back home, nobody sleeps much. There's a lot of rendezvousing in the kitchen in the predawn hours. In the tossing and turning that goes on before that, I try to kick-start my sense of my own good fortune and gratitude. I make an effort to wax nostalgic about things my father taught me, without as much success as I would like. The problem is that I remember few Andy-and-Judge-Hardy-type sessions involving either me sitting still for patient instruction or him sitting still to give it. I am able to list for myself, though, some things I picked up, more or less incompletely, by keeping an eye on him:

How to build, and paint, monster models. How to go easy on the glue. How to enhance the effect of the blood by limiting its splatter. Before Shep, my monsters were like last-stage Ebola victims.

The isolating pleasures, in general, of all sorts of absorbed, small-detail work. Shep has the most appealing tuneless hum in the neighborhood. It sounds like the Bridgeport version of something Tibetan. The closest facsimile I've encountered is a shtick played entirely for comedy: W. C. Fields, as ever henpecked and harassed in a service capacity, keeps some barely restrained customer waiting while humming, just audibly, *Grubbing grubbing grubbing grubbing grubbing grubbing*

grubbing. We watched it together, Shep and I. He hummed as he watched, and to my delight, never made the connection.

We want to bring in other specialists, at this specialist's suggestion. Shep is unimpressed with the idea. How much more poking and prodding do they need? Is this a convention? *This is good enough for me.*

Just before Halloween, it looks like he's finally going to be released. Somewhere in all the information and for their own private reasons the doctors have noted Progress. But on the morning of the big day, having shuffled over to the tiled bathroom rolling his IV stand beside him, his family's arrival an hour away, Shep knows something is wrong. His head is a helium balloon. His chest has been invaded by a plank. Sweat soaks his hospital gown before he becomes aware that he's sweating.

The nurses. The doctors. He needs reinforcements. He needs to sit. As far as whatever hope he's entertaining, the bottom falls out and fear's what's waiting there behind it, all the way down.

He tries the toilet but the lid's slippery, and he tumbles and folds up like a camp stool. I try to imagine his next moments. I try to imagine his next moments, alone on the floor of that actionably narrow bathroom, and something in me upheaves and rebels and inverts itself; something in me that's fundamentally cowardly refuses the engagement. Thirty years have passed and I'm still a timorous figure navigating a makeshift and narrow life. Thirty years have passed without my having addressed my ambition to shape myself into an admirable figure, in his image. My mother has lost the use of her personality. My brother's weeping has stabilized as a form of raging at himself and us. My own inventory – a meticulous examination of the barn door now that the barn is empty – reminds me that I didn't even do my best to love, whatever my best was. When exactly did their *It's good enough for me* become our *I need more*? Why did we let it happen?

Twenty-two years after my father hit the flush tank and then the tile, I fell in love and got married. My wife, a good woman, believes I'm a good man. My children, seven and four, repair my emotions every chance they get. They're both boys. They sprawl. They tumble. They raise hell. They love me. I can see it.

We had our luck and our luck ran out. We got the news when we arrived at the front desk of the hospital. My mother's knees stopped working before either of us could catch her. My brother swept his arms into the air and brought them down and cleared everything from the nurse's station counter in front of us. I gripped the counter with two hands like it was time to steer this lobby somewhere else and thought what I still think now, that all along my father was right: we could fuck up Paradise. We did. We have.

JOHN UPDIKE

MY FATHER'S TEARS

I SAW MY FATHER cry only once. It was at the Alton train station, back when the trains still ran. I was on my way to Philadelphia – an hour's ride ending at the 30th Street terminal – to catch, at the Market Street station, the train that would return me to Boston and college. I was eager to go, for already my home and my parents had become somewhat unreal to me, and Harvard, with its courses and the hopes for my future they inspired and the girlfriend I had acquired in my sophomore year, had become more real every semester; it shocked me – threw me off track, as it were – to see that my father's eyes, as he shook my hand goodbye, glittered with tears.

I blamed it on our handshake: for eighteen years we had never had occasion for this social gesture, this manly contact, and we had groped our way into it only recently. He was taller than I, though I was not short, and I realized, his hand warm in mine while he tried to smile, that he had a different perspective than I. I was going somewhere, and he was seeing me go. I was growing in my own sense of myself, and to him I was getting smaller. He had loved me, it came to me as never before. It was something that had not needed to be said before, and now his tears were saying it. Before, in all the years and small adventures we had shared, there was the sensation, stemming from him, that life was a pickle, and he and I were, for a time, in the pickle together.

The old Alton station was his kind of place, savoring of

transit and the furtive small pleasures of city life. I had bought my first pack of cigarettes here, with no protest from the man running the news-stand, though I was a young-looking fifteen. He simply gave me my change and a folder of matches advertising Sunshine Beer, from Alton's own brewery. Alton was a middle-sized industrial city that had been depressed ever since the textile mills began to slide south. In the meantime, with its orderly street grid and its hearty cuisine, it still supplied its citizens with traditional comforts and an illusion of well-being. I lit up a block from the station, as I remember, and even though I didn't know how to inhale my nerves took a hit; the sidewalk seemed to lift toward me and the whole world felt lighter. From that day forward I began to catch up, socially, with the more glamorous of my peers, who already smoked.

Even my stay-at-home mother, no traveler but a reader, had a connection to the station: it was the only place in the city where you could buy her favorite magazines, *Harper's* and *The New Yorker*. Like the stately Carnegie-endowed library two blocks down Franklin Street, it was a place you felt safe inside. Both had been built for eternity, when railroads and books looked to be with us forever. The station was a foursquare granite temple with marble floors, a high ceiling whose gilded coffers glinted through a coating of coal smoke. The tall-backed waiting benches were as dignified as church pews. The radiators clanked and the caramel-colored walls murmured as if giving back some of the human noise they absorbed day and night. The news-stand and coffee shop were usually busy, and the waiting room was always warm, as my father and I had discovered on more than one winter night. We had been commuters to the same high school, he as a teacher and I as student, in second-hand cars that on more than one occasion failed to start, or got stuck in a snowstorm. We would make our way to the one place sure to be open, the railroad station.

We did not foresee, that moment on the platform as the signal bells a half-mile down the tracks warned of my train's approach, that within a decade passenger service to Philadelphia would stop, and that eventually the station, like railroad stations all across the East, would be padlocked and boarded up. The fine old building stood on its empty acre of asphalt parking space like an oversized mausoleum. All the life it had once contained was sealed into silence, and for the rest of the century it ignominiously waited, in this city where progress had halted, to be razed.

But my father did foresee, the glitter in his eyes told me, that time consumes us – that the boy I had been was dying if not already dead, and we would have less and less to do with each other. My life had come out of his, and now I was stealing away with it. The train appeared, its engine, with its high steel wheels and long connecting rods and immense cylindrical boiler, out of all proportion to the little soft bodies it dragged along. I boarded it. My parents looked smaller, foreshortened. We waved sheepishly through the smirched glass. I opened my book – *The Complete Poetical Works of John Milton* – before Alton's gritty outskirts had fallen away.

At the end of that long day of travel, getting off not at Boston's South Station but at Back Bay, one stop earlier and closer to Cambridge, I was met by my girlfriend. How swanky that felt, to read Milton all day, the relatively colorless and hard-to-memorize pentameters of *Paradise Regained*, and, in sight of the other undergraduates disembarking, to be met and embraced on the platform by a girl – no, a woman – wearing a gray cloth coat, canvas tennis sneakers, and a ponytail. It must have been the spring break, because if Deb was greeting me the vacation had been too short for her to go back and forth to St Louis, where her home was. Instead, she had been waiting a week for me to return. She tended to underdress in the long New England winter, while I wore the heavy winter coat, with buckled belt and fleecy lining, that my parents had bought me, to my embarrassment, to keep me from catching pneumonia way up in New England.

She told me, as we rode first the Green Line and then the Red back to Harvard Square, what had happened to her that week. There had been an unpredicted snow squall, whose sullied traces were still around us, and, at the restaurant where she waited on tables some evenings, she had been given, because she was the only college student, the assignment of adding up numbers in the basement while the other waitresses pocketed all the tips. She was angry to the point of tears about it. I told her what I could recall of my week in Pennsylvania, already faded in memory except for the detail lodged there like a glittering splinter – my father's tears. My own eyes itched and burned after a day of reading in a jiggling train; I had lifted them from my book only to marvel at the shining ocean as the train traveled the stretch of seaside track around New London.

In the years when we were newly married and still childless, Deb and I would spend a summer month with each set of parents. Her father was an eminent Unitarian minister, who preached in a gray neo-Gothic edifice built for eternity near the Washington University campus. Each June he moved his family from the roomy brick parsonage on Lindell Boulevard to an abandoned Vermont farmhouse he had bought in the Thirties for five hundred dollars. That June, Deb and I arrived before her father's parish duties permitted him and the rest of his family, a wife and two other daughters, to be there. The chilly solitude of the place, with basic cold-water plumbing but no electricity, high on a curving dirt road whose only visible other house, a half-mile away, was occupied by another Unitarian minister, reinforced my sense of having moved up, thanks to my bride, into a new, more elevated and spacious territory.

The lone bathroom was a long room, its plaster walls and wooden floor both bare, that was haunted by a small but intense rainbow, which moved around the walls as the sun in the course of the day glinted at a changing angle off the beveled edge of the mirror on the medicine cabinet. When we troubled to heat up enough water on the kerosene stove for a daylight bath, the prismatically generated rainbow kept the bather company; it quivered and bobbed when footsteps or a breath of wind made the house tremble. To me this Ariel-like phenomenon was the magical child of Unitarian austerity, symbolic of the lofty attitude that sought out a primitive farmhouse as a relief from well-furnished urban comfort. It had to do, I knew, drawing upon my freshly installed education, with idealism, with Emerson and Thoreau, with self-reliance and taking Nature on Nature's own, exalted terms. A large side room in the house, well beyond the wood-stove's narrow sphere of warmth, held a big loom frame that had come with the house, and an obsolete encyclopedia, and a set, with faded spines, of aged but rarely touched books entitled *The Master Works of World Philosophy*. When I broke precedent by taking one of the volumes down, its finely ridged cloth cover gave my fingers an unpleasant tingle. It was the volume containing selections from Emerson's essays. 'Every natural fact is a symbol of some spiritual fact,' I read, and 'Everything is made of one hidden stuff,' and 'Every hero becomes a bore at last,' and 'We boil at different degrees.'

Deb used this large room, and the vine-shaded stone porch outside, to paint her careful oils and pale watercolors. When the day was sunny, and heating the tub water in a kettle on the kerosene stove seemed too much trouble, we bathed in the mountain creek an easy walk from the house, in a pond whose dam her father had designed and built. I wanted to photograph her nude with my Brownie Hawkeye, but she primly declined. One day I sneaked a few snapshots anyway, from the old bridge, while she, with exclamations that drowned out the noise of the shutter, waded in and took the icy plunge.

It was in Vermont, before the others arrived, that, by our retrospective calculations, we conceived our first child, unintentionally but with no regrets. This microscopic event deep within my bride became allied in my mind with the little rainbow low on the bathroom wall, our pet imp of refraction.

Her father, when he arrived, was a father I wasn't used to. Mine, though he had sufficient survival skills, enacted the role of an underdog, a man whose every day, at school or elsewhere, proceeded through a series of scrapes and embarrassments. The car wouldn't start, the students wouldn't behave. He needed people, the aggravating rub of them, for stimulation. Reverend Whitworth liked Vermont because, compared with St Louis, it had no people in it. He didn't leave his hill for weeks at a time, letting the rest of us drive the two miles of dirt road to the nearest settlement, where the grocery store, the hardware store, and the post office all occupied one building, with one proprietor, who also managed the local sawmill. We would come back with local gossip and a day-old newspaper, and my father-in-law would listen to our excited tales of the greater world with a tilted head and a slant smile that let us guess he wasn't hearing a word. He had things to do: he built stone walls, and refined the engineering of his dam, and took a daily nap, during which the rest of us were to be silent.

He was a handsome man, with a head of tightly wiry hair whose graying did not diminish its density, but he was frail inside from rheumatic fever in his Maine boyhood. Rural peace, the silence of woods, the sway and flicker of kerosene light as drafts blew on the flaming wick or as lamps were carried from room to room – these constituted his element, not city bustle and rub. During his hilltop vacation months, he moved among us – his wife, his three daughters, his son-in-law, his wife's spinster sister – like a planet exempt from the law of gravitational attraction.

His interactions came mostly with games, which he methodically tended to win – family croquet in the afternoons, family Hearts in the evening, in the merged auras of the woodstove and the mantle lamp on the table. This was a special lamp, which intensified and whitened the glow of a flame with a mantle, a kind of conical net of ash so delicate it could be broken by even a carelessly rough setting-down of the glass base on the table. Reverend Whitworth was ostentatiously careful in everything his hands did, and I resented this, with the implacable *ressentiment* of youth. I resented his fussy pipe-smoker's gestures as he tamped and lighted and puffed; I resented his strictly observed naps, his sterling blue eyes (which Deb had inherited), his untroubled Unitarianism. Somehow, in my part of Pennsylvania blue eyes were so rare as to be freakish – hazel was as far as irises ventured from the basic brown the immigrants from Wales and southern Germany had brought to the Schuylkill Valley.

As for Unitarianism, it seemed so milky, so smugly vague and evasive: an unimpeachably featureless dilution of the Christian religion as I had met it in its Lutheran form –

the whole implausible, colorful, comforting tapestry of the Incarnation and the Magi, Christmas carols and Santa Claus, Adam and Eve, nakedness and the Tree of the Knowledge of Good and Evil, the serpent and the Fall, betrayal in the garden and Redemption on the Cross, 'Why hast thou forsaken me?' and Pilate washing his hands and Resurrection on the third day, posthumous suppers in an upper room and doubting Thomas and angels haunting the shadier margins of Jerusalem, the instructions to the disciples and Paul's being knocked from his donkey on the road to Damascus and the disciples talking in tongues, a practice at which the stolid churchgoers of Alton and its environs did draw the line. Our public-school day began with a Bible reading and the Lord's Prayer; our teachers and bankers and undertakers and mailmen all professed to be conventional Christians, and what was good enough for them should have been, I think I thought, good enough for Unitarians. I had been conditioned to feel that there could be no joy in life without religious faith, and if such faith demanded an intellectual sacrifice, so be it. I had read enough Kierkegaard and Barth and Unamuno to know about the leap of faith, and Reverend Whitworth was not making that leap; he was taking naps and building stone walls instead. In his bedroom I spotted a paperback Tillich – *The Courage to Be*, most likely – but I never caught him reading it, or *The Master Works of World Philosophy* either. The only time I felt him as a holy man was when, speaking with deliberate tenderness to one of his three daughters, he fell into a 'thee' or 'thou' from his Quaker boyhood.

He was to be brought low, all dignity shed, before he died. Alzheimer's didn't so much invade his brain as deepen the benign fuzziness and preoccupation that had always been there. At the memorial service for his wife, dead of cancer, he turned to me before the service began and said, with a kindly though puzzled smile, 'Well, James, I don't quite know what's up, but I guess it will all come clear.' He didn't realize that his wife of forty-five years was being memorialized.

With her gone, he deteriorated rapidly. At the nursing home where we finally took him, as he stood before the admission desk he began to whimper, and to jiggle up and down as if bouncing something in his pants, and I knew he needed to urinate, but I lacked the courage to lead him quickly to the lavatory and take his penis out of his fly for him, so he wet himself and the floor. I was, in those years just before my separation from Deb, the eldest son-in-law, the first mate, as it were, of the extended family, and was failing in my role, though still taking a certain pride in it. My father-in-law had always, curiously, from those first summers in Vermont, trusted me – trusted me first with his daughter's well-being, and then with helping him lift the stones into place on his wall, where I could have pinched one of his fingers or dropped a rock on his toes. For all of my *ressentiment*, I never did.

I loved him, in fact. As innocent of harm as my own father, he made fewer demands on those around him. A little silence during his nap does not seem, now, too much to ask, though at the time it irritated me. His theology, or lack of it, now seems one of the spacious views I enjoyed thanks to him. His was a cosmos from which the mists of superstition had almost cleared. His parish, there in the Gateway to the West, included university existentialists, and some of their hip philosophy buffed up his old-fashioned transcendentalist sermons, which he delivered in a mellow, musing voice. Though Unitarian, he was of the theist branch, Deb would tell me in bed, hoping to mediate between us. I wasn't, as I remember it, graceless enough to quarrel with him often, but he could not have been ignorant of my Harvard neo-orthodoxy; with its Eliotic undercurrent of panic.

In Vermont, my household task was to burn the day's wastepaper, in a can up the slope behind the house, toward the spring that supplied our cold water. One could look across twenty miles of wooded valley to the next ridge of the Green Mountains. With Reverend Whitworth's blessing, I had been admitted to a world of long views and icy swims and New England reticence. He was a transparently good man who took himself with a little Maine salt. It is easy to love people in memory; the hard thing is to love them when they are there in front of you.

Pennsylvania had its different tensions for Deb and me. We had gotten off to a bad start. The first time I brought her home to meet my parents, we disembarked at the wrong train station. The train from Philadelphia was a local. One of its stops was a hilly factory town seven miles from Alton, also along the Schuylkill and closer by a few miles to the country farmhouse to which we had moved, at my mother's instigation, after the war. We were among a handful of passengers to get off the train, and the platform in its tunnel of trees soon emptied. No one had come to meet us. My parents, in spite of arrangements clear in my own mind – I was trying to save them mileage – had gone to Alton.

Now I wonder how, in that era before cell phones, we managed to make contact. But in that same era even little railroad stations were still manned; perhaps the station-master telegraphed word of our plight to Alton and had my parents paged in the echoing great station. Or perhaps, by the mental telegraphy that used to operate in backward regions, they guessed the truth when we didn't disembark and simply drove to where we were. I was a young swain, and Deb, so securely in her element in St Louis or Cambridge, seemed lost in my home territory. I kept failing to protect her from our primitive ways. Blamelessly, she kept doing things wrong.

Though we were not yet married, she had put some dirty socks and underwear of mine through her own laundry, and packed them, clean, in her suitcase. When my mother, helpfully hovering in the guest bedroom, noticed this transposition, she let loose one of her silent bursts of anger, a merciless succession of waves that dyed an angry red V on her forehead, between the eyebrows, and filled the little sandstone house to its corners, upstairs and down. The house of my childhood, in the town of Olinger, a mere trolley-car ride from Alton, had been a long narrow brick one, with a long backyard, so there were places to escape to when my mother was, in my father's tolerant phrase, 'throwing an atmosphere.' But in the new house we could all hear one another turn over in bed at night, and even the out-of-doors, buzzing with insects and seething with weeds, offered no escape from my mother's psychological heat. I had grown up with her aggrieved moods, turned on usually by adult conflicts out of my sight and hearing. She could maintain one for days until, coming home from school or a friend's house, I would find it miraculously lifted. Her temper was part of my growing up, like Pennsylvania mugginess and the hot spells that could kill old people in their stifling row houses and expand the steel tracks on the street enough to derail trolley cars.

Whispering, I tried to apologize for this climate to Deb, while my mother's sulk, which had frozen all our tongues during dinner, continued to emanate from her bedroom down into the living room. The click of her latch had reverberated above us like a thunderclap. 'You didn't do anything wrong,' I assured Deb, though in my heart I felt that offending my mother was wrong, a primal sin. I blamed Deb for mixing up my underwear with hers; she should have anticipated the issue, the implications. 'It's the way she is.'

'Well, she should wake up and get over it' was Deb's response, so loud I feared it could be heard upstairs. Amazed, I realized that she wasn't tuned as finely as I to the waves of my mother's anger. She wasn't built from birth to receive them.

Near the sofa where we sat, my father, dolefully correcting math papers in the rocking chair, said, 'Mildred doesn't mean anything by it. It's her femininity acting up.'

Femininity explained and justified everything for his sexist generation, but not for mine. I was mortified by this tension. That same visit, perhaps, or later, Deb, thinking she was doing a good deed, on Sunday morning began to weed the patch of pansies my mother had planted near the back porch and then neglected. Deb stood uncomprehending, her feet sweetly bare in the soft soil, like Ingrid Bergman's in *Stromboli*, when I explained that around here nobody worked on Sundays; everybody went to church. 'How silly,' Deb said. 'My father all summer does his walls and things on Sundays.'

'He's a different denomination.'

'Jim, I can't believe this. I really can't.'

'*Sh-h-h*. She's inside, banging dishes around.'

'Well, let her. They're her dishes.'

'And we have to get ready for church.'

'I didn't bring church clothes.'

'Just put on shoes and the dress you wore down on the train.'

'Shit I will. I'd look ridiculous. I'd rather stay here and weed. Your grandparents will be staying, won't they?'

'My grandmother. My grandfather goes. He reads the Bible every day on the sofa, haven't you noticed?'

'I didn't know there were places like this left in America.'

'Well –'

My answer was going to be lame, she saw with those sterling blue eyes, so she interrupted. 'I see now where you get your nonsense from, being so rude to Daddy.'

I was scandalized but thrilled, perceiving that a defense against my mother was possible. In the event, Deb stayed with my grandmother, who was disabled and speechless with Parkinson's disease. My rudeness to Reverend Whitworth was revenged when, baptizing our first child, his first grandchild, in a thoroughly negotiated Unitarian family service in the house of her Lutheran grandparents, he made a benign little joke about the 'holy water' – water fetched from our own spring, which was down below the house instead of, as in Vermont, up above it. My mother sulked for the rest of the day about that, and always spoke of Catherine, our first child, as 'the baby who didn't get baptized.' By the time the three other babies arrived, Deb and I had moved to Massachusetts, where we had met and courted, and joined the Congregational Church as a reasonable compromise.

We are surrounded by holy water; all water, our chemical mother, is holy. Flying from Boston to New York, my habit is to take a seat on the right-hand side of the plane, but the other day I sat on the left, and was rewarded, at that hour of mid-morning, by the sun's reflections on the waters of Connecticut – not just the rivers and the Sound, but little ponds and pools and glittering threads of water that for a few seconds hurled silver light skyward into my eyes. My father's tears for a moment had caught the light; that is how I saw them. When he was dead, Deb and I divorced. Why? It's hard to say. 'We boil at different degrees,' Emerson had said, and a woman came along who had my same boiling point.

The snapshots I took of Deb naked, interestingly, Deb claimed as part of her just settlement. It seemed to me they were mine; I'd taken them. But she said her body was hers. It sounded like second-hand feminism, but I didn't argue.

After our divorce, my mother told me, of my father, 'He worried about you two from the first time you brought her home. He didn't think she was feminine enough for you.'

'He was big on femininity,' I said, not knowing whether to believe her or not. The dead are so easy to misquote.

My reflex is always to come to Deb's defense, even though it was I who wanted the divorce. It shocks me, at my high-school class reunions, when my classmates bother to tell me how much they prefer my second wife. It is true, Sylvia really mixes it up with them, in a way that Deb shyly didn't. But, then, Deb assumed that they were part of my past, something I had put behind me but reunited with every five years or so, whereas Sylvia, knowing me in my old age, recognizes that I have never really left Pennsylvania; that it is where the self I value is stored, however infrequently I check on its condition. The most recent reunion, the fifty-fifth, might have depressed Deb – all these people in their early seventies, most of them still living in the county within a short drive of where they had been born, even in the same semi-detached houses where they had been raised. Some came in wheelchairs, and some were too sick to drive and were chauffeured to the reunion by their middle-aged children. The list of our deceased classmates on the back of the program grows longer; the class beauties have gone to fat or bony cronehood; the sports stars and non-athletes alike move about with the aid of pacemakers and plastic knees, retired and taking up space at an age when most of our fathers were considerately dead.

But we don't see ourselves that way, as lame and old. We see kindergarten children – the same round fresh faces, the same cup ears and long-lashed eyes. We hear the gleeful shrieking during elementary-school recess and the seductive saxophones and muted trumpets of the locally bred swing bands that serenaded the blue-lit gymnasium during high-school dances. We see in each other the enduring simplicities of a town rendered changeless by Depression and then by a world war whose bombs never reached us, though rationing and toy tanks and air-raid drills did. Old rivalries are re-kindled and put aside; old romances flare for a moment and subside into the general warmth, the diffuse love. When the class secretary, dear Joan Edison, her luxuriant head of chestnut curls now whiter than bleached laundry, takes the microphone and runs us through a quiz on the old days – teachers' nicknames, the names of vanished luncheonettes and ice-cream parlors, the titles of our junior and senior class plays, the winner of the scrap drive in third grade – the answers are shouted out on all sides. Not one piece of trivia stumps us: we were there, together, then, and the spouses, Sylvia among them, good-naturedly applaud so much long-hoarded treasure of useless knowing.

These were not just my classmates; they had been my father's students, and they remembered him. He was several times the correct answer – 'Mr Werley!' – in Joan Edison's quiz. Cookie Behn, who had been deposited in our class by his failing grades and who, a year older than we, already had Alzheimer's, kept coming up to me before and after dinner, squinting as if at a strong light and huskily, ardently asking, 'Your father, Jimbo – is he still with us?' He had forgotten the facts but remembered that saying 'still alive,' like the single word 'dead,' was somehow tactless.

'No, Cookie,' I said each time. 'He died in 1972, of his

second heart attack.' Oddly, it did not feel absurd to be calling a seventy-four-year-old man on a pronged cane 'Cookie.'

He nodded, his expression grave as well as, mildly, puzzled. 'I'm sorry to hear that,' he said.

'I'm sorry to tell you,' I said, though my father would have been over a hundred and running up big bills in a nursing home. As it happened, his dying was less trouble to me than Reverend Whitworth's.

'And your mother, Jimbo?' Cookie persisted.

'She outlived him by seventeen years,' I told him, curtly, as if I resented the fact. 'She was a happy widow.'

'She was a very dignified lady,' he said slowly, nodding as if to agree with himself. It touched me that he was attempting to remember my mother, and that what he said was, after all, true enough of her in her relations with the outside world. She had been outwardly dignified and, in her youth, beautiful or, as she once put it to me during her increasingly frank long widowhood, 'not quite beautiful.'

My father had died when Deb and I were in Italy. We had gone there, with another couple in trouble, to see if we couldn't make the marriage 'work.' Our hotel in Florence was a small one with a peek at the Arno; returning from a bus trip to Fiesole – its little Roman stadium, its charming Etruscan museum built in the form of a first-century Ionic temple – we had impulsively decided, the four of us, to have an afternoon drink in the hotel's upstairs café, rather than return to the confinement of our rooms. The place, with its angled view of the Arno, was empty except for some Germans drinking beer in a corner, and some Italians standing up with espressos at the bar. If I heard the telephone ring at all, I assumed it had nothing to do with me. But the bartender came from behind the bar and walked over to me and said, 'Signor Wer-lei? Call for you.' Who could know I was here?

It was my mother, sounding very small and scratchy. 'Jimmy? Were you having fun? I'm sorry to disturb you.'

'I'm impressed you could find me.'

'The operators helped,' she explained.

'What's happened, Mother?'

'Your father's in the hospital. With his second heart attack.'

'How bad is it?'

'Well, he sat up in the car as I drove him into Alton.'

'Well, then, it isn't too bad.'

There was a delay in her responses that I blamed on the transatlantic cable. She said at last, 'I wouldn't be too sure of that.' Except when we talked on the telephone, I never noticed what a distinct Pennsylvania accent my mother had. When we were face to face, her voice sounded as transparent, as free of any accent, as my own. She explained, 'He woke up with this pressing feeling on his chest, and usually he ignores it. He didn't today. It's noon here now.'

'So you want me to come back,' I accused her. I knew my father wouldn't want me inconvenienced. The four of us had reservations for the Uffizi tomorrow.

She sighed; the cable under the ocean crackled. 'Jimmy, I'm afraid you better. You and Deb, of course, unless she'd rather stay there and enjoy the art. Dr Shirk doesn't like what he's hearing, and you know how hard to impress he usually is.'

Open-heart surgery and angioplasty were not options then; there was little for doctors to do but listen with a stethoscope and prescribe nitroglycerin. The concierge told us when the next train to Rome was, and the other couple saw us to the Florence station – just beyond the Medici chapels, which Deb and I had always wanted to see, and were destined never to see together. In Rome, the taxi driver found us an airline office that was open. I will never forget the courtesy and patience with which that young airline clerk, in his schoolbook English, took our tickets to Boston the next week and converted them into tickets to Philadelphia the next day. More planes flew then, with more empty seats. We made an evening flight to London, and had to lay over for the night. On the side of Heathrow away from London there turned out to be a world of new, tall hotels for passengers in transit. We got into our room around midnight. I called my mother – it was suppertime in Pennsylvania – and learned that my father was dead. To my mother, it was news a number of hours old, and she described in weary retrospect her afternoon of sitting in the Alton hospital and receiving increasingly dire reports. She said, 'Doc Shirk said he fought real hard at the end. It was ugly.'

I hung up, and shared the news with Deb. She put her arms around me in the bed and told me, 'Cry.' Though I saw the opportunity, and the rightness of seizing it, I don't believe I did. My father's tears had used up mine.

WILLIAM MAXWELL

THE MAN WHO
LOST HIS FATHER

ONCE UPON A time there was a man who lost his father.

His father died of natural causes – that is to say, illness and old age – and it was time for him to go, but nevertheless the man was affected by it, more than he had expected. He misplaced things: his keys, his reading glasses, a communication from the bank. And he imagined things. He imagined that his father's spirit walked the streets of the city where he lived, was within touching distance of him, could not for a certain time leave this world for the world of spirits, and was trying to communicate with him. When he picked up the mail that was lying on the marble floor outside the door of his apartment, he expected to find a letter from his father telling him . . . telling him what?

The secret of the afterlife is nothing at all – or rather, it is only one secret, compared to the infinite number of secrets having to do with this life that the dead take with them when they go.

'Why didn't I ask him when I had a chance?' the man said, addressing the troubled face in the bathroom mirror, a face made prematurely old by a white beard of shaving lather. And from that other mirror, his mind, the answer came: *Because you thought there was still time. You expected him to live forever . . . because you expect to live forever yourself.* The razor stopped in mid-stroke. This time what came was a question. *Do you or don't you? You do expect to live forever? You don't expect to live forever?* The man plunged his hands in soapy water and rinsed the lather from his face. And as he was drying his hands on a towel, he glanced down four stories at the empty street corner and for a split second he thought he saw his father, standing in front of the drugstore window.

His father's body was in a coffin, and the coffin was in the ground, in a cemetery, but that he never thought about. Authority is not buried in a wooden box. Nor safety (mixed with the smell of cigar smoke). Nor the firm handwriting. Nor the sound of his voice. Nor the right to ask questions that are painful to answer.

So long as his father was alive, he figured persistently in the man's conversation. Almost any remark was likely to evoke him. Although the point of the remark was mildly amusing and the tone intended to be affectionate, there was something about it that was not amusing and not entirely affectionate – as if an old grievance was still being nourished, a deep disagreement, a deprivation, something raked up out of the past that should have been allowed to lie forgotten. It was, actually, rather tiresome, but even after he perceived what he was doing the man could not stop. It made no difference whether he was with friends or with people he had never seen before. In the space of five minutes, his father would pop up in the conversation. And you didn't have to be very acute to understand that what he was really saying was 'Though I am a grown man and not a little boy, I still feel the weight of my father's hand on me, and I tell this story to lighten the weight. . . .'

Now that his father was gone, he almost never spoke of him, but he thought about him. At my age was his hair this thin, the man wondered, holding his comb under the bathroom faucet.

Why, when he never went to church, did he change, the man wondered, dropping a letter in the corner mailbox.

Why, when he had been an atheist, or if not an atheist then an agnostic, all his life, was he so pleased to see the Episcopal minister during his last illness?

Hanging in the hall closet was his father's overcoat, which by a curious accident now fit him. Authority had shrunk. And safety? There was no such thing as safety. It was only an idea that children have. As they think that with the help of an umbrella they can fly, so they feel that their parents stand between them and all that is dangerous. Meanwhile, the cleaning establishment had disposed of the smell of cigar smoke; the overcoat smelled like any overcoat. The hand-writing on the envelopes he picked up in the morning out-side his door was never that handwriting. And along with certain stock certificates that had been turned over to him when his father's estate was settled, he had received the right to ask questions that are painful to answer, such as 'Why did you not value your youth?'

He wore the overcoat, which was of the very best quality but double-breasted and long and a dark charcoal grey – an old man's coat – only in very cold weather, and it kept him warm. . . . From the funeral home they went to the cemetery, and the coffin was already there, in a tent, suspended above the open grave. After the minister had spoken the last words, it still was not lowered. Instead, the mourners raised their heads, got up from their folding chairs, and went out into the icy wind of a January day. And to the man's surprise, the out-lines of the bare trees were blurred. He had not expected tears, and neither had he expected to see, in a small group of people waiting some distance from the tent, a man and a woman, not related to each other and not married to each other, but both related to him: his first playmates. They stepped forward and took his hand and spoke to him, looking deeply into his eyes. The only possible conclusion was that they were

349

there waiting for him, in the cold, because they were worried about him. . . . In his father's end was his own beginning, the mirror in his mind pointed out. And it was true, in more ways than one. But it took time.

He let go of the ghost in front of the corner drugstore.

The questions grew less and less painful to have to answer. The stories he told his children about their grandfather did not have to do with a disagreement, a deprivation, or something raked up out of the distant past that might better have been forgotten. When he was abrupt with them and they ran crying from the room, he thought, *But my voice wasn't all that harsh*. Then he thought, *To them it must have been*. And he got up from his chair and went after them, to lighten the weight of his father's irritability, making itself felt in some mysterious way through him. They forgave him, and he forgave his father, who surely hadn't meant to sound severe and unloving. And when he took his wife and children home – to the place that in his childhood was home – on a family visit, one of his cousins, smiling, said, 'How much like your father you are.'

'That's because I am wearing his overcoat,' the man said – or rather, the child that survived in the man. The man himself was pleased, accepted the compliment (surprising though it was), and at the first opportunity looked in the mirror to see if it was true.

ACKNOWLEDGMENTS

Note on all stories for which permission to reproduce has been granted by Random House LLC: Any third party use of this material, outside of this publication, is prohibited. Interested parties must apply directly to Random House LLC for permission.

HAROLD BRODKEY: Excerpt from *Stories in an Almost Classical Mode* by Harold Brodkey, copyright © 1988 by Harold Brodkey. Used by permission of Alfred A. Knopf, an imprint of the Knopf Doubleday Publishing Group, a division of Random House LLC. All rights reserved. 'His Son, in His Arms, in Light, Aloft' from *Stories in an Almost Classical Mode* by Harold Brodkey. Reprinted by permission of ICM Partners, Inc. Copyright © 1988 by Harold Brodkey.

RON CARLSON: 'The H Street Sledding Record' from *A Kind of Flying: Selected Stories* by Ron Carlson. Copyright © 2003, 1997, 1992, 1987 by Ron Carlson. Used by permission of W. W. Norton & Company, Inc. 'The H Street Sledding Record', Copyright © 1984 by Ron Carlson. From *A Kind of Flying: Selected Stories* by Ron Carlson, published by W. W. Norton & Company. Originally published in *McCall's*. Used by permission of the Brandt & Hochman Literary Agents, Inc. All rights reserved.

RAYMOND CARVER: 'Bicycles, Muscles, Cigarets' from *Will You Please Be Quiet, Please?* by Raymond Carver. Published by Vintage Books. Reprinted by permission of The Random House Group Limited. 'Bicycles, Muscles, Cigarets' from *Will You Please Be Quiet, Please?* by Raymond Carver. Copyright © 1963, 1964, 1965, 1966, 1967, 1968, 1969, 1970, 1971, 1972, 1973, 1974, 1975, 1976 by Tess Gallagher, renewed 1991 by Tess Gallagher, used by permission of The Wylie Agency LLC.

GUY DE MAUPASSANT: 'Simon's Father' from *The Collected Novels and Stories of Guy de Maupassant*, translation copyright © 1923, 1951 renewed by Alfred A. Knopf, a division of Random House LLC. Used by permission of Alfred A. Knopf, an imprint of the Knopf Doubleday Publishing Group, a division of Random House LLC. All rights reserved.

E. L. DOCTOROW: 'The Writer in the Family' from *All the Time in the World* by E. L. Doctorow, published by Little, Brown Book Group. Reprinted with permission. 'The Writer in the Family' from *Lives of the Poets* by E.L. Doctorow, copyright © 1984 by E.L. Doctorow. Used by permission of Random House, an imprint of The Random House Publishing Group, a division of Random House LLC. All rights reserved.

ANDRE DUBUS: From *Selected Stories* by Andre Dubus. Reprinted by permission of Black Sparrow Books, an imprint of David R. Godine, Publisher, Inc. Copyright © 1988 by Andre Dubus.

FRANZ KAFKA: 'The Judgment' taken from *The Complete Short Stories of Franz Kafka* by Franz Kafka. Published by Vintage Books. Reprinted by permission of The Random House Group Limited. 'The Judgment' from *The Complete Stories* by Franz Kafka, copyright © 1946, 1947, 1948, 1949, 1954, 1958, 1971 by Schocken Books, an imprint of the Knopf Doubleday Group, a division of Random House LLC. Used by permission of Schocken Books, an imprint of the Knopf Doubleday Publishing Group, a division of Random House LLC. All rights reserved.